"Common Clay, written by a very uncommon person, is remarkable for its rare honesty, illuminating insights, and contagious creativity, making her story both believable and inspiring."

Eugene Nida
American Bible Society

"Martha Emmert, who calls herself COMMON CLAY in her memoir, is anything but common! Like other extraordinarily gifted people who rose to incredible heights from humble beginnings, Martha is a Living Example of what God can do with a life dedicated to Him."

Dr. William R. Myers, Sr.
President Emeritus
Northern Baptist Theological Seminary

"Thirty-five years in Zaire without an art budget taught Martha that when Christ lives in any culture, be it African or African American, he opens people's creativity so that small, common, broken and discard pieces of that culture can be choreographed into the works of beauty, meaning and Gospel witness. "Common Clay" tells the story of this uncommon Christian we all know and love."

Ray Bakke
Executive Director, International Urban Associates
Professor of Global Urban Mission,
Eastern Baptist Theological Seminary

"Your long and faithful service as missionaries to Africa certainly authenticates you as a person to comment on life as missionaries. That very authenticity should make your book quite interesting to a great number of people."

Millard Fuller
Habitat For Humanity

"Martha Emmert's memoirs are a heroic but true example of how faith can lift a life and bring it to fruition."

Raymond K. Sheline
Distinguished Professor, Florida University
Fulbright Professor, Nuclear Physics, Zaire, 1984

"Common Clay is an exciting story of how God can work in an ordinary life to bring about a very creative ministry ... I would highly recommend it as must reading."

Audley Bruce

"It has been a delight to read portions of her life story but I eagerly await the opportunity to read the whole of Common Clay!"

Rev. Robert L. Maase
Retired Chaplain US Air Force

"I found your stories and reflections both moving and inspiring. They are wonderful accounts of how God has been working among the people of Zaire, now the Democratic Republic of Congo, in spite of the great difficulties they have been facing for a very long time."

John A. Sundquist
Board of International Ministries ABC

"Her memoirs .. interesting accounts of trials and triumphs ... her worthy achievements in contributing to the enrichment of many students' lives will serve as a model for others and stimulate worthy achievements. Ms. Emmert's life story offers a parable of her generation, overcoming initial hardships to reach a productive level of competence and dedication to helping others."

Monni Adams, Ph.D.
Associate, Ethnology & Art
Peabody Museum of Archaeology & Ethnology
Harvard University, Cambridge, Massachusetts

"I marveled at the dignitaries she encountered and the lessons she learned as she carried out her call ... I could not wait to get to the next page. I trust she will consider a sequel. I want to hear more."

Gerry Myers

Elderhostel 1998

Martha Atkins Emmert

Eph 2:8-9 Oct 27, 1998

Common Clay

SECOND EDITION

Published by:

Martha Atkins Emmert
3002 Sandarac Lane
Fort Wayne, Indiana 46815
U.S.A.

Printed By:

Copy Solutions, Inc.
Fort Wayne, Indiana, 46804
U.S.A.

Manufactured in U.S.A.
ISBN: 0-9658791-0-0

Library of Congress Catalog Card Number: 97-90787

Author:	Martha Atkins Emmert
Editor:	Anita K. Steinbacher
Front Cover Sculptor:	Dr. Sam Gore
Front Cover Photographer:	Jesse Worley
Front Cover Design:	Amy Breland
Back Cover Design:	Anita K. Steinbacher

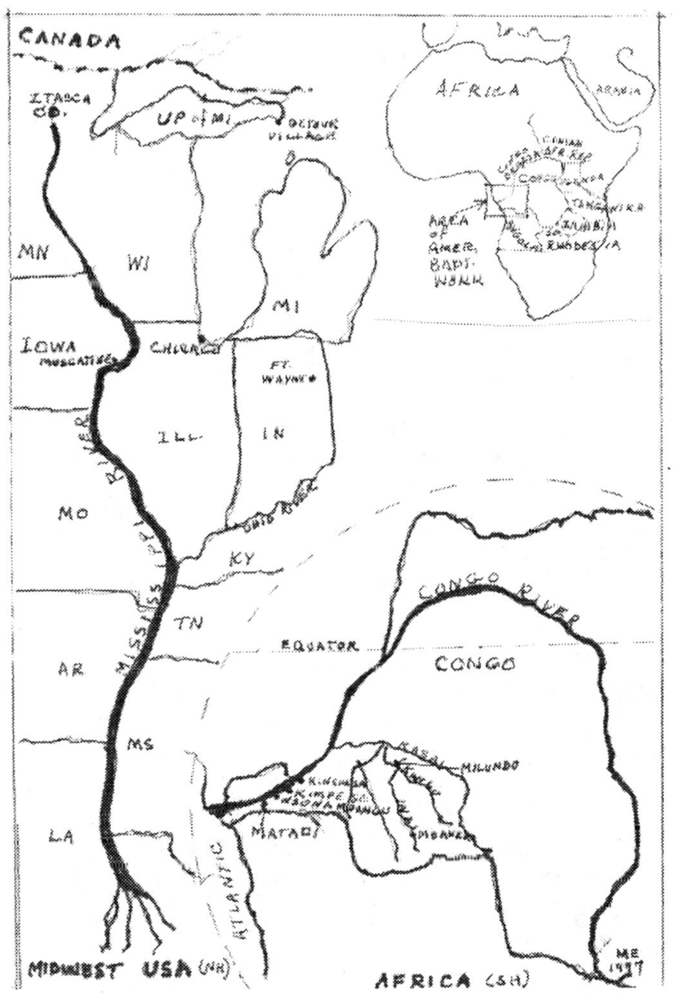

"Martha tells about this journey from along the Mississippi to the banks of the Congo River, in a remarkable way. I would highly recommend it as must reading."

Audley M. Bruce
American Baptist Churches

Dedication

To my family of my first birth
who in love and sacrifice
Preserved my life
Nurturing me in nature's beauty.

And to the family of my second birth
Whose members form ties of love
that encompass the world
defying space and time.

And to my husband, Leon,
my children and their
descendants -- my love and prayers for you
will last beyond the grave.

Martha Atkins Emmert

Table Of Contents

Table Of Contents

(CONTINUED)

Christmas 1927
4 year old Martha Atkins at her Aunt Nellie's house

Part I

"Write down for the coming generation what the Lord has done so that people not yet born will praise Him."
Psalms 102:18 Good News Bible TEV

"Come and listen, all who honor God and I will tell you what He has done for me."

Psalms 66:16

"Now that I am old ... O God!
Be with me while I proclaim your power and might to all generations to come."
Psalms 71:18

"But God chose the foolish things of the world to shame the wise;
God chose the weak things of the world to shame the strong."
I Corinthians 1:27

"Now Jesus loved Martha ..."
King James Version, John 11:5

Introduction

The things I remember seem so far removed from the lives of my grandchildren that it frightens me. I want them to know their roots, to know that life can be good or bad whether they live in better days or in times of crime and violence. We do not choose our era. We deal with it as best we can.

Though born twenty-three years into the twentieth century, my parents stayed back in the nineteenth century just as long as they could and did their best to keep the kids there with them. I always wrote "farmer" in the space that called for father's occupation. Actually, he did not farm all that much. It seemed the simplest answer. My parents were definitely "country," their heroes were the pioneers, naturalists and who knows, maybe the druids.

A stork unloaded me in Muscatine, Iowa, deviating from his migration route. My sister gave me a photo of the house he picked on 408 Lombard Street. I arrived September 10, 1923, the fourth of five children. My sister, was the oldest, two brothers preceded me and, two years later, a baby brother followed to complete our family circle.

My parents moved us at least once a year. My father always in search of a good job, worked as a farmer, bricklayer, mason, woodsman, and button cutter. We usually moved in and around

Muscatine, Iowa. Once we went as far as Pontiac, Michigan. Another time we moved to Illinois City, Illinois, and later to Itasca County, Minnesota for a relatively short time. Never able to get ahead or even to catch up financially, with seven mouths to feed we just kept a move ahead of the landlord, hoping for a job that could support our family.

It was not until we were all grown and gone that my parents finally settled down. My brother Paul's check (from the navy) sent to Mama bought some land and a house for them. Daddy became a partner in an antique shop the last twenty-five years of his life. After both of my parents died, a garage bought their land and it is all cemented over now. No trace is left of the wild flower garden Daddy made of the back yard for Mama, her berry bushes, fruit trees or grapevines.

My earliest memories center on a tent in the wood by a river when I was four years old. I remember the song of a whip-or-will at bedtime, the slap of rain hitting the tent while I watched its walls vibrate in the wind. The trees came alive and spoke in the storm. I listened. I recollect a beloved aunt shampooing my hair, a delicious sensation for me. When my baby brother succeeded to Mama's lap and breast, I recall how jealous I felt. I stood close to her, longing to be the one on her lap again.

I stood on a stool behind Daddy's chair, combing his thick hair while he smoked and read the newspaper at the end of the day. A night of tragedy came crashing into my babyhood. My dear aunt died and everyone cried. I crowded close to Mama's knee whenever she wept behind her veil of long wavy hair, combing and grieving days, months, and even years afterward remembering her sister.

I have happy memories of wood and field, and I, a toddler, following after the family with my little pail to help pick wild berries in the warm sun. I sometimes sat down and ate all I had picked before starting again, calling hopefully to those beyond my sight, "I'se coming Mama, I'se coming!"

I can still see us loading up the back of Daddy's old truck with our bedding, kitchen utensils, clothing and always "Mama's trunk." It held whatever treasures we owned. Her tall vase once filled with roses for her high school graduation, her graduation dress, photo and diploma, rested in the trunk. Her wedding dress, her trousseau and all her beautiful hand tailored clothing later became our clothing as she chose from it to remodel and recreate to provide for our needs. And down underneath the tray, a stack of love letters, tied up in blue satin ribbon, recorded their romance.

The loaded trunk, with a canvas thrown over it, provided seats for children as we positioned ourselves on top and off we would go even if it meant leaving school in session. The new house, usually proved equally small for a family of seven, and was often just as leaky, drafty, and cold in winter. With outdoor plumbing, broken screens, no central heat, and kerosene lamps for light after sunset, the new house never seemed any better than the last.

When electricity became more common, it meant one dim light bulb hanging from the ceiling of a room on a long black wire. The floors held remnants of worn linoleum. We heated and cooked with wood, or coal. All her life my mother washed by hand on a washboard. Soaking clothes in a tub of soapy water, she scrubbed them briskly with a big yellow bar of Fels-Naptha soap. A tub of clear water carried from a pump in the yard rinsed out the soap. She never lived to have indoor plumbing.

Summer and winter we hung the hand-wrung clothes outside on a clothesline and held them in place with clothespins. Only the Amish know anything about that lifestyle now. I remember huge, stiff, frozen winter underwear, overalls, and shirts. If strong enough, the wind could whip them dry. Sometimes they had to be brought in at night frozen, to thaw dripping as they hung over nails, hooks or chairs to dry near the stove.

We never owned a telephone, though we did have a radio of sorts. As a teenager, I remember living for Jack Benny's program at seven on Sunday nights and hoping we could get the milking done in time. That radio brought us President Franklin Delano Roosevelt's fireside chats. How I hung on every word he uttered and had faith that he could see us through the dreadful war that called all three brothers before it ended.

Shy, fearful of strangers, and of new experiences, I dreaded change. I loved beauty, flowers, and quietness. My mother told how I stood silently by garden fences as a toddler, gazing longingly at the flowers until some were offered to me. I loved animals.

I cannot remember when I learned to read. I have always loved words, books, and stories. A catalog in the outside privy, the oatmeal box near the kitchen table, equally enthralled me. Whether at home or at school, a good story blocked out all else. Punished both places for reading at the wrong times, I continued undeterred. Reading brought me happiness, escape, education, aspirations. It both, fed my curiosity, and satisfied it. Books became my dearest friends, my help in stress, my teachers, and my pastors. I cannot imagine life without books – but I run ahead of my story.

I will divide my story into two parts. The first twenty chapters ran merrily along, and were fun to write. The rest of the story is more difficult to relate. Our lives governed by five-year terms and one-year furloughs sometimes repeats itself and rarely runs smoothly and chronologically. I have consequently chosen a series of articles that cover the incidents and memories that marked my life. Although I am not completely satisfied with this method, as it tends to chop up the story and repeat itself in some areas, it seemed the best way to condense our working years.

For better or for worse, this book is my message and my legacy to the family and the generations that shall follow me.

Last but not least, to Anita K. Steinbacher my editor, my gratitude for her diligence and loyalty, without which this book would never have been published.

"Privileges of descent, or relationship never count in the economy of God. The one thing that counts is obedience and the character that grows out of it."

G. Campbell Morgan

1925 - Martha Atkins' earliest picture - 2 years old

Chapter 1

MY FOREBEARS

My brother, Harry, researched the genealogy of our father's family. He found grounds for writing to me to say my daughter and I are eligible to be members of the Daughters of the American Revolution. For most of my life I have felt it presumptuous to trace my lineage. "Better let sleeping ancestors lie," I thought, "for fear of what might fall out of closets." But when good news is found, hey, we can all use family support. This is what he discovered.

My paternal grandmother, Lorinda Burr, descended directly from Benjamin Burre of England, one of the founders of Hartford, Connecticut. He probably came to America with the Winthrop Fleet in 1630, landing in Massachusetts. A monument to his memory and that of other founders is erected in the churchyard of the Central Congregational Church of Hartford, Connecticut, where he presumably lived by 1635, the founding date. Unfortunately, I have never seen this monument.

Described as a well-to-do businessman, Benjamin Burre also had a family. My lineage continues through his son Thomas. Of Thomas' twelve children, our interest falls on the sixth child, Isaac, my forebear (or foreBurr). Isaac Burr I graduated from Yale in 1717. (So I am not the first college graduate in my family after all!) Ordained the second pastor of the Presbyterian Church of Worcester, Massachusetts, on October 25, 1725, he later moved to Windsor, Connecticut in 1744 where he served as pastor until his death in 1752.

Isaac the First married Mary Eliot. Here, the real treasure hides. She is the great-grand daughter of Reverend John Eliot, famous apostle to the Indians. Imagine! An ancestor to read about in the encyclopedia! Isaac I and Mary had seven children. I descend from the second child, Isaac II who became a reputable physician of Hartford, with a restrained brood of two. Isaac III, again a second child, next in my line, served as a soldier in the Revolutionary war. It is kinship with Isaac Burr, the Third, listed in the DAR book, which makes me eligible to join. Isaac III's eighth child, Simeon, born in Vermont, on Sept. 8, 1800, migrated to Iowa with his family and died there in October of 1881. Thus, this distinguished line dwindles down to my humble birthplace.

Before Simeon died, he had one child by his first wife, and six children by his second wife, Sarah Bateman. Among the six were two brothers, Charles Norman and Daniel Burr. These two brothers enlisted in the Civil War together in Muscatine, Iowa, my birthplace. Norman married at the time to Mary Ann Lovell, had one son, Charles. The brothers made a pact.

If Norman should be killed and Daniel survived, Daniel must care for Mary and Charles.

Norman did die in St. Louis, Missouri, August 19, 1863, while still a soldier in the 35th regiment (of the) Iowa Volunteer Infantry. Daniel wedded Mary on September 9, 1868 in Rock Island, Illinois. Dan and Mary had nine or ten other children. Their first child, a daughter, Lorinda Burr (of DAR privileges), became my grandmother. At sixteen years (of age) she married my future grandfather, Eli Delbert Atkins, then twenty-seven years old. She gave birth to thirteen children, of which eleven survived. The third, Harry Way Atkins I, is my father. And I thought the Bible had a lot of begats!

Eli Delbert, my paternal grandfather, was fairly well born since his mother Lucretia Mathilda Way owned properties in Cedar County at the time she became the second wife of Dr. Perry Lewis Atkins. Her husband learned to be a surgeon through apprenticeship to his brother-in-law Dr. Way. He also became a dentist and a minister.

I visited the Tipton, Iowa court house records, and if they are to be believed, this man came near to omnipresence in Cedar County during his adult years. He busied himself healing bodies and souls. As Justice of the Peace, he signed legal papers, as minister he married and buried. As physician, he signed birth certificates for some, death certificates for others. As solid citizen and community leader, he often conferred with the Hoovers in nearby West Branch, Iowa. In his spare time he traveled widely and spoke publicly against alcohol, sponsored by H.J. Heinz, for whom I later worked like a slave in his Muscatine factory. My great-grandfather Perry Atkins lived in Rochester, Iowa. He preached as a minister of the Rochester United Methodist Church. When Billy Sunday held evangelistic meetings in his area he actively participated. Reading the records, one wonders what remained for the rest of the neighbors to do.

While his grandparents lived, my father lived in the same block as his granddaddy's church and attended church with them. Of all these forebears, I can only recall seeing at a distance, Grandpa Eli Atkins. He died when I was eight or nine years old. He did not figure emotionally in my life at all. My sister, his first grandchild, and my older brothers, remember much more. By the time I came along, he had so many other grandchildren, I doubt he noticed my presence.

This large family thrived on annual reunions. My sister says the reunions were always on Labor Day. I remember my greediness for dill pickles and home-cranked freezer ice cream in several flavors. I remember being sick every year as a result. What a noisy, hectic and lusty family we presented each year... such a welter of babies and grown-ups. My father's sisters loomed amazingly tall and sturdy to my infant viewpoint. Now I am the same tall sturdy type. I never did sort them out very well. I cannot recall the family being organized or called to order, or having a blessing said over that vast food collection.

I attended in 1975 with my mother and sister. I took my daughter, married son and wife and my first grandson. In 1993 about 127 (of us) met in Iowa. I went with my nephew, his youngest son, and my youngest grandson, both boys were 16 years old.

I found fourteen or fifteen of my first cousins in attendance, some of whom I recognized. There did not seem to be as many babies as there used to be. Many did not attend.

Mama had practically no family compared to my father's innumerable nieces and nephews. By my memory, only Aunt Clara and her daughter Cleo became an important part of my life. Less is known of Mama's family, in spite of research. My mother's paternal grandfather, James Catterson, had a first wife and daughter Emma before marrying the woman destined to become John Catterson's mother and my maternal great-grandmother. John had a brother Bill, and a sister, Mabel.

All I know of great-grandfather James is that he was tall and liked to play cards, while his wife was short and hated cards. My mother inherited a dislike for cards, so maybe great Grandpa was an Irish gambler with a droopy black mustache and twinkling blue eyes. (I can dream, can't I?) My mother would speak of her Uncle Bill and his son Andy, and Andy's wife

Bessy, but I cannot remember now what she said about them. They are just names to a child who never met any of them.

John Catterson, my mother's "Papa" died long before my birth. In a photograph that I have of him he appears to be a fairly short man with mostly beard. He lathed and plastered houses and served as a caretaker of the Prentiss Estate of New Boston.

Due to John I am one-fourth Irish. Thanks, Gramp! Were you a merry charmer? I wish I could see under that beard. He also, like so many others, used his woodsman's skills throughout his life.

Mary Hannah Staley, my maternal grandmother, born in Germany, had a tailor for a father, reputed to be of some renown. His wife, Martha Springsteen, or -stein, is her mother. The origin of my first name is now discovered. My brother is named Paul Staley, so perhaps that explains the tailor's name as well. It could have been Paul. Who knows now? We heard rumors that a connection exists with the Staley Syrup Company family, but probably that is wishful thinking. Maybe we started the rumors!

The tailor died in Germany. His gifts later flowered most notably in my mother, Jennie, a master tailor, knitter, crocheter and embroiderer. As near as I can tell, those gifts died with her as well, for neither my sister nor myself are famous for our seams, though we love to sew.

The widow and child came by ship to America. The child lost her doll overboard enroute. The young mother met a widower, Hiram Rose, who married her and adopted her daughter, giving her his name. Martha bore him three more children. She also suffered from asthma and my informer revealed that Mary Hannah, my grandmother, being the eldest, did most of the housework.

Hiram became a General in the Civil War (I presume), and has an imposing marble column erected to his memory and hers, at his grave site in the Oquawka, Illinois cemetery which I visited in 1990 and again, in 1995. Did he die in battle? What became of the other Rose children? Growing up I had no memory of this family. Around 1880 Mary Hannah Staley Rose married John Catterson in New Boston, Illinois. They produced six children, but only four survived infancy, the last being my mother.

Nature Speak

From earliest days the rivers spoke
In rush and swirl, past bridge and oak.

The robins sang, the peckers pecked,
While chorused lark and finch bedecked.

Trees rustled in a gentle breeze
Or softly moaned with windy wheeze.

But when I waked to first snow fall
There wasn't any sound at all.

In nature birthed and taught to know it,
How could I not become a poet?

Martha Atkins Emmert

Young Harry Atkins - Martha Atkins Emmert's father

Chapter 2

DADDY'S FAMILY

Daddy had nine brothers and three sisters. Two of his brothers died in infancy. Only one of the thirteen is alive at the time of this writing. Aunt Ruby, 85, is the ninth child in order of birth. The eldest, Uncle Perry, an exemplary child grew to become a Big League baseball pitcher for the Red Sox. According to Mama, he met his doom in alcohol, served at victory toasts. Under its influence, his health declined until his death. When he sobered up, he could hunt and trap with the best, an important skill in his lifetime. Though married to Aunt Laura, he had no children.

Ray, my next oldest Uncle, seemed to be with us a lot. He had a wife and their daughter, my age, tried hard to be a bad influence on me, but God protected me, because I envied her exploits which she reported to me in full. Uncle Ray, during one vacation from his wife, lived in our back yard in a tent. I, being nearly school age, can remember being fascinated by his great hunting hounds that lived with him. The dogs gulped down whole biscuits at a time, as he tossed them. They did not seem to chew at all. Ray lived a primitive life. He popped corn in rendered skunk fat. (See my brother if you do not believe it!) He trapped and fished with my dad. They cut winter ice to store in sawdust for summer sales. Uncle Ray could carve intricate things out of wood. He made chains and little curios, which my brother still keeps. He taught my brothers useful skills.

I remember Uncle Alfred as fairly short and stocky. He married Aunt Ethel and had seven children. Aunt Ethel brought one, Clarence, with her from her first husband. I recall their oldest, Bertha, as a dark and quietly pretty girl. Aunt Ethel's mother, Bertha Kellums, married my widowed grandfather Atkins and usually lived near, or with Uncle Alfred's family after that.

We had great fish fries in their house. Alfred and Grandpa loved to fish, and Aunt Ethel and her mother were great cooks. The fish, rolled in cornmeal and deep fat fried, crunched deliciously as we ate and ate until we could hold no more. As I look back, fish and cornbread were the sole survivors in my memory of those feasts, with the view of "our" Mississippi River swirling past us as we ate.

I suppose the cousin I felt closest to came from that household. Florence, or Tubby, as some called her, walked to and from high school with me in that first year when I lived for a time with my sister, near Uncle Alfred's. We made a comic pair, she short and wide, and me, tall and gaunt. Florence had a bubbly, joyous temperament and I loved being near her. I needed her optimism and cheer, which she shared gladly. I became better acquainted with her big brother, Pete, at that age. I last saw him at my wedding in Muscatine in his army uniform. He stayed in Alaska, at the end of the war and married Clara. They have maybe ten children and more than sixteen grandchildren.

The year I attended second grade, we lived near Uncle Charlie, on "The Island." "Muscatine Island," so-called, in Louisa County, later covered with the massive floodwaters of '93. I remember a fight with Cousin Harvey, when provoked to wrath I chased him around the house twice and broke my pencil box over his head. Mary, the third child, and first of six girls, may be nearer my age. We were in school together, but I recall very little. By then, school had ceased to be fun.

I cannot account for the graphic nightmares I suffered in childhood and youth about wars and bombing and such, except to suppose Uncle Charley and Uncle Roy, two World War I veterans, must have reminisced often. And I, filled with a fearful curiosity, could not stop listening. So even protected children can suffer vicariously. Where my nightmares of earthquakes came from, I do not know ... perhaps books?

Uncle Roy, an upstanding military type seemed more important than the rest of us. He was nicknamed "Jumbo" by his brothers. Jumbo and his wife Edna produced four children. Arnold, who was about my age, started high school with me. Tall and good looking, Arnold later played with the Cardinals, before being sold to the Cubs. Are there Arnold Atkins' baseball cards? I have only rumor and hearsay. Someone said Arnold coaches Bush Leagues. Uncle Roy, a mogul in Veterans of Foreign Wars, secured full military honors for my little brother's funeral, when he died in an accident at the young age of twenty-three.

Aunt Ida had a peculiar nasal quality to her voice. I thought it unpleasant. The first time I heard my own voice on tape in Seminary, I could not believe my ears! I sound just like Aunt Ida. No doubt she also had a deviated septum without the modern relief of nasal sprays and anti-histamines. How people survived without anti-histamines, I cannot imagine. I have lived on them for forty years now. Hay fever and asthma plagued my father's family. My hay fever appeared when at nineteen, I began working in a little button factory near home. Without the proper means of carrying off the pearl-button dust, the shop filled with contaminated air. My allergic reaction became so violent I had to find other work.

Aunt Ida also had hay fever. She had five children, but only four when I remember her best. Pauline seemed to have been near my age. I remember visiting and climbing cherry trees and eating ripe cherries. I remember currant bushes loaded with ripe red currants, which we ate. The memories of the fruit eclipse that of my cousins, I am sorry to say. My sister's memories are very different however. As our families grew older, we became more separated.

Uncle Clifford, next to the youngest boy in Daddy's family, lived in Muscatine with Aunt Cecil. They had a number of babies visible at reunions. Their children, much younger than I, failed to interest me then. Real interest in babies began with children of my own. His brothers called Uncle Clifford, Kissy.

Aunt Ruby is the only living sibling of Daddy's today. Only twelve when her mother died, she is eight years older than my big sister. After her mother's death she may have been mothered by Mama and her sister Nellie, both in the family by then. Aunt Ruby grew to be a beautiful woman, married and had a nice family of six or seven. Her eldest, Sophia (or Skeets), and Donna, the next one, are nearest my age and we played together often.

I particularly remember a spring visit of theirs to Kemper's Island, where we lived, when I turned sixteen. We scoured the woods together for wild flowers. Skeets, a happy, cheerful girl, sunny-faced and tall, made a congenial friend. Donna, younger, very dark and quiet, developed into a real beauty. According to reports, she is a successful artist. Once in 1961, my husband and I crossed the western prairies and by a strange coincidence, we happened to stop at a gas station when my cousin Donna and her family stopped, going the opposite direction. We recognized each other and visited briefly. Our next reunion, also brief, occurred at my sister's Golden Wedding observance.

Except in theory, we did not know Daddy's

youngest sister Emma, or her baby brother, Delbert. They lived with great aunt Ida Creps and did not associate with the likes of us. I cannot remember even meeting them until I grew up. Daddy used to park the truck full of us in the road near Aunt Ida's big farm, and while we sat and waited with Mama, he checked on their welfare. Aunt Emma, renamed Mildred by her adoptive mother, came once with her husband all the way to Northern Minnesota to call on us. She taught school and as an adult, wanted to re-establish family relationships. I remember their visit vividly.

We poor relatives watched from our leaky house while Mama engaged these better class citizens at their car door. I have since wondered a lot about that. Did Mama invite them in? I cannot blame her if she had not the courage. Perhaps Aunt Emma refused to be a "bother." At any rate, after their conversation, the car drove away. It seems both rude and cruel to me now. We lived miles from civilization. Where did they go to eat and sleep? Perhaps they had hampers of food and tents. I am sure I do not know. I know we children were not introduced to her. I think Daddy, away from home cutting railroad ties or something, missed her altogether.

By the time Emma and Delbert were free of great-aunt Ida and integrated back in the Atkins family, I worked overseas. I never knew them. Aunt Emma married a fine man and had two sons, one a lay minister. Uncle Del served in the Second World War on a submarine. He has children, whether they were Creps or Atkins, I do not know. He died fairly young.

These many Atkins cousins, as you can see, I scarcely know. My older siblings of course, have a different viewpoint. My own feeling is that when the depression came on and we grew poorer and older, my folks were unable to sustain a hospitable table. I do not recall much entertaining at any of our many homes. I am not a product of a stable, familiar community. My first community, the overseas missionary community, taught me to cooperate, communicate and be interdependent.

I grew up with feelings, but without the vocabulary to express them. We did not say "please" and "thank you" automatically, if at all. I cannot remember being thanked for anything I did. We felt embarrassed to say such things. We ought to know without being told ... but we did not. Even today, I remind myself in worship, to express gratitude, even to praise... strange word. Mama treated praise as a dangerous commodity, leading to pride, and I do not know what else. I have spent my whole life working for praise and approval from Mama and significant others, who have succeeded her, never seeing my hopes as doomed. Only in the Christian community have I found words to express these things and to hear them expressed to me. Even so, acceptance of them is hard.

How does one believe true what one's own mother refused to say? What a strange mental dilemma governs our vision of ourselves.

"But oh for the touch of a vanished hand
And the sound of a voice that is still!"

Alfred Tennyson

1966 - Martha Marie (Martha's niece), Pearl and-Mama come to visit Martha in Fort Wayne. Michal Rose in front.

Chapter 3

MAMA'S FAMILY

Mama's only brother, Frank, was the eldest of six children. He visited and helped our family until I was four or five years old. A tall, husky, woodsman type, he went to Wisconsin to work in the sawmill. He eventually lost an arm there. He married and had one child, a girl, in 1910. At three weeks, this baby contracted polio and became paralyzed in both legs. The father, Uncle Frank, deserted the family and went to Canada to live and die. I tried once to establish a correspondence with him in his old age, but his letters seemed emotional, excessive, and not quite normal, so I gradually gave up.

I heard stories about poor little Amber while I was growing up... how she never walked. She wore casts on her legs ... had them amputated at age six, replaced them with artificial limbs at the age of eight. At sixteen gangrene and tuberculosis of the bone struck her. In three months she suffered seven operations, each time being amputated higher in the thigh. Although I had never met her, I pitied and felt sad for her often. I did not know that she considered pity, wasted and unwanted. She is very courageous, optimistic and totally committed to others. Destined to play a major role in my life later on, I owe her a tremendous unpayable debt.

Of the six Catterson children, the second and the fifth, Carrie and Rosie, died as infants, leaving Aunt Clara as Mama's oldest sister. Aunt Clara had an aura of mystery and decadence about her. Compared to our house, her house seemed enormous and well furnished. On my childhood visits, I remember being awed by the unaccustomed splendor. Her only daughter loomed tall and strong above me, with a regal beauty. Petite and shapely, Aunt Clara giggled and flirted her way through life. She had lost her first baby and divested herself of two or three husbands before my time. She never lacked male escorts. She reclaimed her family name for herself and her daughter, and only used men for convenience from then on.

Aunt Clara and Cleo made regular visits with the current male escort, bringing boxes and bags of wonderful food, clothing, and other gifts. Like a fairy godmother, she arrived smelling of face powder and perfume when she kissed us. I will never forget her gift to me of the red wool cape. It came with bonnet, socks, and shoes, all red. I, a delighted five year old, became Little Red Riding Hood until I outgrew them, tattered and soiled, a few years later.

Aunt Clara had sparkling brown eyes, and when she laughed, as she did so easily, gold shone from her teeth. I conceived a strong desire then to have a gold tooth some day to give me an irresistible smile. I finally managed a gold cap, but it is so far back in my mouth I have to yawn to reveal it and that is not the same. My first letters were written to Aunt Clara in my baby hand. That hand has now written thousands of letters over the years. Aunt Clara lived to be very elderly. We owed our survival, in part, to her charity.

Of the sister closest to Mama in age, Nellie, my memory is very vague and tenuous. Her presence hovers shadowy and important over my babyhood. Both, Clara and Nellie treated Mama as the "baby" of the family. Babies can be recognized by that pleased little "moue" about the mouth. It comes from knowing you can get whatever you want out of Mama and knowing everyone else knows it as well. My husband has it, and so does my daughter. I should have liked to have it, too, but my little brother ruined that.

Nellie had polio in pre-school years and limped. Her education suffered from it. She had a sweet face and loving ways. She fussed over Mama's children and helped out constantly, sneaking in during quarantine to cook for us. I remember only two things about her, the delicious sensation of the shampoo she gave me, and the terrible night she died. She had two successive husbands and died childless of an abortion when I was about three or four. I have often wondered about it. Was the abortion to please her husband?

With Auntie's death, my mother lost a major emotional support for whom she grieved long after. I always dreaded our annual Memorial Day's visit to the cemetery. When we reached Auntie's grave, Mama's tears would fall long and quietly. In that sense, Auntie's influence lingered for years. Visiting family graves annually is a dying custom. Children have no time or interest in it. At least the children I know feel this way.

Jennie Pearl Catterson - Oct. 3, 1892- May 2, 1979.
Graduated 1911 from New Boston High, New Boston, Illinois.
Taught at Wrayville, IL and Duncan IL .

"Women are twice as brave as Men,
Yet they never seem to have reached the statue stage.

Will Rogers

The Hand's Touch

Our need in human life is such
We wither if denied a touch.

Our glory in maternal nest
Feel baby hand on mother's breast.

Our thirst is quenched, our hopes are fanned
With secret touch of lover's hand.

Strength relied on to the end,
The heart-felt hand clasp of a friend.

And most remembered, most revered,
My mother's touch, by death endeared.

The power of touch we own each day,
Used well, it lightens life's pathway.

Of all hands' touches great or small,
The touch of God surpasses all.

Martha Atkins Emmert

Chapter 4

MAMA

My mother, Jennie Pearl Catterson, is the major influence in my life from birth through my teenage years. I doubt I can contain her in one chapter. Born October 3, 1892, sixth and youngest, she grew up at the edge of New Boston, Illinois, where she completed primary and high school. She graduated Salutatorian in the class of 1911, highly respected as a good girl and a dutiful child. She once told me she had no curiosity about dirty stories and naughtiness. I tried to hide from her how unbearably curious I felt about everything, both good and bad.

My impression remains that she and her mother raised a truck garden and supplied clients in town with the produce. I assume her Papa lived at the Estate, which he managed, only visiting his family from time to time. She prepared for teaching country primary school by attending a summer chatauqua, the custom in those days. She taught for two years at twenty dollars per month, boarding with the Dave Ripley family of Buffalo Prairie, Illinois. Their son, Wilbur, attended her school at Wrayville, Illinois.

When she met my father, Harry Atkins, it was instant fatal attraction on both sides. It ended her career as a paid teacher, though she kept right on teaching her family. Grandmother Catterson knew Harry's family ever since her daughter Nellie had married Daddy's half-cousin. They met Daddy at Nellie's house in Muscatine.

At any rate, Grandmother Catterson forbade the marriage. My mother made her romantic choice. They married in the parsonage of the United Brethren Church of Muscatine by the pastor, Reverend McCorkle, a native of Rochester, Iowa. Mama's wedding dress, which she made, always rested in her trunk, tiers of soft creamy lace in a slender style. I removed the bottom tier years later to wrap around my Bible as a base for the white orchid wedding corsage which my husband bought for our marriage.

Mama never saw her mother again. Due to the distance between Muscatine and Oquawka, as the horse trots, she did not attend her mother's funeral. It is a very short afternoon drive today by car. This had to be a major trauma for her. My sister tells me that in Mama's final years, she spoke often with regret, grieving over her disobedience to her mother.

So, for all practical purposes, I grew up without the influence of grandparents. My mother figured as the center of my life until I became a Christian. I thought her beautiful and sweet. I believed that she and Daddy knew everything. Petite, with dark wavy hair, her pink complexion stayed soft and downy like a peach. She always smelled good. This is remarkable, since I doubt she ever used deodorant, and she worked like a dog. I have heard since, that some few are blessed with scented body odor. I know Mama is one.

I depended upon her emotionally so much that I became ill, if separated, and had to be taken home. I clearly remember an instance when I must have been ten years old. In my late sixties, after Mama died, my sister decided I could handle knowing I had been born a twin, my twin born dead. She feared to tell me before, and Mama never mentioned it, ever. It made me wonder what other secrets, of interest to me, I have never yet been told. I must have been the stronger, to survive. Yet, why have I been so emotionally dependent? It is a puzzle I mull over.

I wish I had known my parents when they were younger. I have an old post card photo of Daddy in a studio sitting on a cardboard crescent moon and above him in big script, "Yes, I'm single. Let's get acquainted." I never knew Daddy like that. Other postcards, some of Mama smiling coyly up, her long dark curls, tied behind in the fashionable enormous ribbon bow, spill softly over one shoulder. She looks so rested.

When I knew her, she often wore Daddy's old overalls, actively attacking the work, whether pulling dead limbs to the house for firewood, or blowing the fire in the kitchen stove to hurry it up for a meal, or cracking the verbal whip to activate lazy children to help her. She hardly ever sat down, or looked rested. In later years she disliked photographs, and I can understand why, now. The years changed and aged her. No time to sit and primp and curl as in those long ago days of postcard beauty. I know them in a depression with five kids to feed.

I asked my sister once, "How do you remember Mama and Daddy when they were young?" "They were happy," she reflected. "Mama always sang, and baked, and cooked. Their house filled with Daddy's many unmarried brothers and sisters." It sounds like a lot of happy communal living. When my first Grandma Atkins died, three years before I arrived, some of my aunts and uncles were quite young. As I mentioned, the two youngest were taken by Grandpa's sister, their Aunt Ida, who later adopted them. Some say Grandpa gave great-aunt Ida the family land, inherited from his mother, to clinch the adoption. If so, I am sure grumbling ensued among his many landless offspring.

By the time my memory kicks in, life no longer blooms with sunshine and roses. The cast now includes hungry children - the scenario, distressing living conditions. I know now my parents' heated arguments stemmed from the pain of living with so few options. You have to fight someone when your kids are cold and hungry and missing out on your dreamed-of privileges and opportunities. Even so, we all knew our parents' love story and the box of forbidden love letters tied up in blue satin ribbons. We saw them embrace warmly each morning and evening as Daddy left and came home from work. We knew they loved each other and us, but poverty, that enemy of peace, dogged our tracks.

Though Mama taught school for two years, she remained as innocent as a rose. Daddy had to teach her all the facts of life after their marriage. She believed in innocence. She kept us as ignorant as she had been, for as long as she could. In a way, I can see why she tried. I never heard of a lesbian, or a homosexual before my early twenties, and then, very vaguely. I feel wistful for my lost innocence.

Mama never needed a haircut. Her hair did not grow to reach her knees, as mine did. She needed no cosmetics. She kept her bloom in spite of suffering and poverty, into middle age and past. I inherited my dimples from her. She stayed slender, as well.

Mama still sang when even I can remember. These are the songs that evoke her lovely soprano voice: "Pretty Red Wing, When You and I Were Young, Maggie, Listen to the Mockingbird, Sweet and Low, Apple Blossom Time." She sang, "Believe Me If All Those Endearing Young Charms," and "Drink To Me Only With Thine Eyes." The song that suited her best started out like this: "We'll build a sweet little nest, somewhere in the West, and let the rest of the world go by."

She taught me to sing. I sang solos in the early primary grades. I remember one long narrative ballad about an Indian maiden called, "The Little Mohee." I sang it at school programs.

When I became an alto at puberty, I figured my singing days were over. Later on, in the church, I learned about alto voices, rejoiced that I had major company as an ex-soprano. I sat next to a strong alto in choir and memorized the part for all the old-time hymns. On some of the new ones I am not as sure-voiced.

Mama lived for her family. Everything else in her life she renounced, or made secondary. All of her incredible talents of tailoring, teaching, cooking, pioneering, she dedicated to our service. This did not prepare her to let go of us easily when the time came for us to leave the nest. I had also to be detached from my children by force of circumstance, in spite of the warning of Mama's example, and my efforts to profit by it.

So many of Mama's quotes are engraved on my brain. "Not failure, but low aim is crime," "Early to bed, early to rise...," "Pretty is as pretty does," "Waste not, want not," (I still save every used bag and envelope). "A penny saved is a penny earned." I have waited a lifetime to have a penny of my own to save ... at last, a pension! "A whistling girl and crowing hen always come to some bad end," (I still whistle. It might help if you happen to come to a bad end). "Sing in bed and the devil dances over your head." I wonder where she got that one! She could quote Wordsworth, Coleridge, Longfellow and Browning by the stanza, and she did. About the time I reached seventh and eighth grade, I remember her trying to write lyrics for popular songs. Her marketing activities continued unsuccessfully for several years.

Mama was a crusader back in the days of universal conformity. She served her family as a Ralph Nader, a Nathan Pritikin and James Dobson, all in one. Although she never marched in protest, she held strong convictions. She never retreated. Her family's well being her primary objective.

Long before the Surgeon General's warning against tobacco, she knew it harmed her Harry. A child smoker, he promised to quit when she married him. He did not. She saved his Bull Durham tobacco bags and stitched them up as bed covers, to point out on what he might better have spent his money.

His strong coffee displeased her as well. She campaigned against his old enameled coffeepot filling slowly with boiled grounds until he had to empty it to make room for the new ones. I think she had a coffee-free and tobacco-free house before he died.

Dandelions annually purged our systems in the spring. Skim milk or buttermilk appeared most often as drink. Meats she served sparingly, to season stews and soups. Before the popularity of health foods, she pared the harmful and unnecessary from the family diet.

In her day, the county regularly sprayed roadside weeds with DDT. Our lane ran past the truck patch and ended at our door. She would have none of it. Alone, she stood the graveled way and prevented having "poison" sprays near her yard, or truck patch. Though she stood barely five feet tall, she prevailed.

As a crusader, Mama resisted the electronic age with full force. She grew up in horse and buggy days, could barely tolerate the automobile, never rode on a train or airplane, and never wore cosmetics, or bobbed her hair.

When old and widowed, a more affluent son sent her a television set by train. She marched it right back to the depot and returned it to him. She did not want the quiet of her home polluted. Much that she fought against, is now prohibited, the rest is recognized as dangerous.

Mama disciplined us. Daddy seldom did. We were born at home and as her babies we nursed at her breast. She kept us healthy with home remedies. She used bacon-rind or bread and milk poultices on boils and infections to "draw them out." We took homemade onion syrup for our coughs and Vicks Vaporub and flannel on our chests for colds. For injuries, we had a bucket of hot water with a bar of Ivory soap floating in it, and a long rest sitting and soaking, hand or foot, or whatever part had been injured. We lived in dread of "lockjaw" (tetanus), rabies, or polio. She took every precaution with us.

To augment Daddy's income, Mama found a use for everything. I remember making mincemeat with her from wild rabbits and squirrels, hominy with dried field corn, and sauerkraut with all the cabbages remaining in the patch as fall ended. The garden, we gleaned thoroughly, cold-packing fruits and vegetables. We harvested wild fruits and berries for jams and jellies. She made our own cottage cheese, breads of all kinds, stews, soups, and cobblers. Too many cracked eggs meant, make jellyroll, or noodles. I have made noodles since age ten, when she designated me to do so. Any stale bread became bread pudding, which I dislike to this day. Ours seemed three-fourths bread and one-fourth pudding.

My mother died in May 1979, fifteen years and one day after my father's death. It happened a month before Michal Rose finished high school in Zaire to begin our fifth furlough in the United States. I was unable to attend the funeral.

Mama was eighty-seven years of age, and nearly blind. My sister had cared for her after my father's death. Mama stayed in her own home as long as possible but spent her final years with my sister Pearl.

"And then you have the shining river,
Winding here and there and yonder.
Its sweep interrupted at intervals by clusters of
Wooded islands threaded by silver channels."

Life On The Mississippi - Mark Twain

High Bridge at Muscatine, Iowa - "The Port City of the Corn Belt" with the Muscatine sky in the background

Chapter 5

DADDY

Harry Way Atkins I, called Colonel, by his brothers and Daddy by us, worked hard all his life. Education, after the sixth grade, proved a luxury his parents could not afford. He matured early. Our poverty can be blamed on the Great Depression, as well as the size of our family, and the fact that Daddy's skills did not match the changing times. He possessed the pioneer virtues of self-reliance and survival instincts. His vast accumulation of nature lore impresses me still. Gifted in animal husbandry, he once saved, during its difficult birth, a bull calf of an expensive sire. Neighbors knew they could call on him for help with veterinary problems.

Daddy showed me how to use leverage, moving heavy logs or sick horses, single-handedly. I have watched him gather wild honey, setting smudge fires at the base of the bee tree, reaching in arms covered with noisy bees, to bring out the heavy honeycomb. I have helped him capture wild swarms of bees by beating pans and throwing water in the air, simulating a storm, causing the bees to cluster on a tree limb surrounding the queen. He then lifted the hive, placing it over the swarm hanging like a huge throbbing bunch of grapes, and pushed them off the limb into the hive. He checked twice to be sure he had the queen, for without her the bees would not stay.

Oh, to go back and spend one more day hunting mushrooms with him. He knew where to find them. I have no idea today where to go to gather morel mushrooms. He knew where the pheasant's nest lay hidden. We borrowed eggs from them for food. Though a hunter, he never killed for sport, only necessity, for survival of his family. He loved animals. He brought home orphaned babies; skunks, raccoons, opossums, birds. We mothered them as best we could, and learned about them.

Santa Claus and the Easter Bunny never failed to revive the child in my father. We believed. Daddy showed us proofs. In houses without chimneys, he showed us cracks in the brown paper covering the holes in the glass panes, where Santa or the Easter Bunny entered. He convinced us. Psychologists marvel at my gullibility. It helped me through childhood. It screened out a lot of misery. I enjoyed the luxury of innocence until I was fourteen. Then it all hit me at once: Santa, the Easter Bunny, and the Stork. The last, was the worst - my life fell into the dismals, during those teenage years that followed.

During no other time but Christmas time, Daddy invaded the kitchen at night. He would boil up the sorghum, pop big pans full of popcorn, butter his arms up to the elbows and proceed to make popcorn balls, which we ate at leisure.

Another thing Daddy always did was clay modeling. Modeling clay appeared mysteriously and Daddy would have an orgy of modeling little wild animals of all kinds. Pheasants and other birds would perch around the house for a while and finally disappear through wear and tear. Years later, trying my own hand at clay in a college classroom, I remembered Daddy, and wondered at the significance of that creative urge in him.

He loved children and they loved him. He also loved simple folk music. After we had a radio, he liked to listen to the Saturday Night Barn Dance. Usually he had an old accordion, Jew's harp, or harmonica. He would sit outside in an old chair on the porch and play and play. I can still seem to hear his favorite tunes: "Darling Nellie Gray," "The Little Old Sod Shanty on the Plains", "Bury Me Not On The Lone Prairie" – all with a plaintive air.

Spring, glorious spring – we knew it had arrived when Daddy came home with the first spray of red bud, the first Mayflowers, the first violets. Off with shoes and socks. We went off to the woods to gather more flowers to fill jars and glasses with the glory of Spring. Later on, he arrived triumphantly, his old battered felt hat in his hand, full of wild strawberries, raspberries, then blackberries. Did I inherit my love of beauty from my Dad? What about my love of flowers? Mama, forced to practicality, spent her time providing food, clothing, and shelter. She promoted beauty of thought, ideals, beauty of needlework. She crafted so well, the wrong side of her garments appear as beautiful as the right side. As for me, never let me catch you looking at the wrong side of anything I sew!

Both my parents read avidly. I can see Daddy in his chair of an evening, the paper before his face, reading out parts of it to Mama, who was sitting sewing nearby. He kept informed politically and socially. He always voted, never revealing for whom, although we knew he esteemed President Roosevelt. He insisted one must vote for the man, not the party. Will Rogers' newspaper columns gave him much enjoyment.

He was too softhearted and generous ever to succeed in business. While peddling melons at the roadside stand, or by truck, his most notable business efforts, if someone hesitated at the price, and Daddy liked him, he got a melon cheap, or free. His last twenty-five years of life, he spent studying antiques. He became part-owner in an antique store in Muscatine, and seemed thoroughly adapted to attending auctions and acquiring pieces for resale.

Daddy, tall, spare, Lincolnesque, had a hairless chest, but an overabundance of hair on his head. I inherited that huge mop and passed it on to my son. Daddy stuttered sometimes, especially if he became excited or angry. He loved peanut butter and crackers. He loved my mother Jenny, whom he courted by rented horse and buggy across the toll bridge ... the old "High Bridge" separating Muscatine, Iowa from Illinois. That toll bridge, featuring hills and curves is now a bygone centerpiece for Fourth of July picnics and fireworks to those who thronged the Riverside Park. During their courtship days, Mama and Daddy wrote each other daily. They visited every possible weekend. Sometimes she went to Muscatine on the riverboat, The Helen Blair. They dated with her sister Nellie, and Daddy's cousin Ike, or his brother Ray and Edith. They picnicked at Salisbury Bridge, now a monument in the Salisbury Recreation Area in Illinois. He did not go to her box social for fear he could not afford her box.

In my childhood and youth, Muscatine thrived as the center of the pearl button industry. Pearl buttons figured significantly in my childhood. My Dad, an artisan button cutter in the days of backyard shops, stood with three or four other men in rubber aprons and boots through the cold of winter. Taking a clam shell gathered in summer, he fit cylindrical saws to a machine turned by hand and under running water cut out blanks of different sizes for buttons. He received so much for each pail filled, as piecework.

In those days women all over town, would be issued a stack of cards, packets of tinfoil squares, needle, and thread and buttons. I have seen my aunts card buttons, swiftly and almost automatically. As piecework, it provided pin or grocery money for the wives. I cannot remember my mother ever carding buttons. She seemed to always be patching overalls, darning holes in socks, or creating something from her trousseau clothing for us to wear. During the Depression, she embroidered linens for the bakery lady in return for day old bread.

My father always claimed to be Welsh, my mother half-Irish and half-Pennsylvania Dutch. I feel I have inherited the melancholy of the Welsh and the emotionalism of the Irish. The German part of my heritage is recessive in me. I have always been proud of my Irish blood, for no reason whatsoever. I imagined the Irish to be carefree, jolly and full of romance, which is what I wished to be myself.

Although emotionally dependent upon my Mother, Daddy's world drew me with greater passion. His world of rivers and woods and fields of corn ... his world of animals and husbandry, and the beauty of bud and flower. By day I followed Daddy's footsteps. When nightfall came, I wanted Mama and stories by a warm stove. I wonder if Daddy ever guessed how much he gave me. It is only lately I have begun to realize it myself.

Daddy died on May 1, 1964 at the age of 73. I learned of his death during my second term in Africa. I served our post of Nsona Mpangu as a short wave operator. The telegram from home had gone astray, and reached a distant Catholic bush post. They relayed it to me by short-wave radio several weeks after the burial.

While I was grieving for my father, the African women out of sympathy for me brought a small money offering wrapped in cloth, which I treasure to this day.

"Sisters are certainly the most satisfying relations.
They are your own age, which your children are not,
your own sex, which your husband is not,
and your blood relative, which your friends are not.
No one else will fill the gap."

Mary Thomas

Big Sister Pearl Speaks

When I was just a little girl
I was my parents' priceless Pearl.
I learned to talk and sing and read.
They said my mind was bright, indeed.

And then a brother came to stay.
A baby we called Harry Way.
O, how I loved and cherished him.
Such memories cannot grow dim.

Soon Harry Way was joined by Paul.
Our family grown to five in all.
Mama's helper I was cast.
I learned to diaper very fast.

I helped my folks along life's route.
Inside the home or peddling fruit.
I barely had the boys in hand.
When Martha came to join our band.
At last I had a sister dear.

I combed her hair, I dried her tear.
I tried to teach her all I knew,
But she dreamed dreams, without a clue.

And then one special Christmas eve,
A gift from Santa, I believe.
Came baby Larry, living doll.
I soon was at his beck and call.

I pleased my father. I was smart,
My selling powers, a gift, an art.
Within the home I worked each day.
I watched my mother turning gray.

And through the years, though wed, of course
I stayed quite closely to my source.
We often read and fed together
through days of calm or stormy weather.

And when at last my Dad went home,
Leaving Mama all alone,
She then became my priceless girl,
For her, I'd named my Jennie Pearl.

And through the memories of our life
we strolled as old and younger wife.

We each had five, two girls, three men.
(Our youngest ones, both dead by then.)

And thus I've lived with Jesus' aid.
I've raised my family, made the grade.
And kids from here to Arkansas,
Call Harold "Gramps" and me "Grandma."

But still a part of ME's a girl.
I look back on that little Pearl,
And think of those I mothered then
Will they come home to me - and when?

Martha Atkins Emmert

Big Sister Pearl

Chapter 6

BIG SISTER

"Put that chair opposite the window!" commanded Pearl, my 15 year old sister.

Eight years old and powerless, I sniffled and whined. "What does 'opposite' mean? I've put it everywhere and you will not tell me where..." and so on. She never did tell me. I must have hit the magic spot at last.

I try to recreate in my mind the fifteen year old girl, who very early in life assumed major responsibility for housework and the care of four younger children. I cannot remember her youthful, or carefree.

I can see her reading to all of us in the dim light of evenings. Mama patched torn clothing, Daddy read behind his newspaper, and the rest of us flopped wherever our fancy chose. Stern even in her reading, rather than repeating our requests, she began at the beginning of Mama's "Big Blue Book" of literary selections, and read straight through. She never skipped "The Raven," or "The Face on the Barroom Floor," or any of the other wrenching ballads, as I begged her to do.

Forced to maintain authority, Pearl could not allow herself the pleasure of giving in to our pleas, or showing favoritism. Sober, quiet, in control, we could not fool her, or manipulate her as we could and did our mother. Later on, she used this training by taking care of pre-school children for working mothers. With her own five, she added a house full ... wall-to-wall toddlers. No pandemonium, however, she ran a tight ship. They knew what they could and could not do. Firm and kind, she believed in discipline and obedience. Many of those children, grown-ups today, write lovingly to "Grandma Martin" as they call her, having found in her care, structure and guidance they lacked elsewhere.

Named for both parents, Pearl Harriet, daughter of Jennie Pearl and Harry Atkins, she bore bravely the burden of first-born; first fruit of their proud, young love. So much was expected of her from the beginning, she seems to have assumed command as fast as it became necessary for Mama to have an assistant.

Mama and Pearl, so very different in personality, always lived in close proximity. Until one day the roles switched, and mother became daughter until Mama's death. There were similarities in their lives. They each ran off quite young to marry against their mother's wishes. They each had five children, of whom the youngest in both cases died tragic, youthful deaths.

Pearl had a fine brow and nose from Daddy, but her hair inclined to wave like Mama's. Her even features, compared to my snub nose and low hairline, decided me very early as the ugly duckling of the two. Even when I grew to tower over her, she retained her psychological supremacy. We were never pals, or buddies. My sister and I grew close after I married and became a mother myself, and saw my sister as another human being. Do I still depend on her emotionally? Probably – she seems dearer each year, and harder to part with after visits.

Pearl became a Christian in 1943, a year after my own conversion. Her husband accepted Christ three years later and has been a constant witness, in church and out, to the saving power of Jesus.

When Daddy died, Mama came first on Pearl's agenda. I worked in Africa, but Pearl lived nearby. Because Mama wanted to feel independent, Pearl let her stay in her own home most of the time. Only when Mama became blind in her eighties, did she move in with my sister. During those years alone, Pearl faithfully checked on her several times a day. She spent evenings reading to Mama and visiting with her as otherwise she would sit alone by her stove. My overseas missionary career depended on Pearl's care of Mama.

Pearl's children and grandchildren too, helped to see if Grandma Atkins had a need. My mother held dear by this large family of my sister, taught them as diligently as ever, her maxims of health and right living. Even my daughter-in-law, who only met her once, respects and honors her still.

Our mother, never easy to please because of her high standards, ("not failure, but low aim, is crime") did not aim low, or give up easily. If she lived with you (or you with her), as she did with my big sister, it meant constant critical comment on childcare, diet, weight, etc. I pitied my sister during those years. My sister reassured me. "I just let it go in one ear and out the other. I forget all about it. I am going to do all I can. I want no regrets after she is gone." In fulfilling this vow, she risked alienating her own children, for often Mama's demands and requirements conflicted with theirs. For instance, Mama vetoed television in her presence, including prime time TV.

When Mama died, she left an old house ready for demolition, and a plot of ground. My sister had earned it a dozen times. With the money from the land, she fulfilled a lifelong dream of having a dining room and table large enough for all her family to sit down together for a meal. Now, when the family gathers on Sundays and holidays, the diners stretch away toward a vanishing point in the dining room's distance.

It is a beautiful depiction of a Christian family, usually numbering between forty and seventy people.

Denied an education, my sister married very young and had her big family. She had the potential to be great in business. Her mind, quick and clever, she excelled in salesmanship and managerial ability. She speaks with authority, is decisive and efficient, and never weakens her position by confiding or complaining. She tries to shield those of us who are feebler, but avoids being managed by others. With cool common sense, she is as severe with herself as with anyone else.

After I screwed up my courage and learned to drive at age 52, my sister finally confessed, to my amazement, she had also feared learning to drive. My fear deterred me from driving for years. "Sure, I felt afraid," she admitted, "and I got lost, but I just did it." I thought her incapable of fear. I lacked that kind of grit-your-teeth guts. Someone else did it for me. I let them. I avoided responsibility. How brave Pearl is, and how free of self-pity.

There is one more similarity between Pearl and Mama. Pearl also devoted her considerable gifts to child rearing, just as Mama did. Who is to say she did not choose the highest good? She endangered her health by having a baby every year for four years. She reveled in babies, but waited seven years for her final baby, my little Martha, my namesake. She took in other babies in need of mothering. Her family crosses the boundaries of blood, spreading her influence farther than she dreams.

Her pace considerably slowed down, she survives today, a diabetic, a victim of several strokes, major surgery, shattering grief and many losses. There is never any doubt in her house full of family, as to who is the boss, and who has the final word. As her children troop home with grandchildren and great grandchildren, she is kissed by one and all on arrival, and when leaving.

To me, her word always ruled, and I am not about to doubt it now. I do get different versions of childhood memories whenever I consult my several siblings. I am old enough to realize that none of us could write each other's story successfully. We each see so differently from our special viewpoint in the family. We bring such different temperaments, different hopes, different fears and they color our memories.

Though we disagree, what we each remember is true. It is true for the one remembering. The impact of its truth marks our lives, though translated quite differently in other memories. How different and varied each of our five stories would be, set side by side. Yet the solid truths of our family remain unchanged, the bulwark around which each of our lives eddied until it found its own resting-place.

Pearl and Harold's baby, Martha Marie married in 1966 to her childhood sweetheart. My husband, Leon performed the ceremony as we were home at the time. Martha Marie had never missed a Sunday in church with her mother. They had never been apart for a day without contact. In October the same year, Martha and Mike were killed instantly by a drunk driver on the way to a prayer meeting. My sister aged overnight. Her hair became snow white. "Would she blame God?" I wondered. No, they kept a brave witness and God led them through the years of grief that followed.

Her oldest son, my first nephew, Harry Thomas, with his wife Claudette, came to Zaire as volunteers for a year in 1988-1989 to work as Mission Engineer and garage accountant. All my Christian life I prayed to be joined by family in serving Christ - Harry and Claudette surprised and blessed us in this glad act of sacrificial service.

1993 - My nephew Harry Martin with wife Claudette gave a year of service as volunteers in our Zaire mission during our final year in the mission field.

I know how a prize watermelon looks when
it is sunning its fat rotundity --
how to tell when it is ripe without plugging it --
I know the crackling sound it makes when the
carving knife enters –
I can see the split fly along in front of the blade
- its halves fall apart – I know how a boy looks,
behind a yard long slice of that melon.

Mark Twain

The Boys during WW II Paul Staley, Larry Daniel, Harry Way Atkins

Chapter 7

THE BOYS

My two older brothers came between my big sister and myself. Born less than two years apart, they enjoyed an ongoing power struggle for supremacy during their growing years. We made great efforts to treat them as equals at all times. They were always together until separated by World War II. My third brother, the baby, arrived before I expected competition. In fact, he definitely displaced me, and as my elders whispered to one another, "Her nose is out of joint," meaning, of course, I suffered from jealousy. I needed Mama's lap and the feel of my head tucked under her chin. I needed her arms free to enfold me. I did not want to be a big sister. I wanted to be the baby. I did not think him cute as the others did. To me, he seemed big enough to know better. I thought of him as spoiled. Others delighted in his sunny charms.

Looking back, I am sorry I let him take the blame more than once for my misdeeds. I even led him into trouble, but Mama cherished him as her last-born. She wanted him a baby as long as possible. She must have nursed him two years.

I remember feeling offended and jealous, watching him claim her.

Photos of Larry reveal a baby boy with blond curls, blue eyes, and a dimpled smile. My sister dressed him in my baby dresses sometimes. "See," she pointed out, "He is cute enough to be a girl!" In fact, he did look remarkably like our cousin Betty, who was about the same age. Betty grew up and as Betty Walters, became the mayor of Buffalo, Iowa. Larry died in 1948.

Larry and I attended grade school, and later, high school, together. He often complained that his studies were not a challenge. Perhaps, his teachers failed to see and meet his needs. His intelligence shone. He grew to be the tallest of us all at six feet two inches, and the handsomest. As a young man he boxed in carnivals to earn money. He entered the Navy at Shoemaker, California where he served as Seaman 2/C. He boxed for the Navy, as well.

Before he left the Navy he married and had one child, a girl. I have never met her, although I have tried to trace her and write to her. Larry, at 21 died in a power line accident while learning to be a lineman. This tragedy occurred a month before my wedding, leaving my parents pale and frail for the ceremony. I can still feel Daddy trembling all the way down the aisle. I buried Larry's death and funeral in my subconscious, deep enough down to be bearable, not to be dwelt on often, or for very long. Whenever I read David's cry, "Oh, Absalom, my son, my son ... Oh my son, Absalom," I think of Larry and grieve within at his early death.

"The Boys," Harry and Paul, were major influences in my life. I spent my childhood being a tomboy so I could be included in their activities. My oldest brother, Harry, tells me he had dreams of being a doctor or a veterinarian. Born in 1918, in time to keep Daddy out of World War I, he had less time than I did to be the baby of the family, before a brother followed him. I idolized my older brothers throughout my childhood and looked to them for affirmation and worth.

I entered into their escapades willingly. When dared to eat a raw egg ... I ate it. I had to measure up. I learned to walk on knee stilts buckled to my legs, as they did. We also used high stilts. On them we could perch on the shed roof. I remember falling from a barn rafter and my overall leg being caught by a nail. I cannot remember how I got out of that. I followed my big brothers to the tops of trees. I followed them as far and as long as they permitted me. The War ended all of that, changing all of our lives forever.

Harry pursued many of the interests learned from my father. This brother also learned to oil paint, do woodcarvings, and many clever crafts. Brother Harry served in the Army with the Military Police and with the 8th Fighter Command. He engaged in the war for five years in England and Belgium, receiving nine or ten decorations for sharp shooting and bravery.

Harry, as oldest, served as our leader. I thought them both quite handsome. Paul, closest to me in age and temperament, usually supported his brother. He served as my champion, nicknamed me Meggy, and did his best to give me the material things I longed for, such as my first locking diary, my first birthstone watch, and out of his first earnings, gifts of jacks and roller skates. When I finally finished High school, Paul gave me my first typewriter. Tender hearted, loving, and sensitive, the war years must have caused him much suffering. He joined the Navy in January of 1941, enlisting for a six-year stint. In the Navy he learned to be a pipe fitter, a profession he has since followed.

Paul married during his Navy years and had three sons. Later divorced, he has a second family in South Carolina. His first son, Paul, Junior by his first marriage is in appearance, a replica of his father. This nephew is very dear to me. He is a fine Christian lawyer near Charleston, West Virginia, and has a happy Christian family.

My brothers and I corresponded at great length throughout the war years. They did not want me to join the women's military. Both boys were cheated out of post-primary education because of the Depression and the War, but they have resumed their education since. Paul at 73, studied for a Bachelor of Arts degree in South

Carolina. Harry, a widower at 75, surprised us by taking a new bride. My father now has a great-great grandson named Harry Way Atkins V.

"I remember the squirrel hunts and prairie chicken hunts –
how we turned out, mornings while it was dark – chilly and dismal
dogs – raced and scampered about and knocked small people down
and made no end of unnecessary noise.
After three hours tramping
we arrived back wholesomely tired, laden with game,
very hungry and just in time for breakfast."

Mark Twain

Mama with Martha, Paul, Harry and Larry (front) around 1931

Chapter 8

HUNTING AND FISHING

Today, although I support laws restricting sales of guns this is not my background. A gun, a dog, a good knife, tools, sons - these prized possessions belonged to the rural semi-pioneer life led by many of my father's generation. Life has not always been fast foods and plumbing. It still is not among the majority of the world's peoples.

To ask today's ecologists to read with sympathy and understanding a life based on wild foods, both vegetable and animal, is a daring thought. I sat in church with one, my grown daughter when a fur coat came in and heard this child of mine, as militant as her maternal grandmother say too loudly, "Rats, where's my catsup bottle?"

To my knowledge, we always hunted in season with a license. We children were taught to handle, use and respect guns. I remember shooting squirrels with a .22 rifle. I confess, I grew decreasingly bloodthirsty with age. I once killed a chipmunk with a slingshot and privately grieved over its little limp body, while being praised for my marksmanship. My grandsons, dismissing my tales of youth as so much hot air, came to attention when grandma hit the targets on their Nintendo game like a pro. I got to say, "I told you so!"

We survived the Depression because we hunted for food to feed a family of seven. Wild meat predominated on our fall and winter tables: rabbit, squirrel, pheasant, opossum, raccoon, and deer. We even ate porcupine, bear and muskrat. I do not recall eating turtles as my older siblings do.

We hunted and trapped for furs to sell. We dried and sent the skins to some fur company. Our attic would fill during winter months with hides hanging, fur inside, or stacked in stiff piles. I learned the proper method of removing pelts of mink, weasel, skunk, beaver, and other animals as well. I skinned many a mink, stretching the fur on a slender board to hang, wondering if I would ever wear one. As it happened, I did wear a mink scarf, a gift from my husband, when I graduated from seminary in 1949. Sometimes I worked with my dad. He cut and I held. The cut must be carefully made, with a very sharp knife, from one hind foot to the other, passing under the tail. Then the hide must be slowly peeled off the tail, legs and body by inserting fingers into the previously made slit. Daddy prepared the boards ahead of time. He whittled and smoothed the edges of different sized boards to fit the shapes of assorted furs. After stretching them tightly, he carefully tacked the bottom edge to prevent shrinkage.

My little brother and I ran a trap line before school when I was about fourteen, and he eleven. We trapped along a frozen creek in holes visible under the trees along the banks.

We enjoyed crunching the creek ice underfoot as we made our way from trap to trap. Sometimes water still ran underneath the ice and we would break through into it, feeling the cold through our boots and socks. Other places, all the water would be frozen, lifted off the bottom, ready to shatter with sharp, tinkling sounds. The clear, cold air and the precarious path sharpened our senses, alerting our whole bodies for action.

I coached my little brother, Larry, "Now, if there is an animal in the trap, do not hit it until I pull it out from under the tree and step back from it, especially, if it is a skunk." We usually caught rabbits and a few weasels. Although rabbit fur had little value on the market, we could eat the meat. Larry and I actually caught a skunk in our trap. He had pulled the trap in under the tree as far as it would go. The big, bushy black and white tail moved around, mixed with the trap, chain and stake. "Now wait!" I cried, trying to be calm and cool in spite of our excitement at catching a salable pelt. "Do not hit until I tell you to!" I yelled excitedly.

I maneuvered the chain around my stick and dragged the skunk out. He reared up snarling at me, and the sight must have triggered something in my brother. Larry whacked the skunk with his stick. The skunk, far from dead, let loose with his ammunition in full force on me from head to toe. What a stink! We finally dragged our smelly loot home and tried in vain to clean up, but I reeked of skunk for days, and had to finally bury my clothing.

In the spring, Larry and I made some money collecting groundhog tails and turning them in for a bounty - ten or twenty cents a tail. We expended great energy digging in holes for ground hogs and carrying water to pour in and "drown 'em out." We caught enough to keep us trying for more. Back then (in the 'thirties) we never heard of an allowance. We talked of just cutting off a small part of the tail and letting it grow back for another time, but I do not think we ever did this.

Woods in winter! What enchantment! Everything transformed. Leaves of faded splendor, rimmed in frost and snow set off each branch with highlights of white. Precariously perched snow fell on our heads with soft thumps while in sheer pleasure we tramped under the trees and bushes. When our grandsons were two and four years old, I took them to a snowy woods to introduce them to the joys of winter. We took a path to fairyland and making a turn, the car vanished from sight. "Grandma," they wailed, "When can we go back to the car? We're scared in here." Scared? In a woods? I could not believe my ears. How could it be? In only two generations, my family had lost its roots in the pioneer living of my childhood, where we found our safest place in our tent in the deep woods. How I loved the sounds, sights and scents of forest living. I want to record it, to make sure it is known, hopefully, understood.

We hunted fish, too. I have so many happy memories of fishing. I have only fished in the simplest, most childish way, with a pole, line, hook, sinker and floater. I started fishing with a piece of string, a bent safety pin and a stick. With worms and a stream to fish in, we always caught something. We ate the fish, even though they contained tiny, needle-sharp bones. I would like to fish again some day, but I am afraid of today's sophisticated equipment.

I want to go back to a rickety little bridge over a clear creek, sparkling and gurgling through sunlight and shade. I want to lean over and rest my arms on a railing, and watch happily and quietly as my worm descends, enters the water, and wiggles. I want to watch what happens as the sunfish sees it, swims over, nibbles the bait, then retreats. I want to feel that tug of life through the line and pole as the bullhead tries to get the food without the hook. I do not really want to catch him today. I am not hungry. I just want to play the game, and remember. I want a reason to bask in the warmth and peacefulness, soothed by the bird song, the rumor of water, the scent of marshy growth. I want to perspire gently and taste the salt on my lips again in the soft breezes of summers past.

Have you ever seined for minnows with a little brother, both in bare feet and rolled up pant's legs? We took our net and held it at the end of a culvert where the creek rushed through. We tried to catch the elusive darting minnows as they shot through the turbulent waters. A whole morning passes in wonderful companionship and total concentration of effort and teamwork. Tired, wet and content, we bring our catch home in an old bucket of creek water, to be used later as bait, to snare larger fish.

When the rivers froze over, we could fish with Daddy through a hole made in the ice. We were allowed to try our hand at spearing or gigging large catfish or carp as they came near the hole. Not as restful as summer fishing, but an exciting, primitive method learned from bears, perhaps.

As a child of ten, I assisted my big brothers in a system of lake fishing in upper Minnesota. We used row boats. Although we knew the water was deep and dangerous. We had no life preservers. On the banks we set trot lines in different places with baited hooks, staked firmly against a possible catch. These trot lines could then be checked from time to time without a boat. From the boat we threw out baited lines tied securely to large corked bottles, which served to alert us as to the location of our lines. The bottle, next morning, if towed a great distance from its launching place, meant possibly a big fish, too tired to fight. This is how we made our contribution to family survival. We had never seen fish as large as the wall-eyed pike, or the pickerel of northern Minnesota lakes.

In the early forties, we lived on an island in the Cedar River, cut off from the mainland by a narrow stream. A flood occurred while we farmed there, and most of the farm went under water, except the hill on which the house and barn perched. To reach the road, we traveled by rowboat for half a mile, or so. We lost crops, but when the floodwaters receded, all the low places on our island held diminishing diminutive lakes in which many fish were trapped. I can still remember them trying to swim and escape with an inch of their back exposed to sight.

We worked very hard to cure the fish we could not eat at the time. For this, we had only salt and smoke as preservatives. My Dad made racks in metal barrels on which we placed whole, cleaned and salted fish. He made smoldering corn cob fires under these fish and covered the barrels with burlap bags, which we called gunny sacks. The salted fish smoked for several days until they were cured and dry enough to keep for eating later.

APPLES

When young and small our apples grew,
Without the spray and picking crew.
And if we had no apple tree,
The ones beside the road were free.

Apples fed us, flesh and soul;
And Spring foreshadowed heaven's goal.
When in a world of pink and white,
We breathed their scent in pure delight.

In summer leafed out thick and green,
The birds and I could hide unseen
And dream about the joys ahead
When those green apples turned to red.

But sometimes pushed by hunger's pain,
Those big green apples, hung or lain,
invited us to try a chew,
Though aches could come, our tummy knew.

When apples spread their autumn feast
we ate and ate, restraint released!
And then when we could eat no more
our mother called us to the door.

"Now, take these pans, and go," she said,
"And gather up each fallen red.
The time has come to save the good:

And store them for our winter's food.

Stirred apple butter by the day.
Peeled for sauce - threw worms away.
Dried on grates both low and high,
and everyday ate apple pie!

Then I grew up, and what a blow,
I worked where apples couldn't grow.
And when I suffered from this luck,
We searched for imports, each a buck!

But now I stand in orchard bright,
The trees all loaded, just my height.
And know again my childhood zeal
for apple scent and sight and feel.

And though the ground is covered red
I need not gather up the dead.
My spirit soars, my heart's aflutter,
No standing, stirring apple butter.

And as we load our van complete
With yellows, reds and cider sweet,
Enough to last the winter through
Our thanks, dear growers, go to you!

Martha Atkins Emmert

Chapter 9

GLEANING

The forest provided another precious commodity – maple syrup. At age ten and later, I helped my dad choose the sugar maples to tap, as soon as the snow began to melt and the sap began to rise in the trees. Daddy made spigots (hollowed pieces of soft wood), which we carried with us as we went from tree to tree, drilling holes with a brace and a bit. We hung a bucket on each tree to catch the flow of sap, which we then collected at regular intervals to prevent the sap from overflowing. Meanwhile, back at the house, Mama mobilized her largest boiling kettles and stirred up a fire in the big wood range in the kitchen.

The run, out of sight of our house, made a fairly extensive circle through the woods, before returning back to the house. To gather sap we took empty pails that we filled at each tree, then carried back to Mama's waiting kettles for boiling down. I cannot remember selling any Maple syrup, but I am not sure. We needed a lot of syrup for our family. When it ran out before next spring, Mama boiled old, hard Christmas candies in water, and we used that for syrup.

In the early spring, we hunted morel mushrooms. Mama hunted her favorite greens - dandelions, sour dock, lamb's quarter, plantain, wild mustard, pepper grass, horseradish leaf, among others. We hunted wild asparagus along fence rows by country roads, available in abundance. We gathered as regularly as we would from our own garden patch.

In the summer mulberries ripened, white and purple. With a cloth spread under the tree, we shook the branches and collected until our pans were full. They were best cooked with rhubarb to add tartness. Wild grapes made a special topping for pancakes, or bread. Mama boiled them then squeezed them through a sugar sack. Thickened with sugar and flour, they made thin syrup. The flavor of wild grapes is strong and distinctive, and needs to be extended to taste best. Grapes stained our hands, tongues and faces.

I do not know if wild plums exist any more, but we used to gather them, plum jam being just about our favorite, and easy to make. We gathered wild crab apples for jelly. Wild raspberries, blackberries and dewberries as big as a man's thumb grew along the edges of woods and in clearings.

When we moved into our present housing development in 1990, I picked enough wild berries for four cobblers. Those bushes are now gone, replaced by lawns, houses and cement driveways. Although commercial berry patches replace a small percent of these lost berry patches, they cost more than the picking. In the wild patches of my youth, Mama taught me never to trample the plants, or vines, always to pick all of the ripe fruit, large or small, and to treat the patch as though it were my own.

The Fall brought outings, when, clothed in our oldest, mended clothing, we searched the woods for bittersweet berries which we pulled out of tree tops, cut up and bunched for sale. We looked through the crisp, scented leaves for butternuts, black walnuts and hickories. We garnered the clusters of hazelnuts from the bushes along the road, later to wrest the nuts from their tough husks before they became stiff and dry. We saved some for winter, and some would go to pay the grocer's bill. On cold Fall days, we could always find two rocks and crack nuts, to relieve our hunger until meal time.

In the fall we hunted ginseng. Even today, I cannot go for a walk in the woods without looking for ginseng. Those horizontal five-lobed leaves are imprinted on my mind. Above the center of the leaves, would be a cluster of white flowers or red berries, depending on the season. I thought my dad knew where every ginseng plant grew, in several counties. I followed him for miles on end, over low and high rises, stumbling on rotting logs, climbing over downed trees, with the scent of fallen leaves in our nostrils, the song of birds in our ears and the cool breeze of autumn refreshing our faces.

If the plants we found were old enough to have large roots, we dug them. The ginseng root is incredibly wrinkled, folded and twisted into grotesque shapes, sometimes wlth one, or several taproots, sometimes with a shape like a gnarled, old man. Thc color is ivory tan, when scrubbed clean of dirt with a toothbrush. I cleaned them for drying. Once the ginseng roots were thoroughly dry, we packaged them and sent them off to some dealer for the Orient, who sent us several dollars an ounce. Once in an African market, I found a tube of ginseng toothpaste from China, which I bought in a fit of nostalgia.

I miss the hunting and harvesting we did as a family. We seemed happiest and closest to one another when we were all occupied, working for our common good. When I returned to Iowa, I looked in vain for the places dear to my memory. Todd's park, which was not a park at all, but a forest preserve along a river, with springs to clean and use, and miles to scour for food, firewood, and healthy exercise has disappeared.

Though Iowa is my home state, I can find no "home place." I know where I feel at home, though. My "home" is Midwestern, providing four definite seasons, each changing just in time to make way for the next. My home must have a body of fresh watcr nearby, for I grew up on the Mississippi River. The rivers of Iowa live as presences in my memory. I feel their absence. To be fully restored, I must have woods enough to walk an hour or two, undisturbed by houses, or cars, or people. Let the trees be oak and maple, alive with birds, and bugs, and small, wild animals. I look for a quiet place where strawberries ripen in the clearings, and berry bushes reach out thorny reminders of treats to come. At "home" I find mosses and ferns, lady slipper and bluebell, violets, daisies and thistles growing freely in season, for my eyes to feast on.

I have found a reasonable facsimile of my childhood home in the Upper Peninsula of Michigan. Sitting at my desk, looking through birch and cedar to Lake Huron, I wonder why I have the privilege of tasting again the peace and joy of nature that I knew in my childhood. Not my goal in life, I did not search for it. God gives in mysterious ways, more than we can ask, or think. Why am I astonished at His gifts, after receiving His greatest? Why me? I do not know. I am grateful. The child in me delights in every sight and sound, for the time allotted me to enjoy them.

"God is the mightiest environment of any human life. God is an Inheritance possessing which all poverty is cancelled and all other wealth made as of no account."

G. Campbell Morgan

Martha's humble birth place and "Mama" in Muscatine, Iowa

Chapter 10

HOMES SWEET HOMES

A row of photographs lay before me, old homes, forlorn, dilapidated, ... the way old houses look when visited decades later. My sister has found and captured them with her camera. She wants me to have a sense of my roots. Uprooted so often, I am reluctant to fix myself in any soil without some promise of permanence. The photographs of my birth-home attracts me, due to flowers in front. Four more to follow, of which I retain no memory. She tries to fill me in, make them live by furnishing addresses. There is still a void in my memory bank when I punch in "Old Home Place."

When tenting is mentioned, my memory stirs. I was three years old, maybe four, I had a baby brother, by then. Whatever we owned as furniture, lived in the tent with our family of seven. My grandfather Atkins, with our step-grandmother, occupied a nearby tent, I am told. The setting, a woods by a river near Green, Iowa, the first home I can remember. We tried to forget the perilous winter, just passed, when over Christmas we were all sick and quarantined with Scarlet Fever, including our baby boy, newborn on Christmas eve.

All that I recall of beauty and comfort seem to go back to tent-camping days along Iowa rivers. We were all close and cuddled in a safety assured by our parent's nearness. We awakened to the scents of coffee, bacon and wood smoke, never-to-be-forgotten aromas. Following my Dad in sun streaked paths beneath giant trees to find food ... scrambled pheasant eggs with wild onions for Easter, fried mushrooms and other delicacies.

From that remembered idyll, we inevitably went back to town for winter. I have a photo of a little girl with tied up braids, holding a big Christmas doll. My doll, was given by Auntie, Mama's sister, Nellie, who died three months later. In that house we said, "Goodbye" to Uncle Frank, Mama's brother, before he went to Canada for good. I remember sitting on his knee, his missing arm with shirtsleeve pinned shut, a vague worry to me. Perhaps, that year, Daddy carried me on his shoulder to the Community Christmas tree where we children received free fruit and candy, and a toy from a jolly Santa Claus.

After Auntie died, Daddy may have wanted to get Mama away from Muscatine and her grief. Our annual migration took us toward Cedar Rapids near Vinton, Shellsburg and Urbana, Iowa. Daddy built a precarious house for us to live in then he peddled melons that summer. Aunt Clara came and clothed us.

By 1929 we were living near Urbana, in a farmhouse, raising green beans for a canning factory. My big sister reached eighth grade just as I started school in a one-room country schoolhouse. She had capably sold melons and produce from a roadside stand all that summer before.

That year, Shep our dog, was hit by a car. He died on the hot, dusty road in Mama's arms. This grief, personal and sharp, stands out in my memory. A happier scene is also etched there. On our way to school, a bridge crossed a little creek. That spring, a sea of bluebells bloomed. The scene returns repeatedly throughout my life. The cool shade, the scent of the bluebells, the vision of the blues, pinks and lavenders called to me as a child, to come and live among them in joy, but school insisted I leave behind the beauty and peace of the bluebell woods.

From there we moved back to Louisa County, on Muscatine Sand Island. This area, reputed to produce excellent melons, also produced sweet potatoes and black-eyed peas. There we planted all those products and also attempted raising some sheep for the first time. We must have butchered, for I can recall the taste of mutton. Mama made batches of fried bread, donuts and other foods cooked in mutton fat, that only our famine could force us to eat. I remember the house having an upstairs we could not use. We found no visible means of reaching it, except through an outside, upstairs window. A haunted house perhaps?

I attended Hopewell School, just across the melon field, without my sister's benign protection. My brothers, so kind at home, would not have me hanging after them during recess. Mrs. Montgomery, a kind enough teacher, had favorites. I did not number among them. Timorous, vulnerable and feeling forsaken, I dreaded school. I retreated to library books. At that school, I remember hearing about the presidential elections for the first time. Someone came to school and at the blackboard, explained the election process and told about candidates. That fall, Hoover won.

I have a small tin cup in the storeroom. I earned money to buy it, working for my dad. Each child had to bring a cup to use at the school pump. I picked ten half-bushel baskets of black-eyed peas to earn the 10 cents it cost. Another job I helped with required sitting surrounded by heaps of rotting muskmelons, or cantaloupes, and removing their seeds to be washed and dried for future planting. In early spring we ate dandelions until we gagged at sight of them. We even tired of "creamed" wild asparagus.

Next we moved back in town to a small home on Sampson Street in Muscatine's South End. We put a garden in the back and morning glories around the porch. Misery loves the city. Daddy, trying to recover from a near fatal bout with hepatitis, went back to cutting buttons. Mama kept us in bread with her embroidery work. The depression settled in for real. My brothers quit school in order to scrounge for jobs to help out. My little brother and I took our wagon and hauled trash to the dump for families who would pay us a few pennies. Sometimes families who were not so poor gave us table scraps, or leftovers. I can remember the browned skin and fat of a large baked ham we carried home. Mama used it to cook navy beans. To survive that winter, we ate navy beans so often, some days I could hardly walk upright to school because of severe gas pains in my stomach, chest and shoulders.

My sister got a job in the new automatic button factory. Machines now made obsolete the back yard artisans who used to cut blanks by hand. Then my sister eloped, plunging our family into tears. How could the loss of one girl leave such a gaping, empty hole in the center of our lives? But it did. Without her, we hardly knew what to do with ourselves. She soon reappeared with her husband, and like Aunt Clara, helped to feed and clothe us. Her declaration of independence was bobbed hair and a permanent wave! That fall, when school started, Minnesota beckoned.

"It isn't so astonishing,
the number of things I can't remember,
as the things I can remember that aren't so."

Mark Twain

Martha Emmert harvests the elusive Virginia strawberry

Chapter 11

ITASCA COUNTY AND BACK

I well remember that October day when Larry and I realized we would never have to dodge bullies or stay in after school with Miss Othmer again. We were soon packed and riding to Itasca County, Minnesota, perched high on the furniture filling the back of Daddy's old International truck. The bright blue sky enhanced fall's blazing colors. Heady with freedom, I reflected Nature's smile.

This time our home really surprised us. An old one-room log house, it had a loft up above which could be reached by a ladder, where my brothers slept. The snow sifted through the cracks in winter. Mama made my bed out of soft pine boughs in a huge packing crate. She padded it with old wool overcoats. Our two cherished puppies, Ginger and Queenie warmed me. Both puppies later met a sad death fighting a porcupine that filled their bodies with quills, which were impossible to remove, though we tried in vain.

In the center of the log house, a brick chimney pierced the roof, serving as a room divider. Attached to this, a horizontal, steel drum heating stove stood on legs. It had a door cut in one end. This held quite long logs and got red-hot. As it cooled, four pairs of wet-shoed feet could fit against the sides to hasten drying. In spite of the crude and difficult living for our parents, we children fed on stories of Abe Lincoln's boyhood, considered it delightful and romantic.

The first winter, snow blocked us in. The food supply dwindled away. My eldest brother nearly died of pneumonia. We could not get through to reach a phone, or a doctor. We had nothing to eat but potatoes, for what seemed like weeks. The temperature reached sixty below zero, making the logs of the cabin crack and pop.

During the long evenings, we listened while one of us read by lamplight. We read the complete works of James Fenimore Cooper, who takes time to describe every leaf and grass blade. That summer I jumped in a mud puddle, in an excess of energy, and cut a sizable gash in my bare foot on a piece of submerged and jagged glass. Out came my mother's cure-all, hot water and Ivory soap. While I sat soaking, I had time to regret my rash and foolish ways.

Our second home in Itasca County we called, "The leaky house," near Kuhn's Lake. We worked for Mrs. Kuhn in her big house, and fished her lake with her boats. We picked raspberries in her patch for pay. Disillusioned with homesteading, my brothers ran away (from our house). Mama cried until we heard from them. They went to the harvest fields of nearby

North Dakota to earn money. This left only my little brother and me to keep my parents happy. Then Larry fell ill with measles, and we waited and watched through the deliriums of his fever. I remember with what joy we received my older brothers back -- with what alarm we listened, as they told of riding freight trains there and back.

From Minnesota we returned to live briefly with my sister. Soon we found a little house near Muscatine on a rural route. Our house, "Schooley's place," appears in the photograph as small and bleak as the others. It did not seem so when we lived there. For a while we housed my sister and her husband, who were expecting their first child. We had two teenage boys as well as my parents, my little brother and myself.

Mr. Schooley, the owner was short, bent, old and blind. He lived in a shed behind our house, cooking and caring for himself. Dismayed and fascinated by his blindness, my brother and I would be coaxed in for company, where we stood poised, ready to flee, as we listened to Mr. Schooley and watched him maneuver with hand and cane to find whatever he needed. He died in the poor house. Mama took us to visit him once before he died. What a horror of vicious odors, a mourner's bouquet of disinfectant, urine and loneliness!

At his place we planted and harvested. Our whole front yard was a kitchen garden, and always there was a place for morning glories, petunias and moss roses. There at thirteen, a gawky, gangly girl still steeped in fantasy and dreams, I gazed entranced upon my first newborn nephew at birth. He was a marvel of intricacy and wonder, mine to care for, examine and hold, with his little head beneath my chin. Floodgates opened within me and maternal instincts poured forth. I adored him. Then he too left with his parents for a new home.

At fourteen my photographs show me as very awkward and gawky. My father unexpectedly presented me with a birthday gift, an unusual event in our family. A real freshwater pearl ring. He had found the pearl himself and had it set for me. It came in a jewelry box, with velvet lining. I accepted it gladly and wore it off and on until I gave it to my daughter, realizing she had coveted it for years. Some wise adult seeing me wear it carelessly, counseled me early saying, "That is a beautiful pearl ... a lovely tiffany setting. No matter where you go, or how many other jewels you may have, that ring will always be beautiful ... take care of it!" After that I wore it less, put it in water for long storage times and had the prongs checked and cleaned regularly.

In that house I became, at fourteen, a woman. I learned the facts of life, though not from Mama. More than some children, feelings and emotions ruled me. Sexual feelings and dreams became prominent in my known pleasures. Never did it occur to me to connect sex with babies. Sexual dabbling as children produced marvelous feelings, true, but if caught, Mother scolded severely.

Sex play continued, but with greater secrecy. That it had anything to do with parenting would have astounded me. About that time my classmates decided to relieve my ignorance. There I first saw pornography, when I snooped under my brother's bed mattress. It made a tremendous impact upon me and lust became familiar to me. Fortunately, my new knowledge of the results of sex served as an effective deterrent. To think that my sister produced a baby under my nose, so to speak, and I never caught on! Instead of thinking "pregnancy," I still dreamed, "Stork."

The time came to move on. This time we lived on Kemper's Island in the Cedar River. We had a two-story home built up on stilts. We had a barn and a chicken house, with a few livestock to fill them. From there I went away to high school with high hopes. To that home I returned when I quit high school, defeated, trying to work away from home so I could attend high school. There we told the boys, "goodbye," as they went off to World War II. There I had my sixteenth birthday, feeling that life had by-passed me completely.

Sounds of Childhood

Tinkling silver catching candlelight
Piano music softly in the night
The bells of telephone and door within the hall
A voice inviting to a gala ball.

Grandfather clock awake in hallowed nook
The squeak of leather chair, whisper of book,
A lisp of silken skirts against the floor
The tap of dancing slippers out the door –

These are the sounds of childhood, so divine,
The only trouble is, they were not mine.

Martha Atkins Emmert

Chapter 12

GO PLAY - OUTSIDE!

It did not matter what the season: summer, winter, springtime or fall, when five children in the crowded house got boisterous, my mother strongly advised us, "Go play outside!" We clattered and tumbled out of doors, and with nothing but our imaginations and the few things we could devise on our own, we proceeded to have so much fun, that barring accidents, we did not return until called home, as night deepened. We played, "Hide and Seek," for as long as it took for each of us to be, "It," with all of the others hiding. Running freely in the sun and breezes ranks high in the remembered pleasures of childhood. I can recall becoming so heated, flushed and exhausted with running I had to throw myself on the grass to catch my breath again.

The boys kept themselves in slingshots made with a forked stick, two strips of rubber cut from old inner tubes and fastened on a square of leather. The rough inner hide was meant to hold the stone to be slung. We all practiced a lot, trying to hit tin cans and various other objects, with the slingshot. I expect we kept the pigeons on the move.

Every boy or tomboy had a pocketknife, usually a gift from Santa. With it we did many useful things. At Halloween, we cut nicks all around the ends of spools so that when we wound a string around the spool, then held it up against a window and pulled the string, it made an agreeably loud clacking noise, causing folk inside the house to jump a little in surprise!

My two older brothers shared an air rifle. It shot tiny lead beads, poured into the barrel and blown out one by one. With the gun came a big cardboard target with a bull's eye, which we tacked on a tree for shooting practice. My eldest brother had seen a wild-west show where the cowboy could shoot back over his shoulder and hit the bull's eye. He could not rest until he was able to duplicate this feat, which he did with the aid of a small mirror.

He coaxed me to hold a walnut between thumb and finger for him to hit. We did this out of sight of the house, but it drew a nice audience of neighborhood children. He performed well, but not being perfect, he eventually hit my thumb, which lost him fifty percent of the act right then. I cannot remember telling my parents, but I nursed a purple lump on my thumb for quite a while.

If an old oak or maple had a straight limb, we made swings. Some had board seats we could stand on while others had just an old tire on the end of the rope. One of the great free sports of childhood, climbing trees, I gave up regretfully after reaching puberty. We had lots of big trees then. Houses needed shade since we had no air-conditioners, or electric fans. We had screened doors and windows so we could leave the wood and glass ones open as far as they would go. We could all climb the same tree and each have a limb, or we could each have a tree and see who could climb highest. We climbed to find fruit to eat. We climbed to hide and read, or to spy on our friends. Perching like a bird, we enjoyed a view much nobler than ground level.

Kite season ushered in the spring. We made our own kites. My brothers did the constructing; I ran and fetched scissors, paste, string, brown paper and rags for the tail. The great moment came when we took it outside, one gripping the tether, one holding the kite aloft and running across a muddy field. Would it fly? What a thrill when the wind caught it, taking it up to breathtaking heights, threatening to snatch it away from us. It reminded us of a fishing line with a live fish at the end, tugging from above, instead of from below. Years afterward, taking our children to Mary Poppins and hearing, "Let's go fly a kite," it brought back the wonderful hours we had flying kites in the chilly March wind.

By the time kite season tapered off to calmer days, we busily collected our bags of marbles. Though chiefly a boy's sport, a little sister could join in when other playmates failed to show. Oh, the grubby knuckles of marble season! If we decided to play for "keeps," we tried to knock out as many marbles as we could from the big ring, drawn with a stick, in the smooth, hard dirt of the yard.

In the spring we transplanted wild flowers and ferns to our yard, near the house. We made little moss gardens with toad stools of bright colors. Made in a tin lid, we brought it inside on a table where we could dream about it, seeing a fairyland peopled with elves living among the ferns. We hunted four-leaf clovers. We braided clover blossoms, sweet and pink for our heads and necks. Among the wild daisies, we picked off petals, one by one, chanting, "He loves me, he loves me not." Spring in the city meant jacks, jumping ropes, hopscotch on the sidewalk and roller skates, if you were lucky.

My little brother and I used to play at farming in the dirt of the back yard. We made fields fenced in with string and matchsticks. We plowed with an old spoon, we harrowed with a bent fork. We worked the earth into furrows for irrigation and raised flat ridges for planting by dragging a stick between our two fingers. Sometimes he would join me in making mud pies. We gathered the brown seeds on the Sourdock stalks because they looked so much like coffee grounds for play coffee.

While we were still small enough, we used to climb inside an old tire, fitting our backs to the inside of the tire. We held on tightly while the older children rolled us down the hill on dangerously exciting rides. At the foot of the hill we would be too dizzy to stand up and walk straight, which amused us greatly.

Winter brought a wonderland of snow. From the first dreamy snowfall, its large, lazy flakes floating down from who-knows-where, to the melting snows of spring, we reveled in it. Snow meant bundling up in layers of warm clothing, mittens, boots and wool hats to go out and make a snowman. With enough children, we could build two snow forts and divide up in opposing forces. We made huge piles of snowballs for ammunition and had long-lasting battles, including in the fray, any hapless intruders on our battlefield.

Snow meant that a simple hill became a playground of the most satisfactory sort. With sleds, cardboard cartons, or any flat objects, we could slide speedily down the hill as many times as we found the strength to climb back up. Many tumbles of heated bodies in the soft whiteness caused our clothes to become wetter and wetter. I can smell the wet wool yet. We would get so warm from the exercise, we had to unbutton our jackets and loosen our scarves.

We made a huge circular track with spokes like a wheel, where we played Fox and Geese as fast and as furiously as our bulk and the snow permitted. We played early and late. Many a mild winter evening, we played by moonlight. I cannot understand the cringing and whining complaints of winter that I hear from children today. We never tired of snow games and the invigorating cold air that made our cheeks and noses so red. Since our homes were not centrally heated, we dressed warmly for winter weather, in the house, as well as outside.

"In 1850: men supplied 15% of energy for work, animals 79%, and machines 6%. In 1960: men 3%, animals 1%, machines 76%."

"A good man takes care of his animals."
Proverbs 12:10

Martha Atkins at 16 beside Cedar River, Iowa

Chapter 13

CHORES

A chore is compulsory, regular work that a child is expected to do, before or after school, or on weekends, without being reminded by a parent. Chores can also be anything else that parents may require a child to do, to help out in an emergency situation. My childhood, being fairly nomadic, did not have anything like a settled routine year after year, but still, each child had his work to do as soon as we located again. My big sister assumed the care of children and house under Mother's direction.

My two older brothers helped Daddy chop wood and carry it in for our use. On a farm, they helped with outside work in field and barn. All of us contributed whatever earnings we gained by picking seasonal fruits for neighbors or hoeing fields of cabbage for other farmers, or whatever odd jobs we found to do for pay.

My little brother and I had the least hard work fall on us, but still, many tedious chores remained to be done. It helped us to consider, "work" a virtue, sincc to survive, we all had to work and to do our part. My parents believed work built good moral character. If I managed to sneak away and hide in the top of some leafy tree with a book, out of sight and hopefully, out of mind. I read with an uneasy conscience while others labored without me.

Activities governing my growing years are totally foreign to my grandsons today. They are city children and I am a rural product. How many hours have I spent sitting on a porch shelling peas, or taking the strings off green beans? Cleaning wild gooseberries took persistence and a dogged patience. We began the work in the truck on the way home from picking. It meant removing the stem from one end of the berry and the old, dried blossom from the other end of each one. We did this after picking them one by one from thorny bushes all day. I spent those hours of my childhood dreaming as I did necessary tasks. In all my dreams I never approximated the adventures destined for me, nor did I guess at the variety of ways they would be fulfilled.

How many children have to pick up chips today? Mama needed a lot of chips to start the kitchen fire and restart it every day. I can still hear my mother calling me to, "Run and gather a few chips for me, and hurry!" I ran out where Daddy chopped wood, and with a leaky, old pan quickly picked up the largest of the bits of wood flung far and wide by the ax.

Besides chips, Mama and I gathered dead branches from nearby woods, dragging them home to break up for kindling. We depended on chopped up trees for most of our fuel. The hard wood, like oak, was kept for the hottest fires, whether baking, or heating.

Without gas or electricity, fuel for heat is a major daily concern, of which most children today know nothing. Their input may not be needed in the crucial task of warming a home or cooking a meal. My job of picking up chips got me out of the house often and gave me an active and important role in our daily survival.

It also befit my minion status to empty the chamber pots daily and scrub them weekly. Mama gave me an old cloth or brush, sent me out near the ash pile, where with sand and ashes I scrubbed them clean, inside and out. After a generous rinsing under a pump, they dried in the hot sun until clean, odorless and covered, I took them in and put them beneath the various beds for night use. Either we use the chamber pot in the night and when ill, or we went outside to the privy, summer or winter, night or day.

In spring we raised baby chickens. I always fed and watered them from their first downy days. Baby animals captivated me. I sat marveling at their adorable ways for hours. All my heart and soul responded to their innocence and need. I am habitually enslaved to needy creatures, feeling rewarded if they stay happy and in health. I miss having pets, but neither time nor space permits me to have them today.

I loved gathering eggs, a typical chore of mine. Our hens did not always lay their eggs in prepared nests in the hen house. Instead they hid them from sight. Hunting through the haymow, I would discover a nest full of eggs snuggled away in the hay. Sometimes a broody hen covered them. She meant to sit on her eggs and hatch them, exhibiting a readiness to fight for the privilege. Daddy removed her, put her in a cage and hung the cage from a clothesline to cure her. Broody hens did not lay eggs. We preferred egg-laying hens. We candled her eggs to see if they were clear and edible.

Of course when spring came, we wanted good mother hens, the broodier the better. A good hen could handle nearly a dozen eggs, turning them daily with her bill, never leaving them chill, day or night, until they hatched. I remember my thrill one morning, when a little fuzzy head stuck out from under mother hen, signaling the time for the babies to peck their way out of the shells.

Lifting the hens and peeking under, I saw chicks lying wet and half-naked amidst the broken shells, peeping and struggling to stand while the mother hen fussed and scolded me for being there. Clucking her comfort to them in special mother hen sounds, she fluffed her feathers into an ample home as she settled down, covering them again. The next day, the chicks, transformed into the softest downy balls, peeped and pecked sleepily here and there about their mother's feet.

While egg hunting, I sometimes found a soft-shelled egg, covered in tough membrane, without a shell. This signaled my mother to buy a bag of crushed oyster shell to furnish calcium in the hen's diets. We also saved our broken egg shells, baking them on the back of the stove until they were brittle and could be crushed and fed back to the hens. While doing my chores I might find a pullet egg without a yolk, or a double-yolked egg, monsters in the nest. Nature provided many wonders for me as I grew.

When we kept chickens and a chicken house, someone had to keep them clean. The chicken droppings that collected under the night roosts had to be removed periodically. This dusty, smelly job often fell to me. Chicken manure will kill plants if applied directly to a garden. We carried it to a compost area where soil and garbage could be mixed in and rotted with it before use. This involved many wheelbarrow trips, to accomplish the job.

One day while cleaning the chicken house, I heard a scratching under the tar paper covering. I ripped off a panel and hundreds of bats flew out. Finding cracks, they had crawled in for daytime sleeping and my activity awakened them.

The baby chicks grew up each year into gawky adolescents who must be taught to go in the chicken house at night and perch on the roosts. We collected them from branches of trees and bushes, chasing and grabbing, or else we herded suddenly stupid birds into their dark house. Catching each one, we perched it on a roost. Usually it kept falling off. This evening chore lasted until after a week or so, they finally got the hang of it. When all roosted safely off the floor, I closed the door and locked them in.

Everyone helped plant, tend and harvest the garden. If we had fields to work as well, the men of the family gave first attention to them. The worst part of the garden I remember as the war on potato bugs. During that season, we knocked innumerable potato bugs off the vines and into cans for destruction daily. We killed them in all stages of their metamorphosis.

I remember other chores. All water must be carried from the pump in the yard to the table in the kitchen. The whole family used the Big Dipper to drink out of, then hung it back on the pail. It took a good many trips each day to provide enough water for drinking, cooking and cleaning. Sometimes we lived near a spring where water came out of the sloping ground under an old tree. Mama and I cleaned out all the dead leaves and sticks, enlarging and deepening the reservoir of water. When the pool cleared, we dipped it up for a cold drink. We sunk jars of milk or churned butter in its depths. I can remember churning a half-gallon fruit jar of sour cream into lumps of butter by shaking it gently and steadily, back and forth.

When the cows calved we allowed them to nurse their babies for a short time before removing and weaning them from their mother. We took the cow's milk and separated the cream to sell. We taught the calf how to drink skimmed milk out of a pail. I had to put my arm and hand deep enough in the pail of milk so the calf sucking on my finger, would also suck in milk. Gradually, I withdrew my finger to let the calf realize he could drink without it. Calves butt when they nurse, so the pail could spill all over me unless I gripped it tightly between my knees.

Seasonal chores required even more of me. At haying time I carried water to thirsty men busy mowing, raking and loading hay on the wagon. When I became a teenager, my dad entrusted me to guide the horse pulling the loaded hay fork up and into the haymow, where it emptied before returning to the hayrack for another forkful. Even today children can learn responsibility through chores. With pet care, lawn mowing, leaf raking, and garbage to take out, they can help parents and make family life happier and easier for all.

"The urge within me to be in the woods and fields or along a stream is such a strong and pleasant desire that I have no inclination to withstand it."
Jimmy Carter

Chapter 14

SHELLING

Most summers of my youth and childhood involved me in what our family called "shelling." This means locating and digging mussels from river bottoms. We called them clams. We shelled by hand (and foot) although there are other methods. The rivers I remember most are the Mississippi, (before dams were put in), Cedar, Wapsipinicon, Shellrock, and the Iowa.

I recall driving with my dad at dawn, some distance upstream from the camp with our rowboat in the back of the truck. We parked, unloaded the boat into the river and waded in, wearing our old clothes. Holding on to opposite sides of the boat, we began working our way downstream toward camp. We had to hold the boat back against the current while feeling for the shells burrowed into the bottom of the riverbed. Once disturbed, the clam's muscles contracted and the two halves closed tightly.

We pulled them loose, sometimes easily, sometimes with effort, and threw them, still squirting water, into the bottom of our rowboat. Daddy knew where clam beds were likely to be. On sand bars we found sand shells, washboards and elephant ears. We used local vulgar names for all of the species we hunted. By mid-afternoon, the bottom of the boat would be covered with the pile of shells we had found. Tied up at camp, I helped carry up bags of clams to be opened. If the catch seemed small, I might sit the rest of the day opening them with a pocketknife. We kept chunks of raw clam meats in a can until it soured, for fish bait.

As I cut the two connecting muscles, I felt excitement, for at any moment I may open the clam to find a valuable pearl. I kept two jars of water near me: one to put pearls in, the other for slugs, or asymmetrical pearl formations. As far back as I can remember, I shared this work. Long before I grew tall enough to go in the rivers and shell with Daddy. I always found the work engrossing. Because of the element of chance, I also found it possible to daydream.

If enough of us shelled the clams, our harvest exceeded our ability to open them by hand. Then we used a cookout pan. Over a long, narrow pit where the fire burned, we placed a flat rectangular pan made of corrugated metal. In this, we put some water to heat the clams in until they opened. We then dumped them on gunnysacks to cool and put more clams in the pan to cook.

When the cooked ones cooled, I again took my place separating, meats, shells, pearls and slugs. Daddy could depend on me never to miss a pearl, no matter how minute. And so the summer passed. In the fall we hauled the large heap of empty shells to town and sold them to the button factories. I remember Muscatine, the Port City of the Corn Belt, as the Pearl City of the past, renowned for the manufacturing of pearl buttons.

This industry folded with the invention of plastics. Today the Pearl Button museum in my hometown records this history. I hope to visit it one day. I recently donated my last two coffee cans of pearl buttons to a junk art mural I supervised in the Uptown Baptist Church of Chicago. They became the wings of a trinity of angels. These serve as the artist's signature of the girl I used to be.

"Here's an adventure; what awaits beyond these closed mysterious gates? Whom shall I meet, where shall I go? Beyond the lovely land I know?
Above the sky, across the sea? What shall I learn and feel and be?
Open, strange doors, to good or ill! I hold my breath a moment still before the magic of your look. What will you do to me, O book?

Abbie Farwell Brown

April 1971 - Bertha McMahon Harbaugh. Martha Atkins' eighth grade teacher at Hope Country School

Chapter 15

COUNTRY SCHOOLS

The September I turned six I joined my two older brothers and big sister in the three mile walk to the country school. Most of these schools are gone, or are in ruins today. Upperstone, located in Benton County, Iowa, was my first school. Today it is preserved as a state monument in a small park.

My teacher Leota Jones, kept the students of all eight primary grades occupied and learning in one room. I remember early mornings ... my sister hurrying me, dressing me and combing my hair in two tight braids. Dragging me between a walk and a trot, she managed to get me to school on time. The four of us set out with lunch pails. We called them dinner buckets. In about an hour we covered the distance through country lanes, arriving at school before the hand bell rang, calling us indoors.

Miss Jones kept the big bell on her desk. She rang it to begin school, to end the noon hour, and to call us in from morning and afternoon recess. Rows of desks in the classroom graduated in size from adult sized desks in the back, to small ones for the first-graders down in front, where we sat under the teacher's watchful eye. This made it hard to enjoy whispered conversations with classmates. If I giggled, or whispered, or both, Teacher sent me to the back, to sit in disgrace, legs dangling, beside my sister in the row of eighth graders.

A boy named Raymond lived near us. He was slightly older than I. He rode a pony to school. I recall rapturous days, riding on his pony, a princess on the prince's horse. His big sister sometimes used vanilla as perfume, dabbing a bit behind each ear. We loved her scent. My first year of country school passed like a breeze. My sister protected me, made sure I learned my lessons, and drilled me in my parts for school programs. She taught and mothered me. I had no inkling of the suffering ahead in schools without the comfort zone her presence provided.

At recess time and at noon we played games and talked. The teacher urged us outside. She needed a little rest. During early spring and early fall we played softball, that great American past time, plus many ball games of our own variations. We girls jumped rope, played jacks, and sometimes we all joined in group games such as London Bridge, or Ring-Around-the-Rosy. On Arbor Day we planted a tree in the schoolyard. Every morning we stood, and with our hands on our hearts, repeated the pledge to the American flag. Armistice Day meant another minute of silence, eyes closed, to remember soldiers of past wars who had died for us. I did not try to pray, nor was I aware that I ought to.

At that school I observed my first Box Social. The older girls and young ladies prepared their most delicious lunch, then packed it in a decorated and anonymous box. The auctioneer then sold these boxes at an evening social gathering at the schoolhouse. Theoretically, the boys and men did not know whose box they were bidding for, but sometimes rumors circulated. Some bid for the food, and some bid for the girl. The highest bidder claimed the box and they ate it together after the auction ended.

During winter we often took jars of soup to school. In the morning we set them with loosened lids in a pan of water on the huge heating stove in the classroom. Near noon, the aroma made us hungrier than ever. One school had a furnace in the basement with a metal grate in the floor above it. We put our little jars of food all around the edges where the heat gushed up in the middle of the room. Lunches varied according to families. Some could afford bananas or oranges in winter. We usually had apples from our fruit cellar.

Mama made a kind of gingerbread that I am unable to duplicate. It smelled heavenly when we came home hungry and she had just taken it out of the wood stove oven. Made with thick sorghum, sour milk, spices and lots of raisins, we ate a heavy moist chunk of it to stay our hunger until suppertime. Taken to school for lunch, we ate it at morning recess.

Our sandwiches most often consisted of plain homemade bread and peanut butter. Farm families had butter. Without it, we used the first invented oleomargarine, which tasted terrible. It came in a white block made of solid fats. My sister sprinkled it with the packet of orange powder working the color in until it looked like butter. It had a repelling odor as well.

We could buy jars of sandwich spread, but best of all, we liked cold left-over meat, whether beef, or pork, or chicken. We had this less often. Leftovers never seemed to be a problem at our house. We ate hot oatmeal for breakfast with a mug of hot postum, which is a cereal drink that is still available as a coffee substitute. This kept us warm on the long cold walks to school.

Mama taught us to read before we started school at six or seven. Kindergartens had not become popular yet. For me, knowing how to read backfired. The teacher let me recite quickly then spent her time with the slower readers. Class recitation became misery, for rather than being permitted to read more, she skipped me. I remember listening endlessly to the stumbling, halting efforts of the poorest readers, while being trapped in front of the teacher's desk, without any means of alternative interests.

My country schoolteachers befriended the students and encouraged them. When I reached the sixth grade, I remember my teacher invited her pupils to dinner at her home in town. We ate huge fried pork chops, mashed potatoes, scalloped corn and apple pie. She knew how to reach our hearts.

This same teacher arranged for her brother, a pilot, to take me up for my first ride in an airplane. At that time I dreamed of being an airline stewardess, so my excitement built until I reached Muscatine airport and climbed in his little yellow Piper Cub, in the rear cockpit.

I can still recreate in myself that feeling of being suspended, high above my hometown, in a thin shell covered with painted cloth. It was so noisy and vibrated so intensely, I could scarcely communicate with the front cockpit. I have flown many miles in African bush planes since then, looking for landmarks, or a break in the cloud cover, enjoying the participation in flying that such planes give.

My eighth and last country school brought me lasting friendship. My young teacher, just beginning her career, endeared herself to me by her Irish beauty as well as her interest in my life. Our visits have been few, but we have corresponded since 1945. She is now retired with her husband who is a farmer. As a hobby they raise exotic animals and birds for school groups to visit. She lives a full life of service.

In later years I blamed my erratic attendance at these successive country schools for my inability to effectually grasp an understanding of math. It did not keep me from my true interests, however, so I now feel it is a personal inability and not the school's fault.

Words

Words can sing and whoop and holler,
Words can earn me silver dollar.
Words can lift me, thrill me, please.
Words can chill me, knock my knees.
Oh, coming in, or going out,
Words are what my world's about."

Martha Atkins Emmert

Chapter 16

THE SPELLING BEE

It is so long ago now, it seems like another life, but The Spelling Bee had a permanent effect on me (bunions never go away!). Announced one winter morning by our teacher, she then passed out the several pages of newsprint covered with word lists for us to study. Each of us seized our copy and tried to estimate our chances.

As an avid reader, spelling came easy to me. I began to feel as though I could quickly learn the unfamiliar words and win that spelling bee. As the newsprint grew soiled and tattered with study, my excitement and confidence increased.

Just as I expected, I easily won the Township finals and took home a certificate as well as a small teapot as my prize. Now I aimed my sights at the County finals. If I won there, and I felt sure I could, I would go to the State finals in Des Moines, Iowa, and I would possibly qualify for the National.

At that point in my plans, an uncomfortable thought arose. "What would I wear?" My remodeled clothes were a trial to me. I realized the importance of packaging. I knew I lacked the means to achieve the image I desired. I yearned to dress in simple off-the-rack cotton frocks and blend in with the other girls in school, but mother had only her oft-plundered trousseau for materials.

In those days a strict fashion dictated the dress code. The holes in my clothing and the old-fashioned fabrics exposed poverty and humiliation. Who guessed that I would set an avant-garde fashion acceptable forty to fifty years later. I certainly did not. Under my droopy cotton stockings you could see the folds of my wretched winter underwear. I felt darned and patched all over. How could I go to the state and national capitals? How could I even go to the county finals? What *would* I wear?

My best school clothes lay buried in the earth because of that sad encounter with the trapped skunk. My scuffed shoes had holes in the bottom with layers of cardboard inside for protection. I could not bear to wear them on a platform before an audience at the County Spelling Bee. I begged and pleaded for new shoes and finally my parents agreed to send a mail order. I chose carefully from the catalog, and as they required, I put my foot on a paper and drew around it to send with the order. I felt better.

My mother created another blouse of some lovely, but outdated crepe. Another garment she made over into a wool jumper which would have been fine today, but back then I stuck out like a sore thumb. At last the shoes arrived. How beautiful and new! I hurried to try them on. My foot had grown. Still, I could squeeze into them and they looked great when I was sitting. When I stood, however they felt too short and narrow. When I walked, my feet hurt miserably. I knew better than to report this to my mother.

The Spelling Bee coming up in a few days left no time to order new shoes. I decided to suffer in silence, one of my unhappy choices, which I have regretted ever since.

The County Spelling Bee came. There I stood in the line of participants, up on a stage, confronting hundreds of strange faces. My shoes were an agony, my clothes, compared to the others were quaint, to put it kindly. I braced myself to spell. One by one the line shortened and I spelled on. Ten of us, nine of us, eight of us, and I panicked. I could not risk the chance of winning. I deliberately misspelled a word and disqualified myself. Too late, I learned the teacher planned to provide clothes for me, if I won. Ever since then, my bunions have reminded me of that failure of courage at the Muscatine County Spelling Bee.

"As you grow ready for it, somewhere or other you will find what is needful for you in a book."

George MacDonald

"I have never known any distress that an hour's reading did not relieve."

Montesquieu

1945 - Martha Atkins. (22 years old)
High School Graduation

Chapter 17

HIGH SCHOOL THE HARD WAY

I graduated from the eighth grade of my country school in exercises held at the West Liberty, Iowa fairgrounds, during the County Fair of 1938. I recall choosing from Sears' catalog a light yellow cotton ensemble, with a rakish hat to match. It was real contemporary clothing. I felt very fine indeed as I received my diploma.

Influenced by my eighth grade teacher and my mother, I felt motivated to go on to high school. I still faced problems. Neither my big sister, nor my older brothers, had the option of going to high school, due to the depression. Now my parents proved willing to let me go, but how would I get there? We lived too far from town to walk. No system of public transportation existed for bringing rural students to the only high school in town. My dad could not drive me on a daily basis. Somehow, his trucks resembled mules, in that they did not always tote on demand and they usually died before they were wholly ours.

Searching for a solution to my dilemma, my parents thought of the gentleman whose land we farmed on shares. He also had a nursery and truck farm at the south edge of town, where he lived. My parents consulted him and made all the arrangements for me to go live with them and "work for my room and board." They lived about five miles from the High School, in South End. Mama made me more clothing, splurging, in order to purchase a green cotton percale with an acorn motif for one dress that she carefully smocked by hand.

When school started, Daddy took me to the Kempers. My debut as a high school freshman arrived, infused with anxiety, about working for my room and board among strangers. Looking back I see myself as incredibly naïve socially, compared to the girls of sixteen today. I was hesitant, introverted, inexperienced, and to make matters impossible, I knew nothing of modern housekeeping. I feared the noisy machines that washed or swept. I shrunk from them. I declined to use them when asked if I could run them. I had never used an electric iron, only sad-irons heated on top of our kitchen stove.

Homesick and tired, after the long walk to and from school, I managed to do the dishes by hand in the evenings and make the beds in the mornings. I am sure they felt unfortunate in their new helper. They would have done much better to have put me to work in the green house or the truck patch where my skills belonged. Housework had never been my thing. But they did not, and I stood idly in the house at times, nervous, miserable and ineffective, wishing for rest or direction.

During that first month from home I remember how hot I felt from the exercise of walking hurriedly all those miles. I had no bus fare. I doubt I had even heard of an allowance. And the underclothes I had to wear! Mama decreed I should now wear a girdle as a basis for my wardrobe. I had grown up free-spirited in loose overalls of my brothers, and very little underneath. Suddenly, I was shackled by an obligatory garment that gripped my skinny hips relentlessly. Above the waist, moreover, I must wear an ill-fitting bra, which worked daily to raise red ridges around the thorax. Penance, indeed! Stockings, too, must be worn held up by the infamous girdle. I soon gave up on the impossibility of keeping the seams straight up the back of my legs.

At school I began Latin, Junior Business which was as far as I could get from math, English and History. I made a few tentative friends, met a black girl for the first time, and liked some of my teachers. I did not feel free to study after school since I knew that I ought to be busy, "earning my room and board." I cannot recall being given any instructions in my precise duties. Before long, the Kempers "needed" my room. I had to make other arrangements. At this point, the High School Dean of Women, learning of my plight, made an effort to place me in a home nearer school.

A middle-aged couple agreed to take me. He owned a sale barn and they lived on a lovely residential street, in a large house. I remember him as hale and hearty, rather breezy in manner. I prepared meals, did dishes and made beds for them.

For breakfast, the husband required a one-minute boiled egg. After I delivered it to his eggcup, he rapped the top off smartly, took his fork and briskly stirred in salt and pepper. He then proceeded to drink down what looked like warm yellow slime. I could not believe my eyes. Just that egg bit, the first morning, made me regard him warily from then on.

The wife gave the impression of being ill. I never knew exactly what her problem was ... it might have been alcoholism. Overweight and extremely sedentary, she bossed me around from her easy chair. I soon learned that she considered beer a necessity. For all I know, the doctor may have prescribed it for her. Pleasantly curious about saloons, of which I had read, I did not blink an eye when she asked me to make the daily beer run. She provided a large market basket, with a towel to conceal the evil sloshing around underneath. I wonder if the Dean of Women from High School who had placed me in the home ever knew about that!

Other features of that home stick with me ... I remember a bloated Persian cat with a nasty disposition and a large green parrot with a vocabulary as vile as mine. Both of them indulged, with their mistress, in beer. The cat treated me like an animal molester and I had to dodge the parrot's attempts to sever my fingers as I changed his papers. Unlike my responsive country dogs, cows, and pigs, they found me too uncongenial to endure. With a growing aversion to my environment, I did not grieve when the ax fell again, and I had to move on.

School that year, only intensified my miseries so familiar to me in primary school. My series of job failures did not improve my self-esteem. Classes suffered under the pressure of my unhappy quest for lodging. Next, I found a room with friends of the family. I had played with Marie, a daughter of theirs, who was my age, when we were small children. She still lived at home.

I came to them at a bad time. The daughter seemed preoccupied with other matters and stayed aloof from me. She cried a lot. At meals, she picked at a little bacon and stewed tomatoes. Sometimes she ran to the bathroom. I had not a clue as to what was wrong. The mother, sober and worried, clearly wished me elsewhere. Before long, my married sister had to try and fit me in. I learned later that my former playmate, prematurely pregnant, shortly became a young bride and mother.

Living with my sister may seem at first, to have been the ideal solution. Why did not I go there in the beginning? At that time they had just had a fourth child in four years, all six living in a house trailer, at the foot of a steep hill, near the Mississippi River, beside my Uncle's family. To add a large seventh person could only be permitted in extremity. Where could I study, or even sleep? I shared a six-year crib with the oldest nephew, about four. I had already reached my full height of five feet, nine inches. I woke up cramped and aching, unable to change position, due to the confines of the crib.

Happily, the Dean of Women again came to my rescue. She found a willing household for me, very close to school. Members of the First Methodist Church, they owned a jewelry store downtown. The lady of the home received me more as a social service than for her own advantage. I bless her still. She provided what I needed most, instruction in how to "work for my room and board," in a modern home. We very quickly felt love and respect for one another.

This gracious lady took me in hand and pooh-poohed my fears. She demonstrated exactly how to dust, cook, clean, do the laundry and operate the mangle, an ironing machine for flat pieces such as bed linens. I learned to conquer the machines I had feared. I grew happier living with this family.

Both husband and wife were friendly and encouraging to me. They teased me out of my worst grammatical errors, particularly my use of "them folks." I loved to listen while Mrs. Barnard practiced piano, her nimble fingers played "Nola" or "Flight of the Bumblebee." I picked her gorgeous African Violets to wear to school in my hair. I cannot now imagine how I came to do such a thing! What amazes me most, she never mentioned it once to me, although she must have known. My ignorance could only have been exceeded by my homesickness for the woods and wild flowers.

When her father came to stay with them in his old age, she did not use it as an excuse to get rid of me. He added a childlike mischief to the household. A frail, tiny sprite of a man, he resembled a little wrinkled gnome with sparkling eyes. He hid in odd corners jumping out at me when I passed. He caught me dusting the stairs once as he came up behind me. He grabbed and squeezed as tightly as he could, playful as a puppy. His strength surprised me. Had I been more petite myself, I may have been frightened.

But the Barnards' excellent help came too late. Failing, or near failing in all of my subjects, I began to fail in health as well. One weekend, near spring, while home for the weekend, I decided to give up. I dropped out, defeated by circumstances. My hopes of a higher education died. My future seemed bleak, indeed. Little did I dream that I had not seen the last of those poor grades, or that I would be given a second chance, three long years later.

"You will seek me, and you will find me because you will seek me with all your heart."

Jeremiah 19:13 NEV

Daniel Leon Emmert, 1990 - Fort Wayne, IN

Chapter 18

THE INNER STAGE IS SET

As soon as I reached high school and experienced more of life's hard realities, including failure and the return home, I began to question my purpose in life. The war, with my brothers' imminent danger, kept death on my mind. Did our spirits die with our bodies, or did afterlife exist? I wished for more information on death's mysteries. At the same time, I despaired over the suffering and injustice in the world... that which I knew about, first hand, and that which I heard about; brought on by the war.

How did one break out of old ruts and get ahead with a successful life? I had watched my parents working terribly hard for the bare existence we lived. Their honesty brought no reward that I could see. I shrunk from the future I saw before me. Must I struggle, stumble, fall and be mortally injured, as so many adults I knew had done?

Such cowardice I experienced as I faced adulthood! Protected from decision making, subjected to the authority of nearly everyone at home and at school, I had no particular agenda of my own. I waited to be told what to do. Let them make the decisions, let them be responsible for the consequences, if that is what they wanted. Without motivation, laziness and lethargy ruled.

My chief aim while growing up was to make Mama happy. To protect myself from punishment, I lied. I stole time from my chores to read books, smell flowers, write letters and dream dreams. I had no real purpose in life. I badly needed a focus and a role model.

Recalling my teenage rebellion, I feel again the anger and frustration of powerlessness in a world where all the cards seemed stacked against me. Scrutinizing my parents critically, I found nothing to recommend romantic love and the marriage trap. What did it get you? Only squalor and endless arguments. Even as a small child, awake in a crowded bed in the night, I heard my mother crying. I detected her despair as she sobbed, "I wish I were dead and in hell."

What a chilling thought for an over-dependent child. Thereafter, I strained to listen in the night, and heard it repeatedly during those depression years. I did not understand why she felt so. I pictured her dead and knew I wanted to die with her. I did not want to live without her. I did not want to let her out of my sight. Would she still be there when I came home from school?

By the time I turned sixteen, I still had no answers. I hid my confusion and fear behind a brave show of profanity. Any obscenity I had ever read or overheard, I now incorporated into my casual conversation. Who I hoped to hurt by this behavior, I am not sure, but I excelled in it. A momentous incident however, cured me. One day, as I was out searching for firewood alone, thinking bitter thoughts, I tripped and fell, cursing freely. Suddenly something stopped me. A fear entered my heart. A thought passed through my mind. "You keep using the Lord's name to swear like that and you are in deep trouble." Just a passing thought, yet someone higher than I had spoken. I never mentioned this to anyone. It cured my language problem of profanity. I had unknowingly experienced the fear of God.

As the anxieties of wartime increased, any pleasure I may have had in life disappeared, the eligible boys had gone off to fight and I felt the unfairness of living in wartime. Many times I asked myself, "Why have I been born?"

Whether or not we recognize it, I know now that God plans and participates in our lives. If anything in life is sure, He is. In later years I read in my Bible,

> *"When my bones were being formed, carefully put together in my mother's womb, when I was growing there in secret, you knew that I was there - you saw me before I was born."*
>
> Psalm 139: 15-16 TEV

Had God been there then, in the Christmas carols that magically dispelled our gloom, turning parents into caring protectors and filling children with obedience and good will?

Did God guide the hands of the unknown pianist in our neighborhood, whose music reached me in the quiet summer evenings of my ninth year, dinning into my head, so I could not forget it? It was a rollicking tune I found years later in a hymnbook after it had come true, entitled, "*Love Lifted Me*."

Is God the One who made Miss Othmer, my third grade principal, write stories of Joseph, Moses and Daniel for me to copy by hand as punishment for tardiness? Would I have found Him if she had written of Jesus?

Did His presence hover at that hushed and hurried wedding, where I, an only witness, stood beside a young bride and heard strange and impossible words being read from an unfamiliar Book.

> *"But from the beginning of the creation God made them male and female.*
> *For this cause shall a man leave his father and mother and cleave to his wife.*
> *And they twain shall be one flesh; so then they are no more twain, but one flesh.*
> *What therefore God hath joined together let not man put asunder."*
>
> King James Version, Mark 10:6-9.

> *"Submit yourselves one to another in the fear of God.*
> *Wives, submit yourselves unto your own husbands, as unto the Lord.*
> *Husbands, love your wives, even as Christ*

also loved the church, and gave himself for it:
So ought men to love their wives as their own bodies. He that loveth his wife loveth himself.
For this cause shall a man leave his father and mother, and shall be joined unto his wife, and they two shall be one flesh."
King James Version, Ephesians 5:21, 22, 25, 28, 31.

Did He shake me out of spiritual sleep as I listened, focusing my thoughts and emotions on a shining ideal? Oh, to live in such a world! This impossible dream settled slowly and silently into the storehouse of my memory – a brief vision whose brightness gradually dimmed.

Unsuspected by me, the greatest transition of life drew near. A spiritual transition that led to more geography than I had ever considered. The borders of my mind must be made to encompass the world.

And thus I stood, on the brink of life, lonely in my inner soul, unable to find expression, with no place to go - and no one near in whom I could confide. God, did you put in my mind a determination to write, "Poor little Amber?" You knew that she alone, of all those known to me, had the answer to my heart's cry.

"When the unlovable finds love and the unacceptable finds acceptance, there is the Spirit of Christ."

Harold Fray, Jr.

"A while ... without food ... I can live. But it breaks my heart … to know … I cannot give."

Kagawa

Pearl's children Harry, Frank, Eugene and Jennie Martin, who led Martha to church at Christmas, 1941.

Chapter 19

THE GREAT DECISION

For the social contact and diversion I desperately needed as a teenager, I turned to letter writing. I wrote regularly and often to my brothers and friends in the services. I remembered Amber whom I had never met. I began writing to her up in Wisconsin and she quickly responded. Little oddities turned up in her letters that I could not figure out. She would add on things like John 3:16, "For God so loved the world, that he gave his only begotten Son, that whosoever believes in him should not perish, but have everlasting life," of which I could make no sense at all.

When I finally decided to inquire into the significance of such names and numbers, her letters increased in frequency and volume. She realized she had a non-Christian on her hands. She began sending tracts, another strange custom I had not encountered. Of course I read them. I read everything around me. Nothing had any effect that I recall, until a certain day when I read one that said, "For by grace are ye saved through faith; and that not of yourselves: it is the gift of God. Not of works, lest any man should boast."

With the reading of that verse came illumination and understanding, like a curtain pulled back to clearly reveal Truth. It appeared relevant to my quest for answers. I had asked some schoolgirl friends once, if they knew how we got to heaven. The only one who seemed to be sure, told me I had to be baptized as a baby. Great news! This, I rejected. What kind of God would punish me for my parents' failures?

However, from this verse I understood that eternal life is a gift that only God can give. He gives it to anyone who will accept it. It comes bundled up in his Son, Jesus Christ the one who died for us. I could not buy it, which was good news, because I did not have money anyhow. When he offered us this gift, He offered it to all people. That meant rich or poor, in or out of church, old or young, ugly or beautiful, educated, or ignorant. How logical and right it seemed, and my categories were all listed. The only catch was that I must receive the gift by faith. To be so close and foiled still! What is faith? Where can I get some? How can I, an ignorant sinner, deal with an invisible God?

I knew of prayer only as a term used in books. I could not recall actually seeing or hearing anyone pray. To be able to pray in faith became the crux of the whole dilemma. What if I tried and nothing happened? I lacked the courage to risk it. I decided to find a Christian with first hand experience and ask that person to pray for me.

I did not consult my parents. At sixteen, I still hurt from my misplaced faith in those childhood gods that they had encouraged me to believe in. I kept looking for a Christian. It did not occur to me to go to church.

When my Dad gave up farming, we moved to the edge of town and planted a truck patch. Nearly eighteen and still in the nest, my mother tried a scheme to get me out. She visited an employment agency and asked for a job. I supposed she asked for herself, which seemed strange, as she had never worked away from home. I bet now, she signed me up. When the call came, Mother decided she felt poorly. Would I take the job in her place? Did I have a choice?

The job I reluctantly accepted concerned a fairly young family named Fisher, consisting of the parents and two grade school boys. The mother, an invalid, nevertheless, ably ran her household by telephone and mail and mouth. I did all the housework following her instructions, cooked and fed the family and served as companion and nurse's aid to her.

We became very dear friends and I must have worked to their satisfaction. When after several months his company moved him to another city, they begged me to go with them. I began with them a non-Christian when I regretfully left them, I knew Christ as my Savior and had committed myself to prepare for ministry. This meant going back to school. If, as my brother believes, Mama and Daddy planned for me to remain a spinster, caring for them in their old age, as many used to do, I never realized it. That would explain their reaction, though, when their youngest and most timid daughter dared to make a very large choice without warning and without anyone telling her to.

This is how it happened: my elder sister and her family lived not far from us. She had four adorable little children, between the ages of four and seven. Though none of us attended church, someone in the neighborhood took her children to and from Sunday School each week. When Christmas came, in 1941, my sister announced we must all go to see them perform in the Christmas program at church.

I found myself in a church, among the hypocrites, something we had always avoided. Crowded together with my family in an unfamiliar setting, a thought occurred. "There should be Christians in a church." This novel idea, striking me for the first time, distracted me from the program. I cast furtive looks about me into the semi-darkness full of beaming faces fixed on their precious performers. "What does a Christian look like?" I wondered. "How can I be sure?"

More and more my attention focused on the presiding pastor. He radiated acceptance, friendliness and warmth. I figured he must be the safest bet, and that night I decided to return the following Sunday and engage him in private conversation.

Sunday morning dawned sunny and bright. My night time fears of death and punishment dissipated. I turned over and slept in. Finally, two weeks later, at a mid-week prayer meeting on January 14, 1942, I found my way back to the church. I slid quietly onto the rear bench, alone. I listened to a handful of earnest Christians gathered around the pastor as they expressed needs and gave thanks for victories. They all knelt in prayer and one by one, prayed with faith, love, and some with tears.

I had never felt so lost and outside of the family of God. God must be true, I thought. An agony of impatience to know God and to be able to talk to Him like that, gripped me. The service could not end soon enough. I stood in the back waiting for people to leave so I might speak to the minister alone. I did not notice, but instead of leaving, the people went to the basement to pray for me.

"How can I help you?" he asked. "I want to become a Christian," I answered.

We again read verses that the tracts had made familiar to me. At last came the time to pray. Across my mind flashed the thought, "This may mean a big change," but this time I did not draw back. We knelt at the front pew. He led me phrase by phrase in a simple prayer.

While repeating the words after him, a shimmering living light engulfed and filled me almost more than I could hold. Peace, joy and certainty came with that Inner Light, visible in spite of my tightly closed eyes. I had not yet heard of Moses and the burning bush, nor of Saul struck blind on his way to Damascus, but I am as certain as they were, who that Light is. And that is how I passed from death to life.

"In a civilization like ours, I feel that everyone has to come to terms with the claims of Jesus Christ upon his life, or else be guilty of inattention or of evading the question."

C. S. Lewis

1947 - Martha Atkins, 24 years, First haircut.

Chapter 20

NO TURNING BACK

Before that momentous night of my first important decision, I had thought much about the possibility of such a transformation and its consequences in my life. I wondered where it might lead. I suspected it would be beyond my strength to be good for any length of time. Did God have power enough for losers like me?

Then it happened! God moved swiftly to make me His. Getting up from my knees that night I felt incredibly strong and new and drunk with joy. My Christian family reappeared from the nether regions of the church to find their prayers answered. With what rejoicing, hugs and tears they welcomed me. Quite late that night I floated toward home on cloud nine.

Passing my sister's home I decided such good news should not be kept until morning. I knocked until she opened the door. "I accepted Christ tonight. I am a Christian now," I announced excitedly.

She frowned a little. "You had better hurry home. Mama will be worried about you." She closed the door. This cast a momentary shadow, but failed to daunt me. I resumed my walk home, eager to let my parents know. How glad they would be. I wish!

Entering our darkened house, I paused in their bedroom doorway. "Mama?" I called. She stirred and raised herself to see me. "Mama, why didn't you tell me that all I had to do to be a Christian, is to ask Jesus into my heart?" I had not stopped believing they knew everything. Now Daddy woke up. "Do you know what time it is? Get to bed!"

Puzzled by this, I still believed their reaction was a temporary misfortune due to the late hour. Surely they would all see what had happened to me and would join me in my decision. I must explain it all very clearly in the morning. I explained it repeatedly in the years that followed. I bent every force of heart and prayer and will to live a transformed life before them in spite of misunderstandings and discouragement.

I learned to pray in the outdoor toilet, on my knees, in the dead of winter, as this was my only place of privacy. I began a lifetime habit of reading the Bible searching for God's personal message each day. I had never read such a book before. It riveted my attention. In that first reading, the Bible seemed alive to me, anticipating my questions, offering comfort, strength, hope.

I have tried to picture how my parents saw me then. Here stood their shiftless daughter preaching to them, presuming to teach them, disrupting family life by a strange affinity for, of all things, a church full of hypocrites! Instead of reading the comics to her mother, she rushed back to her Bible at every opportunity and even bowed her head silently in the pandemonium that often preceded our meals. Try Roseanne Connor's kitchen. Worse yet, she looked happier and livelier than ever before. How frightening! Who did she think she was? The time for an ultimatum was clearly due.

Mama knew me better than I knew her. She remembered my lazy dependent ways and my reputation for homesickness. She decided to crush me once and for all, to break this alien will in her irresolute daughter. She determined to kill in infancy the resolve she saw resisting all her other strategies. So a few months into my new life, she issued an ultimatum. "If you love the hypocrites at church so much – you can go live with them. You can not live here and go to church!"

It broke my heart. I cried. I did not want to leave home. I tried to explain how I loved them more than ever since loving Christ. I wanted them to understand why I could not turn my back on Him. Church offered an opportunity to know Him better. I needed church. I tried to coax and plead, as well as pray, but Mama never backed down. So I must decide: quit church or leave home. I had found a friend in Jesus, and a purpose in life. I could not turn back.

I found an old brown cardboard suitcase to pack a few sad belongings in. Blinded by tears, I walked out the door, thinking I may never come home again. I wandered unseeing, not knowing or caring where I went. I cast myself upon God's care and mercy. Presently, my tears exhausted, I looked around.

There, before me, I saw the house of our choir leader, Vida Grensing, a petite brunette lady who came from the First Baptist Church downtown to help out with choir practice. Often she invited us afterward for popcorn or ice cream at her home. "I'll ask her advice," I thought. "She may know someone I can work for."

I knocked timidly at her door, surely, a most depressing and bedraggled sight. Then the door opened. She saw me, her beautiful brown eyes filled with sympathy. She took me in her arms and holding me close, answered my unspoken question. "This is your home, Daughter," she stated and she kissed me.

God's love also breaks our hearts. We cried together. Then, in the cheeriest way, she found a place for me in her home, already full with two teenage children, Don and Joyce. I wondered what her husband, Fred, would say when he came home from the factory and learned he had an additional daughter. He seemed as pleased as she with their great good fortune.

Vida Grensing, a woman of great faith and virtue, has followed every step of my life since then with her loving prayers, letters, and gifts. I am not the only stray she has befriended. Many of us call her, "Mom." How very much I owe her.

Today in her nineties, her memory gone, she waits in a nursing home for God to take her.

But people asked my parents uncomfortable questions that first spring and summer. "Where is Martha?" And "Why?" My Dad came and asked me to come home again before many weeks had passed. I returned, committed to witness to them. The same thing happened once more, in the same sequence. Finally my parents relented and let me stay home, knowing I planned to return to high school in the fall.

During summers, I worked in factories. First, at a sash and door factory, then making ammunition boxes for the war effort, then at a pearl button factory near home, and my final summer, at H.J. Heinz, a large canning factory near my home.

I brought nothing to God but my trust and obedience. He accepted me. My skills and talents, unknown and undeveloped, I pledged to serve Him wherever He led. My pastor put me through the paces of service in my local church. Sunday School teacher and superintendent, janitor, youth leader, neighborhood caller, assistant pastor, singer at funerals, I became involved.

But further service meant further preparation, for high school dropouts cannot drop in to seminary without some serious backtracking. My U-turn took me back to high school in the fall of 1942. During these years I actively participated in Youth for Christ services which were becoming popular among the Protestant youth of my hometown. Billy Graham's ministry had begun with God's blessing upon it in no uncertain way. Our Youth for Christ group went to hear him at a rally in Davenport, Iowa, early in his ministry. We have thanked God for the ministry and accountability of the Graham team. Beverly Shea will always rank among the great singers in my memory.

Part II

"Once one has seriously enlisted on the side of God and His purpose, considerable spiritual opposition is provoked and encountered. Pull-back is real! Quite apart from one's own tendency to regress and quite apart from the atmosphere of non-faith in which many Christians have to live, the Christian finds himself attacked by nameless spiritual forces."

J. B. Phillips

"I use not only all the brains I have but all I can borrow."

Woodrow Wilson

May 30, 1948 - Leon Emmert's and Martha Atkins' wedding. Lois Emmert, Pearl Martin, Martha Atkins, Leon Emmert, Walter Emmert and Harold Martin.
In Front: Sue and Julie Emmert, Genie Martin

1948, Muscatine, Iowa - back from honeymoon. Sister Pearl and husband Harold, Jennie and Harry Atkins (Martha's parents), Martha and Leon Emmert

Leon and Martha Emmert with Catherine and Audley Bruce at their parsonage in Moline, Illinois

Chapter 21

STUDY, A NEW WAY OF LIFE

Highly motivated, I returned to study with a vengeance. I made up my failures as a Freshman by getting tutoring during the summer. My D's remained, which pulled down my average. For the first time in my life, I really appreciated school. The future spread like a rich feast before me, and at last I hungered for learning. My life had turned around.

Loved with everlasting love
Led by grace that love to know
Spirit breathing from above
You have taught me it is so.

Heaven above is softer blue
Earth around is sweeter green
Something lives in every hue
Christless eyes have never seen.

Birds with gladder songs o'erflow
Flowers with deeper beauty shine
Since I know, as now I know
I am His and He is mine.

George Robinson

I truly experienced these words. To hasten my progress, I filled my High school schedule with classes to the exclusion of study halls.

To help with expenses, I worked before and after school for my Biology teacher, dear Dollie Dulgar. I worked as janitor of my church. I hiked to and from school several miles each way to save bus fare. Nothing seemed impossible to me. I even tried to study piano at noon in case God should require that of me. He did not. The teacher discovered I had no sense of rhythm and advised me to let it go.

Since my schooling did not receive popular support at home, it became my challenge not to fail. On many days I had little or nothing to eat. Some days I fasted in those early years, so that I might pray more fervently. Why did I always have an opportunity for a rare, good meal on fast days?

By returning to high school, I met Catherine Miller, who taught me Spanish and much more during my remaining years in Muscatine. Her ability, enthusiasm, and expectations challenged me. She enlarged my intellectual world in three major areas. She introduced me to the study of world events, to the works of great painters, and to classical music. She served as my role model for teaching. She is still influential internationally. We are still great friends.

Since embarking on my Christian life, I have been very fortunate in finding good friends. My very first Christian friend, whom I still cherish, is Dorothy Bond Allen. She claimed me as a direct answer to prayer for someone her own age to enjoy. I profited greatly from the arrangement. We shared every heartache and hope.

Dorothy not only knew the church language of prayer, she knew her Bible and hymn book. Both were great mysteries to me. She gave me the benefit of her lifetime of Christian experience and belief. She attended Moody Bible Institute while I entered Northern Baptist Seminary, both in Chicago. She served out her career as a missionary in Japan, and I in Africa. Whenever we meet, the years fall away.

I remember my Seminary years as some of my happiest. Relieved of the daily burden of living among those who could not share my vision, I seemed on the threshold of heaven.

Into my first year of Seminary, I crammed all the fun-filled days of youth that I had missed. My fellows in play were the dining room crew, waitresses and dish-washing boys. We explored Chicago together. Riding buses and street cars provided fun and laughter. The serious business of life still lay far ahead at the end of our studies.

In 1945, rationing still plagued us. A real boyfriend stood in line to get nylons, required by our dress code. Today, anything goes, but back then we struggled to clothe ourselves in hats, gloves, purse, heels and girdles. I borrowed a lot. A girl had to be tall and thin for me to wear her clothing. I fortunately found a few. After marriage, Leon used to inquire about certain outfits he liked that I had worn on previous dates, only to learn that they belonged to someone else.

At times my high spirits landed me in trouble. One April Fool's day, a group of us thought it would be really funny to short sheet the bed of the Dean of Women. I volunteered to do it, since I lived next door to her. I do not know how she found out that I had done it. Her sense of humor failed her for some reason, and it did not turn out to be fun at all. She disappointed me with her serious scolding.

I worked on campus, during my first three years at seminary, settling down somewhat. My first pastor, Wesley MacMurray had been head waiter in the dining hall and his wife had worked as a waitress at Northern Seminary. I followed in their footsteps. The seminary paid me 50 cents an hour. I learned to cook breakfast, rising as early as 4:30 a.m. to prepare for the day. I cleaned my dorm and did housework for other staff persons. Some of us poorer students tried to sell our blood, but only managed to give away a pint each.

After graduation, I worked as a posting clerk for Pennsylvania Railroad's Payroll Division at Union Station in Chicago which meant taking the elevated train downtown and back each day. After the birth of our only son, Daniel, in August of 1950, I went back to work at the Seminary for William Griffith in the Public Relations Department.

I found studying with a purpose very challenging and enjoyable. I liked to research all sides of every question. I appreciated coming to my own conclusions, looking to God for direction and wisdom. We had creative freedom to think and use what we had learned during our fieldwork in Chicago churches. During my first year I helped with Junior Church at the Addison Street Baptist Church, using English, while parents and grandparents enjoyed the morning service in Swedish. During other years I served in the Tabernacle Baptist, Wentworth Baptist and Montrose Baptist churches.

Dr. Charles Koller, the Seminary President, became a cherished and revered friend. When my salary failed to cover board and room, I went to him. He readily drew from the student aid funds to bail me out. He became so accustomed to writing checks for my needs, he kept it up the rest of his life – usually at Christmas. He sent telegrams when I married and when each of my two children were born. He shared so many of my joys and sorrows.

Many times during my seminary years I needed financial help. Very often, at those times, I received gifts through letters, unexpectedly supplying the lack. I wished for a great many items a young lady longs for: such as nice toiletries, pretty clothes, and money to buy gifts to treat my friends.

I rarely had money for offerings. On Sunday I emptied my purse into the collection plate, yearning for more to give, sure that if I had more, I would give more. Is sacrificial giving a lost art in my life today? I hope not, for all that I have, or am, comes from God.

During my last year of seminary, as a wife, my husband freed me from work, to study. My grades improved noticeably. On Senior Day I spoke, along with two or three men of my class. When I graduated, my mother and sister came, along with friends from my home church. It remains a proud and happy day in my life. I knew my mother was proud of my accomplishment.

Northern Baptist Theological Seminary at 3040 West Washington Boulevard, served as a place of nurturing and growth for me in my early Christian years. In 1975 the Alumni Association chose me as the first woman Alumnus of the year, and Leon and I together, as the first couple. Dr. Koller and family came for the presentation, making it an even greater honor.

While awaiting overseas service, our studies continued. We went first to the Toronto Institute of Linguistics. There our sample language, Japanese, showed us how to use a phonetic script and an informant. I did quite well at that, and we met the only American Baptist on the staff, Dr. Eugene Nida, linguist with the American Bible Society, and world renowned, even then. We took him to dinner, I recall, and our son humiliated us when he reached in the sugar bowl, and taking a handful of cubes, said, "Here Mama, put these in your purse." What could I say? I took them.

During the academic year of '54-'55 we enrolled for a course in conversational French at Northwestern University in Evanston, Illinois. We cooked and did housework for a divorced man that year, and worked as superintendents of the Primary Department in the North Shore Baptist Church (where we were members until we retired and settled in Fort Wayne, Indiana).

One summer we went to Fayetteville, Arkansas, and took some courses in agriculture and rural extension work. We went out into the areas and observed the work of one of the home extension agents. I remember I made a stool with a rope seat.

On August 13, 1955, we set sail for Europe, for the first time leaving our native land. We said, "Hello," and "Goodbye," to the Statue of Liberty as we sailed past. In those days, anyone wishing to go to the Belgian Congo must spend 365 days of study in the Ecole Coloniale in Brussels. The doctors and nurses studied a similar course in Antwerp. Ten days later, we arrived in Rotterdam, where we were transferred to Brussels by limousine and trailer, the same day.

I have never studied more intensely than I did that year. We attended classes six days a week, with a half-day off on Saturday. My professor, a huge, burly man carried a large stick with which to hit the floor for emphasis. He used the psychology of fear and kept several of the women in tears.

"Emmert," he roared in my direction. Recognizing my name, I got to my feet and murmured, "Oui, Monsieur." He then motioned me to the blackboard and said something unintelligible to me. On the front row sat a series of sweet Spanish nuns. I looked at them helplessly. I understood their French. In whispers, they repeated what he wished me to do. With much help, I got through my ordeal. Later a classmate translated his comments to me. "Usually Catholics and Protestants do not get along so well together."

I shall never forget the dreaded orals, the tearful sleepless nights spent pacing up and down a cold and clammy apartment, memorizing pages of information in French, in the hope I would recognize the questions they answered. How we feared failure, and being turned back, unfit to serve. Again, God achieved the impossible and on September 5, 1956, I received the precious certificate of proof that I had succeeded and all systems were, "Go," for the Congo. About this time I wrote in my diary: "It is almost a year now since we came to Belgium. Before that time Belgium was only the place told of by returning soldiers after World War II. Now Belgium is a year of my life.

Many times during the year, I have stopped in front of our wall map of the world and moved myself consciously from our Midwest United States to here, until at last in my mind, I have arrived."

"This is Belgium. I whispered to myself as I've walked alone in early morning mist down quiet cobble streets to the Colonial School. I am here preparing for you, Lord. Whoever would have thought that I, Martha, would ever be here seeking knowledge in these ancient streets which bring distant history alive."

"All adventure lies in meeting You, God. Your presence is adventure. Without You travel could be boredom. For You, it has meaning and purpose and lessons along the way. Thank you, Father."

God made Belgium, meditation on the move, communion in corners, prayer while preparing meals, hungrily reaching up for help. Certain memories are etched on my mind; mail on Sunday, workers in wooden shoes, ladies in Paris fashions, children sailing boats at the fountains, and my own child saying, "I'm Belgian now." He was so eager to breech the barrier of nationality among his playmates.

Belgium is music met and loved: the pure, angelic voices of the Vienna Boy's Choir creating a special evening, far from the day's trials. The concert music and the conductor's smile to his musicians as he leads the lilting theme of Capriccio Italien, breaking upon me for the first time, too lovely to forget. I remember the unexpected tears upon hearing a beloved hymn sung in our own English by a dear colleague.

Belgium is a romantic land where flowers and candy say, "Thank you." In everyday life, flowers received and given, were an etiquette, a habit, giving a touch of beauty and youth to each today. I will always remember: the roses of apology, the tulips of congratulations from our tutor, the Lilies of the Valley on my door on May Day, the hostess chocolates and mixed bouquets that brightened our rooms. And every day the street corners bloom for my benefit tended by a special order of flower ladies draped in somber black.

Belgium is made up of quiet towns, panoramas of orange tile roofs sliding past car windows, the church spires in the blue mist, soft and indistinct. And at the Channel, where boats come and go, and the tide washes in and out, Belgium is sun hungry pale people, baring themselves to the warmth, while sheltering from the damp wind. In the Ardennes I found Belgium in the beauty of its forests where my brother fought and other brothers died. These tree-clad hills, haunted with horrors of recent war.

The plains of Flanders stretch flat and green now, manicured meticulously. No small plot is wasted, but each is found in a panorama of living shades of green. The quiet old rivers flow along, carrying their centuries of wisdom.

But more than sensory experience, Belgium is joy in achieving communication of Christ to others, a high purpose of learning language giving past, present and future new meaning. Our year filled with greeting and good-byes, as the stream of missionaries came and went. We learned in the dreary Belgian winter that sunny days were no longer necessary for sunny dispositions.

We saw America through the eyes of others, heard their evaluations, felt our individual responsibility for our country's actions, our appreciation of it compared to other cultures, grateful for our mother tongue.

Yes, Belgium is a year of our life. A year of learning, packed in, pounded down and stored away for use later. A year of hard work sustained by virtue of divine commission and a clearly defined purpose. Though I never see Belgium again, a year of it is part of me now.

Once arrived in Belgian Congo, I had work assigned me, it is true, but did that mean an end to study? No. Whatever else I must do, I could not neglect the study of Kikongo, the language of the Lower Congo, used in church services. I obtained a Kikongo Bible, hymnbook, grammar and tutor. Told we must pass four major language exams during our next four years, we had no time to lose. Otherwise, we may not be invited back.

Our experience of tutoring in Belgium turned out to be quite different from being tutored by an African. The Congolese tutor, more subservient and polite, seldom corrected us and left the initiative for our progress entirely up to us. It became my least favorite method of study. Had it not been for another missionary, Rose Uhlinger, we may never have found time to complete our language exams. She did the requisite prodding.

Language study persisted throughout our career. When we worked in the capital city of Kinshasa, we studied Lingala, the trade language in favor with the government, but it took less well than Kikongo. We taught in French and dealt with the government in French. We studied more French on our second furlough in the United States.

We spent two furloughs engaged in formal study, one at St. Francis College in 1965, and the other at the Indiana University/Purdue University campus in 1970, both in Fort Wayne, Indiana. I remember McDonald's Restaurant in 1970 offering a free hamburger for every A on the first semester report cards. We took four report cards in and came home with a whole bag of hamburgers. What fun! Leon needed to learn new math, and I desperately needed art courses so I would know how to grade, evaluate and teach art. Those classes as an adult proved invigorating and very uplifting to me.

One of my colleagues in Africa, Joy Stabell, took Greek by correspondence and offered to teach me as she learned. I got a good start, but one of those tenses became quite complicated, and I withdrew. I suppose a major portion of my education comes from continual and intensive reading. Not only easy books to relax and enjoy, like Georgette Heyer's delightful comedies, but books to push me beyond my limits, such as Thomas Merton, and some of C. S. Lewis.

"Love is a product. It is a thing to be created by mutual service and sacrifice. Real love is a slow growth coming from unity of life and purpose."

Elton Trueblood

THE BRIDE'S COLORS

O, I am the bride that's soon to be
And one of the customs that comes to me
Is choosing my colors, my favorite two
So I sit and think of the years I grew.

I think of the yellows of youth and fun.
Balloons and balls and the winter sun,
The fuzzy yellow of bumblebees.
The yolk of the egg, the yellow of cheese,
The straw I wore on a summer's morn,
Butter melting on yellow corn,
Jonquils and sunflowers, baby's curls,
Dandelions braided by little girls.
The finch and the birch, fall's matching sight.
My yellow pad on which I write.
And I think to myself, from winter thru' fall,
Yellow's the loveliest color of all.

And what of the second? A lilac tree?

Its smell so sweet, a rapture to see –
I recall mornings of lavender skies,
Of lavender lids on infant eyes.
Or lavender silk with a lavender scent,
Wisteria hanging from vines all bent,
And lavender seems to mean life and age.
It haunts me and grows to fill a page
I know that my yellow, that heedless hue,
Must mate with a delicate lavender blue.

O, I am the bride who made that choice.
Yellow and lavender spoke with my voice.
I sit rethinking it after these years.
I think of the sunshine, the lavender tears,
As our Golden Day nears with its chance to rejoice,
Yellow and Lavender still is my choice.

Martha Atkins Emmert

1953 - Leon, Daniel and Martha Emmert appointed for service overseas

Chapter 22

TEAMING UP FOR SERVICE

In the six years since deciding for Christ, I saw a number of couples who seemed happily married. Gradually, I admitted marriage as a possibility for me. I did not jump at the chance to make my way in the world alone. I felt the need of someone strong in the faith, and able to make the right decisions and take family responsibility. I had great fun dating within our happy, heedless dining hall crew, but marriage needed someone special. I looked for qualities I lacked, in the fellows I knew. If I were to have children, I did not want them to be limited by my genetic pool, reinforced by someone similar. I asked God's help and guidance in such a choice and depended on God to answer.

In my junior year, (1947-1948), Leon Emmert came to the seminary from a farm in Northeastern Indiana. Mature for his age, his control and discipline caught my attention. I asked Audley Bruce to find out if he was too old for me. He reported that Leon had been born seven months after me. That proved a shocker, why, he already had a few white hairs at his temples. He seemed like the ideal pastor to have around, but he had not noticed me.

Another new boy had come that year. Fred Lewis was less bashful, and had begun dating me. An opera buff, tall, blond and handsome, he came with opera glasses and a box of chocolates to take me to my first opera, "Carmen." I enjoyed being coached in the beauties of classical music. I loved his attentions, as he murmured tunes in my ear, but there again, I felt that there was no future together.

By October of 1947, Leon intervened and I had to make a choice, or at least I thought I did. Unlike some girls who could balance numerous beaux simultaneously, I tended to have a one-track mind. For our first date, he asked me to go to Moody Church to hear a sermon. Not quite the giddiest date I had ever had, but I agreed. He came with a mutual friend, Audley Bruce, who had failed to secure a date. I offered to check and see if my roommate Catherine Kinnee was free. I found her available for the evening, and it became a double date. We remained a foursome to be reckoned with until her death in December 1994.

Audley and Leon borrowed Catherine's Sears' employee card, and selected identical diamonds for us in a surprise proposal by each on the same day, January 22, 1948. When we girls compared notes that night in whispers in our dorm room, we discovered we had both become engaged – a scary business. The four of us decided to keep it a secret until we could announce it at a party on Valentine's Day.

Leon's mother, Vida Emmert, came for the party. That day, he delivered to my dorm a chest of Rogers silver plate, "Adoration" pattern. Tied up in a large red ribbon, it impressed all who saw it, and it certainly impressed me. I grew up with a spoon holder in the center of the table. We only used necessities. We have used that silverware for forty-eight years with care, and it is still lovely.

Audley and Catherine married in Detroit on Saturday night, May 29, 1948. Leon and I were married the next day in Muscatine, Iowa. My home church, Lincoln Boulevard Baptist gave me my wedding reception, with punch and cookies, instead of cake.

My pastor's wife loaned me her wedding dress, to which I added a flounce for length. For our attendants, we chose my sister and her husband, and Leon's sister and brother. His nieces, Julie and Sue, and my youngest nephew Genie also served in the wedding party. I had planned a very long and thorough service of songs and scripture, to be sure that all my family attending would hear the Gospel clearly. An interminable affair, it is recorded on wire, the newest thing in 1948, now effectively silenced by obsolescence, and the lack of a machine on which to play it.

All of Leon's family came. Leon preached that Sunday morning. We were married in the afternoon, and borrowing Father George Emmert's new Ford, we left on our honeymoon. In Detroit, we picked up the Bruces and continued on to Niagara Falls and Pennsylvania, before returning to Indiana to the farm. In the fall, we returned to seminary for my senior year, and Leon's continuing education.

The realities of marriage set in. We had grown up with almost nothing in common. Our engagement period did not allow time for in-depth acquaintance. From the little we knew about each other and trusting God's guidance, we felt we had found the right person with whom to best serve God. Through the years, this sense of rightness has grown.

Working side by side, with our eyes on Christ, went very well. As a team, we spoke in churches, parented our children, and taught in African schools. Each supplied what the other lacked. God gave us what we desired most, a partner for service.

As most newlyweds, we began to truly know each other and ourselves in the stress and strain of real life. Both of us worked early and late to achieve our education. After Leon earned his Th. B., I continued working at the seminary to help him get his Masters degree in Education from the University of Chicago. He needed a profession other than missionary to qualify for work in Northeast India, Assam, but that visa did not materialize in 1953.

I think we both were dismayed when we realized that in most decisions outside of career and work, we unfailingly disagreed. We even belonged to different political parties. It is not amazing that we disagree, given such dissimilar backgrounds and upbringing. The miracle is that we have any shared tastes.

In those days, nearly everyone recommended that the Christian wife defer to her husband in disagreements. Having grown up deferring to others, I opted for the familiarity of powerlessness in the interest of harmony, and the view I understood of the Christian way. I still feel real responsibility for my children. Perpetual deference, unless sincere, can leave a residue of discontent and mounting rebellion, with attendant side effects.

Still, being a new Christian believer married to a man who could not remember being anything else, troubled me. How could I have such opposing views? He had to be right, I concluded each time. He thought so too. It did not help when his mother told me how well he behaved as a child. He grew up without a spanking. In fact, she seemed to think, he exhibited nothing but perfection until he married me and let himself be led off to the ends of the earth, away from her. I hope she forgave me for it. She made up as a grandmother what she lacked as a mother-in-law.

For thirty-five years Leon and I worked as a team in Africa. We served as teachers and directors of schools together. The Zaire government later awarded each of us three medals of Civic merit for those years of service. We served the church as fraternal workers in whatever capacity they needed.

During our second term, at remote Moanza in Bandundu Province, we came the closest to never being heard from again. We had almost adjusted to a crisis a year occurring since independence in 1960. Still, we were shocked early one morning in 1966 when the soldiers arrived. We were alone on the post, except for our African colleagues. Our missionary colleagues, the Chapmans, had already left for vacation. The soldiers informed us we were under house arrest.

Leon was due to attend a conference on education in Nairobi. The children and I planned to stay with the Uhlingers in Kinshasa until he returned. Then we would go to the Coast together for a rest period.

We had scheduled a flight out, but no plane came. Instead, the soldiers demanded a search of our homes. They took our short wave set and cut down our aerial. The fact that the Shaba rebellion at that time used mercenaries put Europeans in jeopardy. Public radio urged Africans to take up hoe and machete and drive white invaders from their soil.

In French, mercenary and missionary sound a lot alike. We thought deeply, praying about the protection of our station and ourselves.

We wrote a letter to our leaders to let them know what had happened to our short wave set and sent it by commercial truck. Days and nights of listening for plane or truck continued.

Did the letter get through? Would the soldiers return? Would rescue come in time?

The sound of another truck alarmed us one morning after eight days of waiting. We stayed inside expecting soldiers, when to our joy we recognized our Catholic colleagues from Kimbau, our nearest mission. Close to Moanza as the crow flies, it took tedious hours by the road over and around the hills.

Brother Joseph drove the truck. He was one of the German brothers from their boys' school. With him we saw Sisters Nuria and Maria from a Spanish order in charge of the girls' school. They had brought us a roasted cut of beef, in case we had to travel soon and offered to take us back with them since we were stranded and alone.

We were touched and overwhelmed by their loving concern and prayers. Our faith in God's protection grew. We felt very close as we had coffee and prayed together in meaningful and warm communion. They left, promising to say Mass for us daily.

Eventually, our Mission truck came and formed a convoy with other outlying families as we returned to the capital city. As we traveled, we ate beef sandwiches, ecumenism had passed the test.

During our years in the capital city of Kinshasa, Leon served as Mission Correspondent and Associate General Secretary. He also became involved in Habitat for Humanity.

Millard Fuller had spent a term with his family in Zaire, trying out his theory of community building for the poor. Clarence Jordan and his wife had also come to Zaire and we became convinced of the good scriptural basis upon which this entire movement is based.

Leon helped our church in Zaire to sponsor a Habitat project in Kinshasa and to choose leaders for it from among Christians. I contributed many trees and shrubs, plants and vines to the project. It stood on a hillside and needed help to prevent erosion. Habitat is still one of our favorite charities.

*"Blessed is he who has found his work;
Let him ask no other blessedness."*

Carlyle

Congo Madonna - wife and child of Dr. Reuben Diambomba, former student of the Emmerts. Taken on the front steps of the Emmert home on the Congo River in Kinshasa, Zaire

Chapter 23

TEACHING – TOUCHING OTHER LIVES

If in my grade school years anyone had said to me, "You will be a teacher when you grow up," I would certainly have disagreed, to the point of combat. I saw teachers as ogres who made life miserable, who sprang fully and malevolently formed, without a childhood. Wreak humilities on helpless children? No way!

When I acquired a Christian perspective, I began to find teachers more engaging and human. Still, I would not have consciously chosen teaching as a career. I walked into it as a reasonable and necessary service of my new life.

No sooner did I become a regular at that little church, than I found myself the teacher of the Junior Boys class in Sunday School. There they sat six to eight obstreperous young offspring of the church family. We had no classroom, we met in a nook behind the furnace. I worked to cover my ignorance, they knew far more about the Bible than I did. We hit it off just fine. My years as a tomboy and growing up surrounded by brothers, kicked in. I like to think I had some influence on those boys, but I have lost track of all of them.

After my freshman year in seminary ended, my next teaching experience took me to the Black Hills of South Dakota. With my friend Grace Davis, a classmate from seminary, I traveled there to provide daily vacation bible schools for the several churches of the Black Hills Parish, an enormous area served by Pastor Wallace Schumann. Why there? I became involved in Elmer Strauss' Challenger Club that first year in seminary. He and his friends held Bible schools in various states and then provided correspondence courses for the children contacted in this way. Elmer, now retired from a career in Cameroon, again leads the club in great exploits. When summer came, Elmer's influence sent us to his friends in the Black Hills.

We each taught school five full days a week. On Friday night, we gave a closing program for the community. We then moved on to the next church in the parish. With my brief but sincere piano lessons, I managed to learn three simple hymns for our use, just enough for marching in and out with one left over to sing during the day. For other choruses we sang a capella with motions.

I remember one Saturday night in Scenic, South Dakota when our arrangements for transportation required that we spend the night in the post office. The locals did perceive one danger; Indians from a nearby reservation spent Saturday nights in town for drink and excitement. Since I had hunting experience, someone loaned us a rifle that Grace said I must use to protect us if they should storm the post office to capture us. We heard lots of commotion and did not sleep much. Now that I think it over, I wonder if they were not putting us on. I have a shameful history of gullibility.

We had a wonderful time. The land, filled with colorful cowboys and rattle snakes, provided romance and danger. We lived on ranches, attended rodeos and waded in rivers made famous in cowboy songs. The friends we made that summer, have lasted a lifetime.

For fieldwork in Chicago, I taught Sunday School classes in a different church each year. During some summers I served as a camp teacher – where I received my first camping experiences. Camps prepared us for the school experience in Africa, where the students live in dorms surrounding the staff housing and we cared for all their needs. We held classes six days a week with required church services on Sunday.

As soon as the year in Brussels ended, our mission flew us directly to Leopoldville, Belgian Congo. In 1956 prop planes flew passengers. The ecumenical education center at Kimpese needed a couple immediately to replace two teachers who had gone home for a year. Our designation came as a surprise, but we agreed to help out that first year in Belgian Congo.

I read my assignment and laughed in disbelief. Ancient History ... I had studied American, European, Church and Baptist - never

Ancient History. Psychology ... I had no indication of which species of psychology - and no text. Since it was a class for pastors, I assumed pastoral psychology of which I had a smattering. Causerie ... What in heaven's name could that possibly be?

Moving from the Theological school, I saw myself listed as an art teacher in both the Secondary and the Monitor's school. In Africa for only two days, I was already in need of a miracle. Searching my memory, I could only recall one Art experience in third grade, when I did a watercolor of a goldenrod. Not at all the success I had hoped. Why did they not teach me art in seminary - or at least, warn me? I regretted offering to baby sit in the park while my companions visited the Louvre that day in Paris. (I did not get back for my visit until six years into retirement.)

However, somebody had to teach Art. It remained a required course even after Independence in every year of school in the Colony whose systems of education came straight from Europe. No wonder Europeans think we lack culture! Most of them are knowledgeable about great art and music. A lot of them unashamedly dabble in art themselves. Americans can and do complete their education without ever being required to study art or appreciate it, or without ever entering a museum. So many of us suffer from spiritual malnourishment without being aware of it - our priorities are unbalanced.

How grateful I am now, that God planned my life better than I ever could have. After two terms of teaching art, I wanted to study it at home. I learned I had artists in my father's family - not famous, but nevertheless salable talent. During my fourth term I taught church art to the theological students, and with them I did major projects for the school, churches and other buildings in Kinshasa. My forte, became no-budget junk art. I refined it. My childhood had exquisitely prepared me for scrounging and saving every possible discard from being wasted. Put me in an art supply depot and I am paralyzed with choices. Drop me off at the dump and – watch out Picasso!

In 1978, I was chosen to design the logos for the Centennial of Protestant work in Zaire. Printed on all the programs, stamped on the tee shirts of a thousand voiced choir, it also graced the covers of student cahiers or notebooks.

To help me with my Kikongo language study, the school director graciously provided me with afternoon classes teaching sewing to pastors' wives from every language area, except the one using Kikongo. I knew neither the language, nor the subject. I spent the hottest parts of each day grimly ripping out everything I had no words to correct. That class tested my faith beyond anything else.

When classes (or lack of classes) permitted, and no smiling tutor came over to apply more pressure, I rounded up my six year old son for his first grade lessons. He had enough freedom from my classes to learn both French and Kikongo from his new friends long before we did and he learned it with a purer accent. During my second term I served as language advisor on our post, tutoring newly arrived colleagues.

Just knowing grammar in a foreign language does not make for proficiency. Vocabulary and more vocabulary is an absolute necessity. Every night I worked to translate lessons from English to French, taking my next day's vocabulary list to bed with me, hoping by some miracle of osmosis to acquire the vocabulary I desperately needed.

Before too long, our first students were studying overseas in universities and colleges; some were even studying in the United States. They received doctorates in education, economics, business, theology, and medicine. They surpassed us in qualifications. One student, an outstanding scholar is Phi Beta Kappa in Economics from Stanford University; another is a heart surgeon from Northwestern Medical School in Evanston, Illinois. From my art classes, some trained as architects at the school of Fine Arts in Kinshasa. One of my students became a fine water colorist and taught at the School of Fine Arts in Kinshasa.

Those students from our past now write or phone us from Geneva, Johannesburg, Quebec, Paris and Pittsburgh. They send us copies of their books and theses. We first met them coming out of equatorial grasslands. Some were barefoot. They made the mental leap from village subsistence living, to space age technology. Looking back, I can see them still. The forest teems with earnest scholars bent over thick texts in French. They pace the prairies murmuring theorems, or theatrical parts. We sit in the state jury exams and watch the seniors explain in word and diagram the construction of atomic reactors – these forest youth who have never yet seen a train!

I can see again the rainy day I took our portable radio to class. They gathered around my desk to hear about the first landing on the moon. While we waited -- hushed and listening, it happened. The first astronaut stepped on the moon's surface.

"How do they know it is the moon?" one whispered. "Is it raining on the moon?" another asked. Teaching works both ways. At times, I felt quite sure my calling had been designed primarily for my own personal good, because the growth in me seemed the most astonishing.

The African is congenitally religious, believing firmly in spiritual realities. I could teach no subject that did not lead to questions about God. "What?" They asked me, puzzled, "Prayer is illegal in American schools?" How could I explain it to them? Must I lie to excuse our culture?

There is no doubt about it. The mental effort teaching provided in order to meet my student's needs, enlarged and enriched my life. Undoubtedly, someone else might have done better than I did. However, had I stayed in the United States, I would not have had to stretch mind, heart and body beyond my abilities. Would I then have dared the deeds we did had I not been the one chosen to lead on, or let the vision die?

Take the ceramic mural, for example. It was another case of "biting off much more than you can chew," and then having to chew it. The brick factory in Kinshasa gave clay to schools, I heard. I had taken a craft class while I was on furlough, dabbling in a little of everything, including clay. I became fired with visions of what we might accomplish at the theological school.

Obtaining the clay, my class of future pastors had to be convinced that sitting on the cement outside, working the clay and carving it, fit into their station in life. We conceived and drew a huge pattern on the theme, "Whatsoever you do, do all to the glory of God." We thought of all the ways by which our Zaire Christians earned a livelihood and my students each chose one picture to draw. They then had to fit it into the master plan.

The plan then must be translated into clay pieces, small enough to dry and fire. The class would end and I then hollowed out the backs of the pieces so they would not break while firing and I put them under damp cloths to dry. Then the brick factory fired them for us, but informed me they could not fire the glaze. In the meantime, where could I find the glazes?

My son purchased some glazes and sent them out with a traveler. They were all transparent. A transparent blue on a piece of orange clay is a disappointment at best. Finally, my supply grew versatile when a former student, Norman Kamosi, who had become a vice president of Air Zaire, brought me some opaque glazes from Belgium (of course, none of this funded by an art budget).

It took two years of unremitting struggle to achieve that Mural. I finally found Matetu Baku, a Ceramist with a kiln which functioned. He could only promise space for a piece or two at a time, which meant numerous long trips to his location to check and see if more were ready. Finally, all fired and laid out, mapped and numbered, I spent an interminable day with the workmen plastering it into the outside wall of the Chapel. That was the first and last Ceramic Mural, I was ever to supervise.

"Whenever you are fed up with life start writing: ink is the great cure for all human ills, as I have found out long ago."

C. S. Lewis

Student deaconesses with Communion trays at Nsona Mpangu

Chapter 24

A TEACHER'S PERIL

I left class convinced one student really disliked me. It worried me a lot. Most of the high school students in this central African country seemed to accept the new teacher. At least no others were so actively antagonistic as this one. Not that he committed punishable infractions or that he was not an excellent grade-earner. He was just difficult and uncooperative. His attitude got to me.

The problem persisted like a recurring toothache. I dreaded facing his class. A daily reminder of my personal failure to engage his interest, his belligerent stare upset me.

"I will be extra nice to him," I thought, "even though he doesn't deserve it." He grew grimmer still and I even gave up trying to hide my dislike. My own attitude revealed my wish to punish him. I tried hard to avoid conflict or confrontation with him. His rebellion and disrespect threatened and humiliated me.

"He really is unbearable," I thought. "If only he were a more endearing type." Thin, secretive, habitually wearing an expression of chronic distaste, he rarely volunteered an answer in class. When called on, he gave the impression that I only questioned him out of ignorance.

The conflict between our personalities seemed deadly. I felt burdened and defeated. I knew I could never be happy unless this particular student and his teacher could be reconciled.

One day in class we studied the sense of smell. I took my bottle of cologne to pass around. Each student must sniff it three times noticing how the sense weakened with repetition. I grew tense watching the bottle progress toward my antagonist. I realized I had created an opportunity for him to disregard me publicly. Sure enough, he passed it on to the next with barely a glance at the bottle. He may as well have said, "Your foolish ideas are beneath my intellect and dignity."

"You will come to see me at 3:00 this afternoon, if you intend to remain in my class." I spoke before thinking. Immediately I regretted my hasty words, now too late to withdraw. When I thought of facing him alone, I nearly panicked. What would I say? How could I overcome his dislike and command his respect and obedience? After class, I opened my Bible in search of enlightening counsel or correction. With little hope and a heavy heart, I prayed for guidance. What a miserable confrontation for a young teacher. I hoped neither three o'clock, nor the student would arrive – they both did.

He came to the office. The door closed. We watched each other silently. His unpleasant expression sunk my spirits even lower. Tired of fighting, I determined to confront him. "I know you dislike me. I don't know why. Your attitude continues to be belligerent. I have tried to love you and treat you with respect. You refuse to respond. We can't continue like this. One of us will have to go. What reason do you have for hating me?"

The chip fell from his shoulder. He looked like a lost child. "I can't believe you like me. The whole class knows you bear me a grudge." More bitterly still, he continued, "All my life I've been poor and had to struggle. Others have more than I. They are the ones you like. It makes me pretty sad."

Now I felt desolate. What a tragedy of misunderstanding! Out of our subsequent conversation and prayers, grew a mutual awareness of our warped perspectives, our persecution complex, our neurotic obsession with our own egos. Our own inadequacies blinded us to the truth of each other. Fear and self-pity built an enormous barrier of enmity without foundation.

Routed by true communication, resentment and anger gave way to affection and a desire to accept one another. From the source of my deepest failure, as a young teacher, came the riches of mutual understanding and a key to good relationships.

"... for age is opportunity no less
Than youth itself, though in another dress,
And as the evening twilight fades away,
The sky is filled with Stars, invisible by day."

H. W. Longfellow

Martha Emmert before the Ceramic wall, Chapel ISTEK (Evangelical Theological Institute of Kinshasa)

Chapter 25

CROSS CULTURE - NO ART BUDGET

"One package of construction paper? That's it? I have 250 students in eight classes to teach with one package of construction paper? There is no budget for art supplies? How can I possibly teach so many with so little?"

These were my questions in the 1970s when I began teaching art at Milundu, Congo. Our new assignment was to a public high school of two sections. One section gave four years leading to University, the other gave four years preparation for teaching primary school.

From the beginning of public education, the government entrusted it to missions. Belgian and other missions staffed and administered the schools but the government paid the salaries of the teachers. (Missionary salaries from the government were used to improve the quality of teaching by funding school libraries, labs, maps and other teaching aids.)

Our salaries came from our sending churches in America and we could not accept pay from other organizations. Their government paid our African teachers.

The schools were required to follow the state program of education, based largely on the

European system. Art and religion is required in all grades from primary through high school. So, from my arrival in the mid-fifties, I taught art to African students in various high schools, and later I taught it in the Seminary.

I was learning a great deal and developing my own philosophy of art. At Milundu my great test was to begin. The answers to my questions didn't encourage me. "Yes, you must teach art to 250 pupils per six-day weeks – and no, there is no budget for art supplies." From then on I learned to excel in begging, borrowing, scrounging, collecting and saving. And what glorious horizons opened up because I was forced to diversify and consider all possibilities available in the creation of classroom art.

Art for the artist is a way of life. Even for the classroom artists it can be a way of viewing life, a way of expressing life, or faith, or sin, or failure. To be honest it must be at least as personal as a toothbrush. This creative expression and personal freedom are not concepts with which our students usually come equipped.

Tribal structures encourage rather strict conformity. Anyone standing above or below the norm is viewed as a threat to strong unity. Personal independence or initiative is not valued as a cohesive factor in the African society. Their emphasis is upon the authority of the elders and the obedience of the young.

Art in primary school as taught by the African teachers probably meant copying a drawing made by the teacher on the blackboard. The closer to this model the child made, through imitation, the better the grade. Failure to achieve a good grade weighs heavily on the memories of those that lack confidence and are afraid to try.

What we enjoy aesthetically in traditional African Art was created for the practical and serious purposes of religious necessity. Whether the object was artistic or not, it was valuable and fulfilled its purpose. This traditional art is no longer necessary in modern African life. The artists' profession has fallen into disuse. His formerly indispensable role is evaporating in urban societies where the tribal culture is breaking down. It is no longer dominated by animism, with the ceremonies and secret societies served by traditional artists. Christianity would not accept the artistic objects of animism, such as fetishes and charms. The contemporary African artist waits for the church and the society to find a use for him or descends to tourist art. The need must be felt before the artist can rise up to meet it. He is still there.

The average student brings to art class very little esteem for what is solely aesthetic. His life is dominated by the hard facts of survival. The powers of observation are there. He can identify every kind of edible plant or animal. When it comes to distinguishing colors, these same powers are strangely dormant.

The local languages have words for ripe and unripe, black and white. No other colors were necessary to know, for physical survival. The world of color for pleasure is a great awakening for some. They become aware of the enrichment that art can bring to the spirit and to the emotions. When cloth prints become available to the African, what an explosion of color in market, village and city, as they learned to dress in their chosen colors and combinations of color.

I taught my classes with the materials at hand. I hoped that my pedagogy class would be able to use some of these ideas. They too, would be unable to indulge in many imported supplies. We used paper maché made out of old magazines and wormy flour paste. We used egg shells, match boxes, vines, twigs, roots, leaves and anything else that hand and eye could find that fires the imagination and transforms itself into an art form.

With dyed and broken eggshells we made mosaics on paper-covered wood panels. Coated with shellac, they shine like jewels. On one we depicted many of the symbols for Christ found in the Bible. The water of life pours from a pottery jug of African design. The lily is one that grows in the nearby forest.

With a large bare branch suspended in a corner of the classroom, we added a collection of deserted birds' nests and then made reed and tissue paper birds of Africa to sit on nest or twig, or to fly below, or hover above the branch.

With inexpensive scraps collected from the community we made embroidered book covers, cassava root print designs on cravats and scarves crafted by the pupils. With broken crayons and candle stubs we made wax resist masks and batiks. Strings and yarns were finger-woven into belts.

Science classes made models of cell division using balloons covered with paper maché; then cut in half and fitted with the simulated parts from found objects. We made meter sticks and cloth wall maps with the pedagogy seniors as well as puppets and portable stages for future teaching through stories.

Mosaics of colored broken bits, buttons and old jewelry set in cement decorate school walls. We cut up tin cans to make sculptures. A beautiful flight of 43 birds still adorns the chapel. Each bird required three four-liter powdered-milk tins to make it. It is a fixed sculpture. All birds are flying in the same direction with outstretched wings. The wings are attached to the body with tabs such as paper-doll clothes use. Students and teacher often were amazed at the results.

My teaching method was to introduce a subject of local interest, something exciting, happy, relevant. Exploring it together we stimulated one another to remember and visualize. Then the materials were provided. Each student was reassured anew of his freedom of expression. Uniformity, clichés, formulas and copying are put aside. Those who show courage, daring and joy in creating are rewarded with an attractive exposition of their efforts. There is among students a marvelous simplicity of design, a spontaneity and gaiety of form and use of color. As surface designers they truly excel.

African art inspired the cubists with its simple geometric volumes and surfaces. The symmetrical figures often had exaggerated details. This symbolic exaggeration is seen in class work. Jesus is drawn in a scale to dwarf the lesser disciples. His hands, nailed to the cross are larger than life – great disproportionate hands full of suffering.

This sympathetic and intuitive treatment comes with freedom and encouragement. I could not teach them this form. I could only rejoice in the expression they achieved, more moving than any prose which they could possibly employ.

Our classes sought to create offerings of beauty and meaning to enhance our school. One center of our interest is the chapel. The top classes design and execute art projects of surprising beauty and originality. A pair of Christmas banners evolved from our first timid and tentative try. They were to visualize the symbols from the Bible account. The star was not symmetrical nor was it five-pointed. The Madonna's hair is strictly village style, worked in scraps of cloth and yarn on denim, I did encourage women's groups in America to send materials.

These banners, hanging in pairs, add a medieval dignity and a youthful blaze of color to the gray cement block interior of the chapel. Encouraged by the success of the first pair, we eventually completed four pairs featuring uniquely African symbols. For instance, the leopard's skin and spear replace our traditional crown, as the symbol of royalty. The great commission to become fishers of men uses the symbol of line fishing for men and of basket fishing for women, as it is practiced in Africa. In the creation of Eve, three dark hands, representing the Trinity reach out of the clouds hovering over the sleeping Adam to create Eve. Noah's Ark had a handsomely thatched roof, African style. Pentecost is beautifully expressed as the dove descends and flames rise from bowed heads symbolized by half circles with closed eyes, in repetition.

The most ambitious project is a mobile of enormous proportions for the nave of the church. For both the students and myself, it was a first experience. We learned armature making from jungle material. This was covered with layers of paper maché and enamel was applied as a finish. We talked of the church – its place and importance, its authority and its life. Seven symbols were chosen. The Holy Spirit in dove form at the top representing the Church's guide. Below we put an earth, moon and three stars, and an Apollo spacecraft. These represent the church's space age responsibilities. Nearest the congregation are the open Bible, printed with

"The Word was God," representing the church's authority. Lastly a pair of African praying hands, symbol of prayer as the life of the church. This mobile, in constant movement creates new forms and changing patterns and speaks of the youth and activity at the school.

All art projects presented to the school were made in a cooperative and giving spirit, with our best efforts and abilities combined. They beautify the community by all they represent.

Students are formed here to serve throughout their society in the spirit of an indigenous Christ. Life in Africa is not yet divided into the religious and the secular. All of life is permeated either by the belief in pagan spirits or by a belief in God. If Christ has been born in the heart of any African, then He has taken on Himself the flesh of that tribe and nation. The African Christ, and the African Madonna express this spiritual truth. As long as He stays a white stranger from a strange land He does not belong to them in a way that matters daily.

This is a concept I have taught and I find illustrations of this in all of the various cultures where Christ has made Himself at home. The artwork of our African students attests that Christ is no stranger among them. He could be a member of any of the eight to ten tribes attending this school. He not only gives meaning to our milieu but to our lives as well. Like Him, we have been able to salvage discards and with

His gift of creativeness transform them into works of beauty bringing joy and blessing to all. The lack of budget was the beginning of the challenge. Through our work together, cultural doors were opened and insightful understanding gained by both sides.

"If there is no restoring force,
no healing and rehabilitating Spirit,
no extra-human source of goodness and compassion,
then many of us are indeed undone."

J. B. Phillips

1965 - Leon, Michal Rose, Martha and Daniel Emmert

Chapter 26

A WORKING MOTHER

I never intended to become a working mother. I feel strongly, that compared to our life span, the time our children are home is very brief. I did not know what lay ahead. I did not really think through what having a baby might mean. Committed to study and service, what time would be convenient to have children? At twenty-six, I felt an emptiness only a baby could fill. We decided that the time had come.

No sooner did we decide, then it happened. Tall and thin, I studied my body after a bath, wondering where a baby could fit, and how it would change my shape. Through the weeks of nausea into the weeks of growing hunger, I worked at my desk in the Union Station of Chicago. I hung on the elevated straps to and from work until the zero hour. Railroad retirement offered good maternity benefits, coverage of all costs, and a three-month leave with pay.

We went to West Suburban Hospital in Oak Park, Illinois where the school doctor practiced. Oak Park was a training hospital, and my delivery turned into an excruciatingly traumatic experience. Once admitted to the labor room, friends and family were denied access on grounds of hygiene. While I lay boarded up in a darkened room in fear and pain alone, my husband sat isolated in the waiting room, not knowing what was going on.

A procession of interns passed through, each doing a rectal examination during a contraction. I am not sure whether that caused my first hemorrhoids, but for nearly two weeks after that I could not sit up without fainting from the pain. I cried and called for Mama and for God quite a lot. Nurses came and went in the twilight of my room. Some were kind, some were notably cruel. One in particular told me to stop complaining. "When I have a baby," she asserted, "I'm certainly not going to be a cry baby." That was easy for her to say!

I heard other women coming in to other labor rooms, and after a brief crescendo of effort, I heard the baby cry, and soon the woman and baby went to the maternity ward. Why didn't my baby come? Hour after hour, the pain went on and on. Finally, when total exhaustion came, they gave me an anesthetic and took the baby by forceps.

I wish I could do that birth over. In Congo I watched a baby being born ... the mother gave birth without any anesthetic. She got off the delivery table alone, and did her own washing up! I could not believe the simplicity of that birth. Why had my experience been so dreadful?

Dan, our first child, suffered the brunt of our devotion to our calling. We did no worse than any other parents who left a baby in someone else's care, in order to secure our education. It became my turn to work. I chose work at school in order to be near him, but neither he, nor I wanted to be separated. He cried when I left him and I cried inside.

I became ill, but not ill enough to stop working. After a year of testing, the doctor decided that my chronic diarrhea resulted from the antibiotics. The illness was psychosomatic. Now extremely thin, I lived on yogurt for another year and fought to recover my health so I could pass the required physical exams necessary for me to continue working overseas.

We either left him behind with grandparents, or with other children whose parents attended our conferences, study programs and orientation courses. When we enrolled in the French course at North Western University in Evanston, it meant that at four, Danny must enroll in Miss Speck's pre-kindergarten child care center.

Very shortly afterward, in Brussels, a truly frightful regime awaited him. Because we had classes six and a half days per week, at five years of age he was enrolled in a kindergarten that followed a similar schedule. We took him to huge gates in a walled enclosure. The doors opened and a gatekeeper ushered him in and locked him from our sight. All of the children came from Flemish speaking homes, except our son, who was the only English speaker there. The children were taught French for the first time. Danny learned the Brussels' French, spoken with a guttural accent, recognizable by European French speakers. In the evening, we called for him again.

How could we be so cruel? We did not know what else to do. Danny told us he did not like school. We did not particularly enjoy ours either. He begged for a little brother or sister. He turned to God and sincerely accepted the help of the Savior. "I'm worried about school," he repeated to us. "God will take care of you. See those flowers? They do not worry and God takes care of them," I responded. "But they do not have to go to school, Mama," said Danny.

What could we say? He suffered intense loneliness. That whole year we went to a gynecologist trying to have a sibling that would share his life. We took a few trips together, and had Sundays and Saturday afternoons, if we were free from study and kept promising better times ahead.

Once we arrived in the Belgian Congo and were arrayed with the all-encompassing schedule of teaching, I promptly became pregnant. I had names chosen and dreams dreamed when suddenly, as November ended, the dreams also ended in the miscarried fetus. It seemed a major illness at the time, and the doctor came to stop the hemorrhage. Dr. Carrie Sprague worked over me administering morphine and injecting blood-clotting serums. I remember being jocose, "This one is named for you, Miss Carrie!" She smiled grimly and kept working.

For the next four years of that first term of mission service, I kept trying for that second child – but other pregnancies ended the same way, although none with the drastic effect of the first. Then, like a miracle, it happened once more and I decided not to pamper myself or stay in bed to forestall a miscarriage. I would go ahead with my schedule as usual. This time my daughter arrived during our first home leave.

When we fled the Congo in 1960 with other refugees, we considered ourselves normal people returning for home leave on schedule. Being five months into a pregnancy, everyone, who knew my history, feared a disaster enroute. But this baby was to be born at her convenience and not before. In spite of travel by train, truck, plane, dugout and on foot, she did not budge.

We settled into an old home in LaGrange, Indiana, next door to the primary school and awaited her arrival. Shortly before his sister's birth, our ten-year-old son began to realize the advantages of being an only child. "It's alright, Mama, I do not mind being alone," Dan said. I assured him he must be prepared to share.

At Thanksgiving time, due to the baby's position, she could not be delivered normally. I spent the night on the delivery table in readiness. An X-ray the next morning showed a C-section must be done. That Thanksgiving I feasted on blood transfusions, while the rest of the family ate turkey at the farm.

We returned with a one-year-old baby to a newly independent Congo. The stores were empty, the local markets sparse. Even the normally plentiful peanuts and bananas were hard to find. I had no food to wean her to, so I nursed her for another year, and finally weaned her on weak tea and powdered milk with bread and sardines, among other things. We hurriedly made a food order, but it took months to arrive. One of the things the Africans most liked about me, is the fact that I nursed my baby in church as they did. I lived in a nylon knit Shelton Stroller, that year, with a zipper up the front and a large bow to hide baby and breast. It kept her quiet and gave her a good, healthy start.

Two years later, back in Congo we went with the family to visit another bush station. There I suffered a final miscarriage. I felt sure it would end my life. The short wave radio did not function for some reason and the head nurse left on a trip. I lost so much blood, the nurses propped the foot of the bed extremely high and I am not sure what else they did. I know I worked to keep my eyes open, for I felt sure if I closed my eyes, I would be gone, leaving my two children without a mother. I promised God if he would keep me alive to raise the two I had, I would never ask for more. He heard and answered. The nurse returned and I took iron and vitamins for a long time after that.

During our daughter's second year and our son's eleventh, I stayed home to teach him sixth grade and to feed her and wash her laundry, myself. By the time the school year ended, Dan felt ready to return to boarding school. At eight years of age, he had first gone away to study in French at a Belgian school in Leopoldville (capital of the Belgian Congo). Living with house parents and other little boys from bush stations, I cannot recall those years without tears and pain.

It did not help our son, but due to his unhappiness, we determined never to force our daughter to go to boarding school. We arranged for correspondence school classes at our post. We even made her repeat fourth grade in the United States to make sure she understood math and to delay her leave-taking for one more year. She, however, felt it was a hardship to be kept at home.

This girl knew what she wanted and usually got it. She seemed born with those skills. Once weaned, she cast me off like an outgrown shoe and never returned for the cuddling that I missed. She never confessed to homesickness of any kind. She claimed independence very early.

I understood my son's struggle for emotional security, which was so like my own. To be needed by my children is a kind of comfort, yet living in unsettled conditions, I wanted them to build their independence on self and God. I tried to free them, but in reality I could not let go until I learned a difficult lesson.

When my daughter reached Junior High, I felt I had lost her altogether. I tried every way I knew to hold on to her. My son at Judson College in the States did not write because it made him homesick. My husband spent most of his hours in meetings. My daughter seemed to hate me. Like Job, I turned to God and asked to die.

God is very clever, and unusually surprising. "You want to die?" I heard clearly in my mind. "Try dying to self. Forget that you need her, give her some space, show her your love by letting go."

This shocked me out of my depths of self-pity and pain and God drew near to give such grace and help that it is one of my mountain top experiences, which lasted several years. All of my mountain top experiences slowly wear off and faith becomes blind again, but the memory of His meeting me in my need never fades.

As a working mother I missed many occasions in my children's lives. I missed my son's wedding and my daughter's graduation from college. Their school affairs went by without us because we worked in the bush and due to our schedule were not free to attend.

We lived in the capital city of Zaire, Kinshasa during our daughter's final years in High School, I volunteered in the high school library, getting acquainted with her friends and teachers. I taught as a substitute teacher in science and art in her school. I learned to drive so I could take her to school and to church. I wanted to fulfill the normal duties of a teenage girl's mother.

I am sure I did one thing right. I read to my babies almost from birth. Until they left me, I read at naptime and at bedtime. We can still share the memories of loved books read together. Today, I treasure those hours, which no one can take away from me. Although I have retired from a career overseas, I have never retired from motherhood. As parents our love and concern for our children continues. We are now free to think, pray and care for them in all the appropriate ways.

Our son Dan met Carmen, a Mennonite missionary's adopted daughter from Puerto Rico whom he married in December of 1973. After Leon's family died in a fourth of July plane crash, we returned to Zaire in September after the funerals and estate settling and were unable to come back for the wedding. The Bruces came to Fort Wayne and Audley performed the service and tried to take our places.

To make up for our absence, we gave Dan and Carmen tickets for a visit to Zaire in May of 1974. We held a reception for them inviting our Missionary and Zairian friends. Dan and Carmen visited all of our American Baptist posts before returning to America.

By 1978 they had two beautiful boys and a new home built by Carmen's father and uncle. Their sons are now nearly adults. The youngest, graduated in 1996 from Snyder High School in

Fort Wayne, Indiana. There has been much heartache and suffering which others touched by the disease of divorce, know all too well. We pray, struggle, and daily do what we can to meet their needs. In July 1996, Todd joined the army and is presently at Fort Carson, Colorado.

Our daughter, Michal Rose, chose her mate while on her visit to Zaire from Indiana University in the summer of 1981. She met Larry Hart, a Habitat for Humanity volunteer, committed to two years of service, building houses in Zaire. They married the next year at the Kimpese Hospital guesthouse where we worked. The wedding was very beautiful and Larry's mother came for a month to assist. Afterward, they returned to her studies at Indiana University in Bloomington, Indiana by way of India and the east. Michal Rose earned her Master's degree in Art Therapy and presently works in the Staunton, Virginia School system. Dan lives and works in Fort Wayne, Indiana.

"I will send an angel ahead of you to protect you as you travel and to bring you to the place which I have prepared."

Exodus 23:20

1966 - Martha Emmert in her "rooster dress" with Michal Rose (5) and Dan (15) returning to Zaire on SS Princess Margriet

Chapter 27

THE BONUS OF TRAVEL

Though my family kept moving, at twenty-three due to reading books, my mind traveled more widely than my body. Once given a purpose in life, and a Lord to follow, life beckoned me in ever-widening geographical circles. When my first pastor, Reverend E.W. McMurray returned to visit Iowa from a pastorate in North Carolina, he and his wife kept saying, "Ya'll come see us now, ya' hear?"

I got in their car and went back with them. The truth is, I wanted to believe them. I figured if they missed me a fraction as much as I had missed them, they surely meant what they said. After I got there I heard the same thing repeated by the most casual of acquaintances. This farewell is a commonly used phrase in the south. How embarrassing! They were good sports, warm hosts, and I got to see the Great Smoky Mountains, and other historical places I had read about.

While there, I stayed home with their boys and one day a girl my age came to the door. She motioned languidly to me and drawled, "Would y'all give me a poke?" I almost did. Imagine calling a paper bag a "poke." The McMurrays are still a very present part of our support group, though mostly by phone and usually only an annual visit. We enjoy their youthful spirits. I always feel like a much better person when I am with them.

I saw the Black Hills and Mount Rushmore back in 1947 when my girl friend, Grace Davis and I spent our first summer from Seminary teaching a series of week-long daily vacation Bible schools. Armed with snakebite kits we met all day with the children in little country churches, with a closing program on Friday night. Mount Rushmore came upon us as part of the wilds of the Black Hills. No paths were laid or tourist facilities built. No fences inhibited our movements and no loudspeakers polluted the air. We could pick up rose quartz scraps, if we chose.

We toured the Badlands and marveled at the barren splendor of tinted spires thrusting into the air. We met wonderful cowboys and tried riding and shooting. We saw prairie dog towns with inhabitants peering out or sitting up to welcome us. We drove through western towns fraught with frontier lore; Spearfish, Belle Fourche, Deadwood, Lead.

After my first rodeo, at one of these towns, our escort ordered steaks. I did not know about rare steaks, then. I thought it was the mistake of a poor cook. I felt very sorry for him, and tried to eat all the edges, at least. Since then, I have met the filet American of Belgian-ground steak, prepared raw of which my husband is very fond. I have been corrected.

My assumptions from early experiences and reading have been constantly adjusted and set right by travel and the enlightenment it brings.

On our honeymoon we ventured into Canada, leaving the United States for the first time. We encountered the friendliest of foreign countries. I had been acquainted with the Niagara Falls on the Shredded Wheat box for years. When I stood on the brink of the Falls in 1948, I saw how far short of reality that picture is. Those enormous Falls in twilight fell deafeningly far below. The rushing current threatened with inexorable power. The crash and smash of the mighty falls banished forever, the tranquilizing effect of that cereal box illustration. I drew back in awe and fear, all of my instinct for self-preservation fully activated.

I first saw the Rocky Mountains in 1953 when sent to a convention in Denver, for our commissioning to overseas service. Afterward, we went by bus to Estes Park, up into the mountains. To me, mountains are beautiful at a distance, or on a calendar. Once into them, their height and sharp curves frighten me. The next mountain constantly limits my view. As a Midwesterner I am accustomed to long clear vision, seeing farms twenty miles off. I think the flat cultivated prairies are more beautiful in pattern, fruitful in produce and hospitable in accessibility. These gracious farms and fields stretch to low horizons dwarfed by truly spacious skies. I can contemplate distant snow capped mountain beauty. I am never "at home" in the mountains.

I lived for thirty-one years without ever seeing an ocean. Sent to speak in a number of New Jersey churches, I arrived in Long Branch, on the Atlantic seaboard in 1954. I stayed with Dr. Alice Baker, a missionary who had retired from China. I remember being very eager to see the ocean. At sunset I finally stood at our eastern coast and gazed across the heaving waves as far as I could see. I thought of crossing that water and wondered at my commitment. Salt spray flew close enough to taste, as waves crashed against the shore. I watched. Pictures faded for good in the face of a living ocean. How frightening and determined those huge, muscular waves appeared as they searched unceasingly for ways to grip and rend that shoreline. That same voice of the ocean that was speaking to me roared unsilenced through the ages. It threatened my forebears braving the dangers they faced to come to this continent. Even books and photos did not completely prepare me for the shock, of reality. I thought, "This is the ocean - dare I cross it?"

Later, returning as a guest in Dr. Baker's home, she looked at me and said, "You are too young and beautiful to be a missionary." I did not know what she meant. I had not yet learned to accept compliments. I discounted it, as usual. I did not see what looks had to do with anything.

I still do not see. Perhaps her own youthful beauty, worn out in China, came to her memory. Who knows? However, it stuck in my mind as an enigma.

America is a wonderful land, and mine by birth. Thousands of people risk their lives and lose them to try to come here. I have traveled all our states except Louisiana, Mississippi and Alaska. I did not know my country's faults until I learned them from citizens of small European countries who often knew more about our government than I did. I did not once think, "I am from the most powerful nation in the world." But this too, forced itself into my consciousness by the prestige and power I saw granted to us by others.

Just as many Americans think all Africans are savage or intellectually inferior, most Africans believe that all Americans are rich. It takes interest and interchange and energy to correct stereotypes. They are so easy to use, so convenient to believe. I tried to tell my students of my childhood poverty. You could see them looking at each other, nudging, smiling, as though to say, "Yeah, she was poor – right!"

Travel is an extra bonus that those in Foreign Service enjoy. We travel the shortest distance between two points and always tourist class - - anything beyond that we pay for out of our own pockets. Even so, for an untraveled girl full of curiosity starting out from Iowa, life led me in undreamed of paths within and outside of my own country.

A day came that did not figure in my childhood dreams. We stood, my husband, son and I, with a group of our colleagues at a ship's rail on August 13, 1955. We watched Manhattan move quietly away. As we gazed upon our own dear Statue of Liberty, it receded and shrunk in the distance. Our native land disappeared from sight, and as the day ended, the immense ocean surrounded us on every side.

For nine days we pondered seascapes of every variety, we tasted it, smelled it, and felt its motion keeping some in bed the whole trip. We thought fearfully of its depths when caught in a storm. The heights of those massive waves towering and breaking over us, lifting first and then plunging our ocean liner, as though it were a toy. In a way, it seems immoral to obliterate the awesome reality of that ocean by jet flight. Should people be permitted to cross it, watching movies without once thinking, "Ocean," and ought others to go through life and never notice beauty?

Inside the cabin, more strangeness met us. A small porthole framed the rise and fall of the waves. Four dozen roses emphasized, "This is 'Farewell'." A big basket of fruit underlined the thought, while boxes of unaccustomed candies sweetened the severance of ties that bound us to home.

We arranged trunks, suitcases, hand baggage. We read our stack of letters and telegrams. We settled in and found serenity and repose. It is the greatest of all ways to travel.

How we regretted it when air travel became cheaper and compulsory. No decks to walk, no rails to hang on, no sun and sea air to absorb, no blue-green waves to send up porpoises and flying fish and salty spray.

A glimpse of England's cliffs brought us all to the surface of the ship as we entered the Channel. As the S.S. Maasdam came into homeport and berthed, we took our first step on European soil in Rotterdam. All that I had read of Holland came rushing to mind. As a third grader, I remembered the story of Hans Brinker - his story so gripped me I could not leave it. Before I knew it, the teacher arrived, yanked me up, shook me like a trapped rat, let me go and took my story, right in the middle of an exciting paragraph. I had a hard time forgiving the teacher for making me wait so long to finish my story.

We scanned the Dutch landscape for the canals and windmills. We found them. We saw tiled roofs and window boxes overflowing with flowers, backed by lacy white curtains. But the dikes! How could that boy have plugged up a hole in these gigantic constructions with his hand, or arm, or even himself? I had imagined a levee like those of our Mississippi River, maybe a little larger. These were like gigantic elevated highways stretching an entire coastline, protecting this tiny country from a raging sea's assault.

Cook's Agency loaded us in three limousines with trailers for baggage and sent us off to Brussels, a three-hour drive. Unaccustomed to such chauffeured luxury, we enjoyed our trip immensely, through Holland and Belgium, arriving at the Hotel des Colonies on Tuesday, August 23, 1955, ten days after leaving New York.

Before classes began we had time for a quick trip of eight days to London, north to Edinburgh and back to Brussels. Leon's mother was Scots and a Roy. We checked the phone book in Scotland. We found whole chapters of Roys. That ended our whim of calling a possible relative.

From time to time, during the year, our Belgian professors escorted us to nearby sights. We went first to Bastogne, where 76,890 Americans, killed, wounded or missing in action between December through January of 1945 are memorialized on inscribed pillars where the battle of Bastogne took place.

We toured Antwerp, mainly to see Pierre Paul Ruben's home and many of his paintings. We took a trip to Ghent. In the spring, we bussed to the Keukenhof Gardens in Holland by way of Rotterdam and The Hague. At the Gardens we spent two hours of pure pleasure before our bus returned. In Bruge we saw canals and the famous lace makers of Belgium. Twenty-six years later my daughter wore a Brussels lace veil for her African wedding.

We met and became friends with several Belgian families. Once we visited in Malines in a home bordering on chateau status. Each spring the garden, its paths, its form and its plants were carefully plotted and redesigned with an eye to aesthetic beauty.

Another time we went to a vacation apartment in Ostend on the windy channel with Belgian friends searching for the sun's rays on the beach behind windbreaks, after a cold, damp winter. We dressed our son for school in the short wool pants and jacket and beret of his schoolmates.

With another family we traveled through the country sightseeing, as far as the Chateau of Bouillon sitting high like a fortress on a cliff overlooking the river. We toured this home of Godefroid, chief of the first Crusade, later king of Jerusalem.

With Dan we visited nearby Waterloo, climbed the 226 steps of the monument where the British lion proclaims Lord Wellington's victory over Napoleon. Another winter day, two busloads of us joined the three day annual festival in Binche, Belgium. The costumed revelers called Gilles or clowns threw oranges to the crowds. In this way they celebrated early Spanish explorers exploits among the Aztec in Mexico. The symbolism still seems fuzzy to me but our own expedition proved hilarious. We laughed and played in the snow, ate "frites" (French fried potatoes) out of newspaper cones and tasted street-roasted chestnuts for the first time.

Holidays offered further opportunity for travel. During Christmas of 1955, we joined a small Belgian tour to Nice, France via the train through Paris. How astonishing to at last view the Mediterranean Sea to find not sand for Dan to play in, but large black pebbles on the beach. At Cannes, a U.S. Navy aircraft carrier lay in harbor. Later we visited with some of the homesick sailors on shore leave.

We followed the Cote d'Azur through Monaco as far as San Remo, Italy before having to return to Brussels for classes. Prince Rainier of Monaco had gone to the U.S. to court Grace Kelly at the time of our visit. Aristotle Onassis' beautiful yacht lay at anchor near Monte Carlo - lit like a Christmas tree at night, before the Kennedys were thought of.

During Easter vacation in 1956, we rented a small Renault with the Charles Stuart family and headed from Brussels for France. We visited Versailles, Chartres, Fontainebleau and toured Paris. We walked down the Champs Elysees and on Easter ate snails for dinner in the Eiffel Tower. We visited the left bank and some of us saw the Louvre. On the trip back to Brussels we stopped in Compiegne where the 1918 armistice signing took place. We visited the birthplace of John Calvin and gloried in the beauty of the Amiens Cathedral. At a U.S. Military cemetery in Flanders fields we stood by the grave of Jeannette Stuart's uncle.

As our year of study drew to a close, there were other short vacations and brief forays into Europe. With the Stabells we took a three day trip to Bitburg, Germany to a U.S. Air Force base, to visit a friend, Chaplain Robert Maase and family. With the Maases we explored Luxemburg and Trier, the oldest city in Germany. We examined the Twelfth century window in the St. Mathias church and the ruins of Roman Baths.

Later that month, we joined another missionary couple Joe and Ethel Forcinelli on a train trip to visit Aix-la-Chapelle, or Aachen, as it is called in Germany. Charlemagne's octagonal church still stands. Charlemagne, imagine! Gazing on the mosaics, everything seemed unreal. How can such experiences, incorporated into our mind and body, fail to change us? How could I keep up with the transitions required of me?

We continued on to Cologne, on the river Rhine, the city appeared very new and modern. Then we saw bombed out parts where only a half of a third floor home hung exposed to sight while all about lay ruins, and I realized our allied bombers did this. Cologne cathedral, though damaged, had scaffolding all about it. Painstaking repairs progressed day by day. We still have the small souvenirs purchased there so many years ago.

Classes ended, we completed written and oral exams. We flew from Brussels airport, August 29, 1956, with stops in Lisbon and Kano, Nigeria. In Kano we visited for forty-five minutes with Delta Bond, a girl from my hometown and the sister of my best friend from there. Delta Bond is a nurse and worked in the famous Eye Hospital of Kano. We boarded the plane, our next stop was Leopoldville, Belgian Congo.

For the next four years our travels were confined to the Lower Congo nearest the Atlantic Coast. For each four-year term we had a month vacation. During our first term we vacationed in the Far Eastern part of the Belgian Congo. Friends from Northern Seminary lived on many posts there and we enjoyed their hospitality as we discovered a very different part of Belgian Congo, the Kivu. There we saw the snow-clad Mountains of the Moon, at the Equator, the volcanoes where the Gorillas lived, the National Parks full of wild African game, the lovely lakes, the lava highways, the water falls, and tea and coffee plantations.

On that trip in 1958 we drove into Uganda to shop at an Indian store in Kisoro. We landed at Usumbura airport in Rwanda-Urundi, Protectorates of Belgium. We traveled by car or across the lake by small passenger boats. We met pigmies of three and a half feet height, Watutsies of seven feet, and Bahutu tribesmen of average size.

We stood high on a mountain reading a sign that read "Equator" and shivered in our wool sweaters. Driving a Volkswagen Bug through the National Park at dusk, we nearly collided with what looked like a slow moving gray mass. Elephants were crossing the dirt road, too tall to distinguish. We braked before colliding and sat and held our breath, remembering the stories told us of Volkswagens being picked up by elephants and tossed off into the bush.

Our last night in Kivu, we sat in velvet darkness on a mountain top watching a new volcano come into being on the opposite mountain, near Bishushi. We observed a river of bright red moving and spreading as it burned a path down through the jungle. We could hear the noise of its consuming fire, smell the smoke, see the trees falling as the flames crackled loudly. It was an unforgettable sight!

Returning, we stopped in Stanleyville where Dr. Paul Carlson lost his life in the sixties. The next chapter relives our travels then.

Rainy season blues with clay roads in Zaire. I push!

Crossing the Kuilu River in a dugout canoe at Vanga, Bandundu, Zaire

Iowa Corn Fed

Oh, I was born in Iowa,
And I am Iowa bred,
And nothing seen in travel
Has ever turned my head.

With corn meal mush for breakfast,
And corn bread hot for noon,
Then succotash for supper,
With ham or roast raccoon.

I've eaten mushrooms a la grecque,
And snails in Eiffel's Tower
But give me corn roast on the cob,
Picked in its finest hour.

With appetite of youth and age
We have examined Europe
And failed to find hot pancakes
Afloat in good corn syrup.

O kidney pie and boiled cod
In England are just fine,
But pork chops fried a sizzling brown
Have nourished me and mine.

Once in old Vienna, we ate
Kraut and wiener Schnitz.
We never thought in Iowa
Our kraut was for the Ritz.

Common Clay

Round melted cheese in Switzerland,
Dipped bread with outstretched arm.
It can't compare with headcheese.
Made on an Iowa farm.

We munched fried rice in Hong Kong,
Drank sake in Japan,
Ate curry served in Bombay
So hot it burned your hand.

Danish crepes I ate one time,
All rolled in lingonberries
And longed for childhood's Iowa
Pies of handpicked wild gooseberries.

Italian Pasta, eaten there -
Not just a bite, but oodles
I'd trade as fast as lightning
For Mama's home made noodles.

In Africa we're offered
Some grubs or caterpillar -
For empty places that remain
Chikwangue is used for filler.

The Africans eat termites
And even meadow rat -
If only they'd use cornmeal
And fry in bacon fat!

I long for Mama's gingerbread,
Her cobblers of wild berries
With (gone from life forever)
Thick cream from Iowa dairies.

Then smothered chicken on the farm,
With green beans on the side,
And lots of mashed potatoes
In gravy glorified.

Yes, I have traveled round the world
And nibbled at its best –
But corn-fed back in Iowa
Is where I end my Quest.

Martha Atkins Emmert

Chapter 28

AND MORE TRAVEL

In 1960, due to military unrest following Independence, we and other Americans wanting out of Congo, were ferried to Congo/ Brazzaville and air lifted out in flying fortresses of the U. S. Air Force. Flown to Accra, Ghana, our U.S. Ambassador and his wife met us at the plane and took us to their home for comfort and feeding. Reporters swarmed around taking photos of us, which appeared in their newspapers as refugees fleeing the Congo. The following Friday, our weekly Pan Am flight picked us up. On board we met colleagues from our nearest posts, with only overnight bags, ready to give details of attacks we had been spared.

Our next trip of note came one year and a new baby later. With two other families we boarded the freighter Lusambo, sailing from New York to Matadi, Congo. On this crossing our daughter took her first steps and celebrated her first birthday as we docked in Matadi after twenty-four days enroute.

We learned about the Portuguese Cape Verde Islands when we stopped and toured them. We docked first at Luanda, Portuguese Angola, to discharge cargo for a day or so. While in dock there, we toured the city by taxi and called on our U.S. Ambassador, whose car had been thrown into the Atlantic, the day before, in protest of U.S. criticism of Portugal's colonial policy. We also saw a Methodist mission church, whose windows had all been shattered by Colonial authorities. We heard the story from the American wife and children living near the church, while her husband lay in prison somewhere. Later, when he got out, they came to our area and worked with their Angolan refugees flooding Lower Congo.

In 1965, with our two children, we enjoyed a month's travel returning to America via Nigeria, Egypt, Greece, Italy, Belgium and England. What a privilege to have our children with us, whenever they dozed, we prodded them awake, "Wake up," we urged excitedly. "Look at Greece!" We did not want them to miss a thing. The fifteen-year-old surely retains more than the five-year-old.

Michal Rose only five that trip could not remember coming out by ship. Her memory held only the tropical sun on the green hills and rivers of Zaire and the faces of her playmates left behind.

I had spent hours preparing her for the trip to America. I showed photos and told her about her waiting grandparents. I made matching clothes for her and Cookie, her doll. They were both present when riding our first camel, Mr. Cadillac, or seeing the mummies in the Cairo museum. They looked for babies in the bull rushes when we sailed on the Nile.

Cookie's great adventure came in Greece. We had taken a cruise of the Greek islands for the day and were just coming in sight of Athens again when Michal Rose cried out, "Mama, Mama, Cookie's drowning!" Sure enough, Cookie floated far below us in her pink Sunday dress. Would she sink? Would the ship stop? Neither one happened.

A man got in a little rowboat on shore and came our way. Our ship docked. We landed and watched the man until he stopped, reached over the side and rescued Cookie. What a reunion and the kind Greek gentleman refused a reward. It was a Kodak moment, but we forgot to preserve it in a photo.

Highlights of that trip for me include the dye pits of Kano, Nigeria where cloth was soaked in deepest indigo, while men tended it. In Cairo, the Pyramids and Sphinx of our textbooks, surprised us by seeming so familiar, set in the blowing sands of the desert. We spent hours in the Museum, guidebook in hand. As I recall, we had the place to ourselves. In November 1991 when I returned to Cairo for a second time, the Museum featured wall to wall tourists with each guide trying to yell louder than the ones enmeshed at the borders of her group. We saw very few items, having to wait and take our turn. We felt very foreign and visible that first visit.

The signs in Arabic did not help us. The tour guides took us short distances, demanded money, and turned us over to other greedy guides. With much arm-waving and facial grimacing, we notably failed to communicate. Perhaps due to Lumumba's death, there seemed to be an anti-American climate.

Greece is everything I imagined it to be while studying and teaching ancient history during my first term. The air was clear, light-filled and lyric, and fell on ruins of sublime beauty. The Acropolis, the Olympic Stadium, the Museum, the Delphic Oracle were steeped in historical significance. The Corinthian canal was so modern, and the ruins of ancient Corinth were so reminiscent of the Apostle Paul and his letter to its inhabitants. The very air we breathed seemed pregnant with myth, legend and the Truth on which we feed. In later years, the air in Greece became polluted. Smog hid the treasures of the past and damaged them. What a pity, for out of all of the places we dreamed of, Greece came the closest to fulfilling our dreams and expectations.

We journeyed on to Italy, visiting Rome, Naples, Pompeii and Florence, which contained so many roots of our government and education. There were so many warnings for us. Rome did not fall in a day, neither will the United States, but what a lot of resemblance there is with Rome's last days, cropping up in our permissive culture. Vesuvius, like Mt. St. Helens, stands in the distance and smolders.

Our trip back to Africa via Europe in 1956 aboard the Holland-American ship, SS Princess

Margriet, proved a happy experience. I met a businessman from Holland who grows wheat in our Midwest. This astonished me. He had just made the trip to visit his fields. Somehow, it upset me to think of pieces of America belonging to foreigners. Maybe, it prepared me for the Japanese purchase of Rockefeller Center. Of course, I realize that Americans are notorious for buying land that pleases them, all over the world.

Thinking of that voyage reminds me of my little black dress. I had taken a lovely piece of cotton batik home. It was black with alternate squares featuring large African roosters. It sounds strange but made up with a square, low neck and long tight sleeves it felt quite dressy. I had worn it at a smorgasbord in Fort Wayne before sailing. When I passed some diners on the way back to my table, one man, like a muffled explosion burst out, "My God, there's a rooster on the back, too." The suave Dutch businessman aboard ship remarked with a smile, "Isn't it ironic that the best-dressed beauty on this ship should be you?" Ironic, maybe, but it was the kind of flattery I soaked up like water on a parched desert.

We left the ship in Rotterdam and rented a small car for the trip to Antwerp. Once there, we made arrangements for our baggage to be transferred to the MS Charlesville. We stayed with former student, Norman Kamosi, married and attending university there. On July 28,

1966, we sailed away on the second lap of our third voyage, to Africa.

We docked on Tenerife at Santa Cruz, in the Canary Islands, a Spanish possession, after five days at sea. The ship provided box lunches and chartered taxies for us to tour the Island, around the beaches and through the mountains. I still have chunks of pumice stone I picked up there, and Spanish Toledo swords that we bought in a roadside market.

As we sailed on, following the African coast south, we watched Flying fish and schools of dolphins accompany us, leaping loose from the water in lovely patterns. This time, when we docked at Matadi, two former students who were officers in the army, drove up to the ship in an army Jeep and though other friends had been kept off the ship, they marched stiffly aboard with salutes and fanfare, to welcome our family back. In a military dictatorship, such an occasion adds a great deal to one's consequence. We tried to stay humble and gracious to other less notable passengers.

Our next trip to remember came in 1968 when our son graduated from the American High School of the Capitol City of Congo/Zaire. We took him home to college. As his gift, we planned a trip to Switzerland, where he helped as translator from French to English in the Baptist World Alliance Youth Congress in Berne.

We landed in Geneva, and in the days available before the Congress began, we toured the picture-perfect Swiss landscape. I had dreamed of seeing Venice with its gondolas and singing gondoliers, so we decided to drive to north Italy.

Should we go by tunnels or overland? It seemed foolish to us to go underground. We had come to see all we could see. I lived to regret that choice. One pass in the Swiss Alps is sufficient to impress me. The fact that those peaks pierced cloud covers as we flew over in the eternal sunshine of the stratosphere, might have alerted me to the height of the passes.

I looked ahead and up and saw a tiny notch against the sky. I knew it was the pass we were headed for. How many times did I cower, tremble and hide my eyes, before Leon's courage and fortitude brought us safely over every pass and we reached Northern Italy?

Venice disappointed us, somehow. We found no one who spoke French, English or Kikongo. The gondolier we met took us straight to a glass factory outlet without singing and brought us back where we got on without touring St. Mark's or any of the other sights of Venice. We had no friends there to guide us.

For me, Verona is the highlight of North Italy. A lovely village; we spent the night there. The next morning carts and wagons of garden produce and flowers began to trundle past to the market place. We saw a town come alive on the weekly market day. Every part of Verona charmed me.

In 1970 we took our daughter home through Spain. We wanted to get home quickly to be with our son again. We landed in Madrid and by now, my interest in art and artists took us to the museums as well as to El Greco's Toledo, of the threatening skies.

We decided we should see at least one bull fight. After all, what else do Spaniards do for entertainment? One bullfight, did I say? I wish! We paid for our tickets and climbed into the grandstands. There, we endured not one, but three or four ceremonial deaths. I decided that costumed specialists before a paying audience, (bringing quite a good price per pound) must slaughter most of the beef of Spain. I do not recommend watching a bullfight as a fun afternoon.

In 1975, my daughter and I came home ahead of Leon. We had an hour or two in Doula, Camerouns, got stranded in Switzerland and missed a flight somewhere in Ohio. We drove into Fort Wayne at last, some time after midnight, with a happy group who decided to rent a car rather than sit and wait in Ohio for a plane. My husband's last parting assurance, "You will not need money, everything is taken care of."

That fall our daughter returned to Zaire, for school in September. My husband came home in October, after putting her in our children's hostel there. In January, we returned to our work. With only two of us returning, we decided we could afford to go back via Israel. A former colleague and friend, Wes Brown, taught third world students in Jerusalem, and we could accompany him on some of his bus teaching tours.

That remains a memorable trip. Layer upon layer of history lies in every inch of that soil. I recall running to keep up with Wes – up and down the archaeological sites called tells, taking notes, photos, soaking it all in. I tried to visualize Christ's birth and death in modern Bethlehem and Jerusalem. I thought Nazareth a small hill town. It threw me by being a pretty big metropolis. Accretions of topsoil must be mentally removed to find the actual soil on which His feet trod. But the Sea of Galilee, the Jordan River, the mountains where He stood, the lilies of the field of which He spoke, these gave great emotion and blessing as I remembered Him in the land He loved and called His home.

After retirement, I returned again to Israel in 1992 with my friend, Catherine Bruce. We saw other places, swam in the Dead Sea, drove from Jerusalem to Egypt. I saw how hard and how successfully the Israelis have worked to build a prosperous land of their rocky desert, all the while living tensed, vigilant, armed to protect themselves against enemies sworn to destroy them. I saw the Dead Sea Scrolls and the Holocaust museums. I read Michener's "The Source," and Jimmy Carter's "Blood of Abraham," again. I pray for the peace of Jerusalem.

When our daughter finished high school at the American School of Kinshasa in 1979, we planned a trip home for her as we had for her brother when he graduated. First, we flew to Athens, refreshing ourselves with the sight of its beauty. We then took a bus up the eastern coast of Greece into Turkey as far as Istanbul. Again the weight of history descended and I tried to remember all I had read of Constantine and the division of the church.

We faced language difficulties in Turkey. We could neither read the signs nor understand what we heard. We felt an uneasy climate. Soldiers stood on corners with guns at the ready, as though for an uprising. Relieved, we flew out of Turkey and into Vienna.

Already charmed with the idea of Austria, from the "Sound of Music," the Vienna Boys' Choir and the famous Lippenzaner horses featured in National Geographic, another surprise awaited us when we landed. There, beside our runway, as big as life, sat Air Force One. "Of course," we thought, "The Salt II talks are on. President Jimmy Carter is in town to meet with Leonid Brezhnev."

As we wandered through the streets of Vienna, the possibility of seeing Carter close-up excited us. Our animation fueled by watching Walter Cronkhite do a news broadcast in the street kept us on the sidewalks. We saw Barbara Walters with her bus full of supporting newspersons. Our eyes scanned each official car and our ears listened for escort sirens in the hopes of glimpsing Carter.

On Sunday, we went to the little church where the Vienna Boys' Choir sings. We found it had been sealed off early for the attendance of the Carter family and those cleared by security. This lack of foresight excluded us. We, stood in a cold drizzle on the outside warmed slightly by the tourist bodies accumulating around us.

At last the service ended. Secret Service men hopped and danced about. They opened doors, swung wide the gates and shielded the Carter family as they entered a limousine. They surrounded the car as it slowly emerged from the churchyard and entered the avenue. We could see the President smiling and waving. Rosalyn, came into view doing the same. Amy sat in the back reading a book and trying to forget the mob staring at her.

We tourists busily photographed but did not get much. Cameras held high above jostling heads for potshots do not guarantee best photos. Suddenly, the car halted, the door opened, Jimmy got out and the crowd cheered and thickened. All surged forward as everyone tried to converge on that presidential handshake. I surged as well, sure that my hour of glory had arrived. Clutching my trusty Canon, I tried to let the pushing and shoving crowd head me toward Carter. I should have been more aggressive. By the time I reached him he faced the other way. How could I shake his hand?

Instead of yelling, "Hey Jimmy, I'm back here!" I opted for a timid tap on the shoulder to get his attention. Wrong move. It did not. My tap aborted in mid-air by the iron grip of a secret service man. Neither gentle nor polite, he really excelled at hurting. I feared for my arm and my camera. I now realized one did not tap a Presidential shoulder while mobbing him. Neither could I move away fast or far. Plastered in place by the pressure of people, I retrieved my injured arm and daringly took one close-up of the back of Jimmy Carter's head. I then squirmed full speed back to my family. That photo signed by President Carter hangs in my library.

The boys' choir came outside and sang for the congregation refused entrance earlier. We thrilled to see the Lippenzaners do their stately dances and we rationed ourselves to only one expensive meal in a country with such a high cost of living.

Michal Rose wanted to see Bratislava, a Communist country, and a city of Polish and Czech history. We spent hours touring on foot, our passports held hostage, watching hungry people line up for wilted cabbages and trying in vain to find a decent souvenir to buy in the drab, empty stores. What a contrast to Vienna!

Copenhagen revived memories of the film musical of Hans Christian Andersen, which we had seen in Paris in 1956. We took a boat tour of the city. The little mermaid is much littler than we thought. We visited Tivoli gardens Amusement Park, finding our lovely souvenirs. By train we traveled to Elsinore for our daughter's contemplation of the castle made famous by Shakespeare. We took a boat to Helsinborg, Sweden, had lunch, walked about and later in the day returned to Copenhagen. We flew home from Brussels to New York.

My Library

A dream of mine has now come true
Visit me, I'll show to you,
A quiet room, below, above,
A library of books I love.

My journals are here near the floor
Then all my crafts and wild life lore.
The art that has enriched my soul.
And authors drawn from pole to pole.

My Bibles, old and new, now rest
Together here with books addressed
To problems of the heart and mind
For theologic answers find.

I've humor, history, fiction, truth –
The books that cheer, instruct, bring youth
I've C.S. Lewis and his friends
Where Merton, Michener, Muggeridge ends.

I've Sayers, Seuss, St. Johns and Shute
With West and Wodehouse, Wouk, to boot.
And back up here Bombeck and Buck,
Cosby and Keillor, Goudge, what luck!

There's Charles Schultz, Heyer and Greene,
Then L'Engle with some new between.
This shelf holds Websters, Strunk and White,
The books that help me when I write.

And here's my file of manuscripts.
This folder's for rejection slips.
See scrapbooks of my work. Now let
Me point you to the famed I've met.

I have them framed upon this wall.
There's Nixon, Nunn, B. Bush and all.
Mother Theresa smiles for me,
Her smile, a blessed one you see.

That's Mama in the photo near –
My son and daughter, babies dear.
And here is where I pray and read
And think of loved ones, those in need.

Awards, certificates, Diplome –
All saved and gathered and brought home.
To grace the walls of my book room
Defining me from womb to tomb.

Thank you God, I've this retreat
Which in the night I close to meet
With other minds and Maker, too,
As here we seek what's best to do.

Martha Atkins Emmert

Chapter 29

JUST PASSING THROUGH

I know this world is not our home, but how nice it is to get acquainted with our little plot of land here in Fort Wayne ... to burrow in, make a few ruts to live in. This is the first house I have lived in longer than three years. When our son, a toddler, traveled with us, he once prayed, "Thank you, dear Jesus, for bringing us safely ... where are we, Mama?"

To return to "the same old place" seems a luxury and a rest. I remember how the loss of each house I had made a "home," felt like a small death, orphaning the rose bushes and other flowers and trees I had planted. In the long African dry season I knew they would die without my care. Most of them did. To this Leon would remind me, "We are not here to garden."

The trip we waited for the longest, we took when Leon reached sixty-five and our career in Zaire ended. We wanted to complete a first tour of the world. When we finally headed west traveling east on March 14, 1989, we had the good fortune of being together with Jerry and Lee Weaver, long time friends and colleagues. The first lap landed us in Nairobi.

Earlier, we had visited our former student, Norman Kamosl, while he served as a representative of Air Zaire in Kenya. We stayed in the guesthouse of his gracious Nairobi home and he had driven us to Mombassa through the game parks. We had stayed with him at the Leopard Beach Hotel at his expense. This time, on our own, we stayed at a Union Mission Guesthouse in Nairobi.

From Kenya, the four of us flew to Bombay. An Indian friend, known to us in Africa, had left instructions for us at the airport telling us how to come. We, therefore, took a taxi to Poona. Much to our surprise we drove one hundred miles. We had been thinking of Poona, as a suburb of Bombay. Anil had arranged everything, from the rest in our hotel, a restaurant breakfast as his guest, rides in rickshaws, to little treats and tours of the city. We visited the house in Poona where Gandhi had been detained under house arrest and saw his grave there. That night we ate as guests of Anil's family and his aunt, Kamala Damaraj whom we had known well in Africa. They presented leis and flowers and wore the most sumptuous saris.

Returning to Bombay by train, we stood on the shore of the Bay and saw great arches where colonial powers landed during their rule of India. I saw India as frightening, incredibly vast, so full of exposed poverty, suffering, homelessness, resignation and defeat. Obvious as well to the traveler, are the proud monuments of an ancient civilization, culture and history.

India's heroes such as Gandhi and Nehru, light up our present historical era. We had seen the film, Gandhi, several times. India also has Mother Theresa. In Calcutta we accepted a gift book, *City of Joy*, from a British Jew, who was there to photograph Mother Theresa for a book about "Love".

In 1952 we sent our luggage to Calcutta, hoping shortly to follow. We wanted to go to Jorhat, Assam, where we could work with people like my dear friend from Seminary, Imchaba Bendang Wati, of Nagaland. The government of New Delhi denied us a visa, which was a major disappointment. Our freight returned to New York and waited there until we sailed for Africa.

In Calcutta we took tours and visited Indian church leaders who had studied in the United States. We saw William Carey's church where Adoniram Judson asked to be baptized after his long voyage to the East. By chance, we met Mother Theresa. We felt the benediction of her inner peace and intense love. Her caring gaze looked deep in our hearts, her hands held ours, she smiled up at us and blessed us with her interest and questions about our life and work.

We visited Mother Theresa's Orphanage and saw rooms of babies, gathered up in the night by her nuns from refuse heaps. What a beehive of volunteers there were from all communities of faith, and from all over the world. They are organized and function in the happiest, most diligent way to meet the needs of all these babies who are readied for adoption as soon as possible.

She asked us to visit her home for the dying and destitute, her first love, which we did. There we saw the dying on cement slab beds, the men in one room, women in another. They are bathed lovingly and dressed in clean garments daily by the smiling nuns of Mother Theresa's order. India is not an easy country to visit. India is more like a crucible, trying you in every way, causing you to examine your culture and values.

From Calcutta we took a four-hour train trip, on a relic from the colonial past, to Balasore in Orissa province, along the eastern coast of India. We visited our friend, Sue Powers, from seminary days and through her, delved deeper into the culture and kindness of the Indian people. One of the marvels we saw there, the incoming tide of the Bay of Bengal. Very far in the distance, we could see the tidal water standing up like the parted Red Sea, slowly advancing across miles of shallow beach, with the intent of long practice, to eventually cover the wet sands where we walked and leisurely gathered shells. It arrived long after we had quit the shore.

Another train ride took us back through those continuous rice paddies to catch our plane from Calcutta to Bangkok. We toured this thriving city with friends. Being Easter weekend, we spent most of our time with the American community, some of whom had formerly worked in Zaire. The Gerald Weavers were to return as volunteers for two years to the guesthouse where we stayed in Bangkok.

On Easter Monday we flew to Hong Kong, where we were met by western fast-food chains. We embraced McDonald's, Colonel Sanders and a pizza parlor. It took about a day to get our fill of that. We toured the slums, which were rapidly being cleared, and saw the brand new high-rise communities, into which the slum-dwellers were being transferred, with neighborhood stores and services, built into each complex. We walked the flowering parks surrounding them.

A young pastor who had trained in America, showed us places for study and sports for youth, and described the work being done with drug addicts and other needy persons. Everyone seems to be ''at work'' in Hong Kong. We loved seeing the "Junks" in the waterways, and finding some "rice china" to buy, each grain visible in the fired porcelain. We rode the tram to the top of Victoria Hill, toured the song bird market, watched them take birds in cages on walks and even to a certain restaurant, where hanging above their owners, their songs drowned out the conversation going on below. Though our visit ended very soon, the tailors still had time to measure Leon and make him a new suit. The bustle and crowds prepared us for Japan.

March turned to April in Japan, the cherry trees burst into full bloom, two weeks early. We reveled in them. The bus from Tokyo airport deposited us at the feet of a waiting friend, Dorothy Noyes, in Yokohama, after a two-hour drive. She took us to her home, ordered in hot food, and showed us how to unfold our futons to make sleeping on the floor a lark.

Dorothy, the ablest and most caring of hostesses, provided our every need, from warmer clothing to wonderful meals. She took us to Kamakura to see the Temples and a seven hundred year old really BIG Buddha, weighing 121 tons. We toured Sogo, a large department store overlooking Yokohama harbor. On the roof we enjoyed a whole nursery of bonsai, dwarfed trees in bloom. Not many women in the city wore kimonos, although the store featured the bride's red kimono. We saw a lot of bowing back and forth between folk. In May of 1992 we examined a traveling exposition of priceless antique kimonos from Japan at the Chicago Art Institute, conspicuously guarded by their Japanese chaperones.

We felt a strong dependence upon Dorothy, given the language barrier, both written and spoken. Floods of busy little people mingle with hordes of bicycles. All of them were in a big hurry to get somewhere else. We visited Soshin, a Christian Girl's School in Yokohama, Kanto Gakuin University and the Tokyo Peace Church at Waseda University. Our colleagues worked in each of these schools. Every morning we ran out and looked toward Mt. Fuji. We saw a lot of haze.

Regretfully, we left the blooming bushes of Camellias and stuck close to Dorothy as she led the way by train back to Tokyo, putting us into the hands of Mary Jean Gano. Mrs. Gano, proceeded to present us with a series of impeccable Japanese meals, each with a different table decor and a different set of dishes.

Before leaving Japan, my girlhood friend, Dorothy Bond, married to Dr. Shelton Allen, both career missionaries in Japan, came to collect us and take us to their home where she spread before us a real mid-western roast pork dinner, in the suburbs of Tokyo. They followed us shortly to the US for their own retirement.

Strictly speaking, when we passed through U.S. Customs in Honolulu we had arrived home. However we still considered Hawaii an exotic and foreign land. Eleven wonderful days of exploration changed that. Three of the Weaver children live there and Joel met us with leis in hand. We visited all three, and before we left we welcomed a new Weaver grandchild. With them we toured the two islands of Oahu and Kauai, including a visit to Pearl Harbor where my brother Paul had served in the Navy in World War II.

The weather being stormy for most of our visit, the seas piled high and roaring, the beaches did not beckon as I had been led to believe. Big signs warned of rogue waves, which could run right up on land and snatch you. Well, I had read Michener's Hawaii; I knew all about that. I discovered in myself wariness, induced by the unaccustomed phenomena of being surrounded by unfriendly waters on islands you can almost see across. In the markets I searched to find a purchase that did not have "Hawaii" stamped across the front. They sure know how to advertise.

Finally, on April 17, we landed in San Diego, completing our first world tour. There, we lived with Frank and Joan Andersen for awhile in Escondido, while Frank took care of Leon's medical problems and I had a physical. I learned I had cancer and before many hours passed, I had submitted to a mastectomy. In shock, I girded myself for another kind of journey ... the journey through chemotherapy and hopefully, back to health. The transition to home and the attendant trauma consumed our first year and led up to our official retirement in March 1990.

The major travels are now listed. At last count we had visited 34 countries plus a few Caribbean islands. Whether the future holds others, it is hard to say. We are occupied at the moment in grand parenting. In this chapter we have dropped some big names. More will follow in the next chapter.

"Austerity has always made me happy, and its opposite, miserable. I find it strange that knowing this I should so often have inflicted upon myself the nausea of over indulgence, and had to fight off the black dogs of satiety. Human beings as Pascal points out, are peculiar in that they avidly pursue ends they know will bring them no satisfaction; gorge themselves with food, which cannot nourish and with pleasures, which cannot please. I am a prize example."

Malcolm Muggeridge

Nov. 1982 - Martha Emmert presenting a floral tribute to Barbara Bush at the American Embassy residence in Kinshasa

Chapter 30

BIG NAMES MET IN PASSING

It is a curious paradox that when you leave the world behind and go to serve in some remote area, you end up as I did, meeting and greeting the most unlikely people. This surprises no one more than myself. I went to Africa, divesting myself of furs and the best coat I ever had, prepared to die like David Livingstone, in the heart of darkest Africa. I end up meeting celebrities.

Sometimes while carrying out my duties these coincidences happened even here in the States, while we were on home leave. I remember our biennial convention, which the church held in Kansas City, Missouri in 1970. There in the hotel corridors one day, who should come strolling down the hall but an aged Harry Truman, being assisted by thirty-nine year old Jack Benny. Well, I have nothing against Harry Truman; he is a fellow Democrat, after all. In those days we thought his language a mite salty for a Baptist, but compared to today's sitcoms and talk shows, he seems as chaste as a Quaker. At any rate, I had to make a quick choice. I chose Jack Benny.

I can not say what Harry Truman did in those gloomy war years when, as a pre-Christian teenager, I balanced morosely on my milking stool in a dank and drafty barn, milking Old Bossy with my weary head resting against her warm flank. I recall reflecting that all the sauce and piquancy had gone out of life since the dispersal of my brothers and their friends into the far-flung fields of World War II.

The only bright spot left to me came Sunday night at seven, when, if we were lucky, we could hear a half-hour of The Benny Show on our malfunctioning radio. I owed Jack Benny some thanks and a warm hand-squeeze for the few laughs that we had in those days. I will not deny it thrilled me. I still treasure the memory of meeting Jack Benny.

Speaking of chaste Quakers, I have a photo of me taken with Richard Nixon. At the time, he figured as a politician whose name we all knew. He was not as well known as he is today. A group of us stood in the hotel lobby catching up on our deputation stories, when Nixon, stopping at the same hotel, decided to be folksy and mingle with us. As possible future votes, we may have been a disappointment to him, since we seldom stayed in the States at election time and who knows when, if ever, those absentee ballots arrive.

I consider meeting Muhammad Ali, the world's champion boxer, a gift straight from heaven. I did not ask for it or seek it. Again, it just happened in the line of duty. Both he and

George Foreman flew to Kinshasa for the great boxing match of 1974. You must remember. Publicity flourished. But meet him? Me? How could I possibly contrive such a thing? I ask you? The answer is, I did not.

It happened like this. I drove to the Intercontinental Hotel in Kinshasa for the regular monthly meeting of the International Woman's Club. I functioned as Chairperson of the Welfare Committee and thought only of the report I had to make. After our business we had a very good program, and with our minds still bubbling with that, a colleague and I made our way through the hall into the hotel lobby.

We stopped stock still. There before our eyes stood Cassius Clay/Muhammad Ali holding a press conference. He had gathered up some wee African in his arms and between newsworthy statements, he planted kisses on top of its head. This gesture immediately activated all the flash bulbs held by the cameramen grouped around him.

He really is beautiful. There is no denying it. My friend and I goggled and even giggled in spite of being matrons. We both felt a motherly inclination to fuss over him, he looked so boyish, so innocent and so sweet. Talk about the All-American boy! Just to look at him warmed our hearts. We sort of hung around near the exit, gazing at him, until the press conference ended. Unimpeded, he made his way straight to us. He stuck out a large hand and in a soft voice inquired, "How do you do, Ladies?"

We told him. We prattled like teen-agers all the way to our car. He heard where we hailed from in the States, what we did in Zaire and who knows what else, all the while basking in our admiring smiles and motherly concern for him. We decided capriciously, that he must shake both hands of both of us before we could let him go, which he graciously did.

Well, I will tell you, it may seem foolish now, but he pre-empted the Club program in our minds and conversations for the rest of that day. It was a big day. I still remember it vividly.

After researching his enormous tome containing everything you ever wanted to know about the Boer War, Thomas Pakenham came crawling out of the African Bush and just happened to come to my door for food and lodging. I admit he did not have much choice. Motels and hotels are hard to come by outside of Kinshasa. But I am so glad he came. An Irish nobleman, he lives in a castle. The one-fourth of me that is Irish rushed to predominance as I hostessed him to within a centimeter of his life. It is a very rare treat to have a houseguest as handsome, as tripping-of-tongue, as entertaining and as cultured as Thomas Pakenham.

I had always heard that truly noble persons knew how to put common folk at their ease, and it is true. I felt as close to Thomas as a Country Cork cousin. I admit we have not maintained that closeness. Months after he left, I received a packet containing autographed copies of the first two volumes of Malcolm Muggeridge's autobiography.

After much effort I puzzled out the inscription written in Muggeridge shorthand. I still could not explain the windfall until I remembered the merry tales told me by the Irish nobleman who knew Muggeridge as a fellow journalist. I had expressed my great admiration for Muggeridge.

When we passed through Copenhagen, I looked at the palace and wondered what would happen if I knocked at the door requesting an audience with Prince Henry, the Queen's consort from France. By another of those odd quirks of fate I met that most charming of Princes. He looks like a Prince lifted right out of fairy tales of childhood. How ever did we meet? I will tell you.

Leon, the Field Secretary of our Mission, received invitations to one of our bush stations where the Danish Red Cross had allotted financial aid. The Hospital and Medical School buildings had been enlarged and representatives from Denmark were coming to the official ceremony commemorating the use of those funds.

On the appointed day, we dressed in our poor best and headed by auto towards the country post in question. No sooner had we turned onto the main highway leading out of town, than we realized we had unwittingly joined a cortege of cars, flanked fore and aft by motorcycle police, sirens in full cry.

It was a heady trip for a humble missionary. We never once had to halt or hesitate. The way cleared. Cars fell in ditches in their eagerness to give us the right of way. We thus proceeded for the first and last time in our long career, to drive unhindered for the complete eighty kilometers from Kinshasa to Sona Bata.

Once we arrived, the station leaders designated the reception areas and explained protocol. We discovered we had not only arrived with the Danish Ambassador to Zaire and the Red Cross officials of International stature, but had been enjoying the special escort of Prince Henry of Denmark. He came to do his duty for his wife and Queen. She stayed home. I later heard some foolish bystander ask if I were the Queen. Probably those navy blue pantyhose I wore, left to me by some tourist, had impressed them. At any rate, as we greeted Prince Henry and made socially acceptable conversation after the ceremony, we females were thinking wistfully of being Cinderella with a Prince like Henry riding out in search of us.

George and Barbara Bush, at that time our Second Couple, also came to Zaire, and as it turned out, we are numbered among those who attended the reception for them at the American Ambassador's Residence. We remember the fine meeting we had with Barbara Bush and her gracious response to our delegation from our post at Kimpese. Her two-page hand-written "Thank You" to us, later that night, remains a choice possession.

In 1976, President Mobutu of Zaire held an open house and reception for all Americans in Kinshasa. For this gala event he chose the center of a military camp which housed his elite paratroopers and personal guard. This celebration honored our Bicentennial. The invitation stated formal attire. The evening featured refreshments, music, dancing and a reception line to meet the President, personally.

Some visiting bush colleagues had come to town unprepared for high society. A great skirmish for long gowns and suitable male clothing for everyone ensued, most of us hoping to keep our best clothing for ourselves. Shortly after being transported to the soiree, we passed through the reception line. We met a very personable and friendly man in the President. We then stood aside watching as others arrived and met him. Bulbs began to pop and it occurred to a couple of us early birds that the news media had missed us. There would be no record of our having met President Mobutu. As we grumbled good naturedly about this, pretending to be serious, Citizen Karl I Bond, directly in front of us in the receiving line, turned and said in perfect English, "Why do you not go through the line again?"

What a novel idea! Most of my colleagues refused to entertain the thought. I found one game fellow with whom I could go along as his moral support, or vice versa. Of course this proves just how memorable the hoi polloi can be. We could have gone through ten times, no doubt, and still be unrecognized each time. Anyhow, irony of ironies, just as we neared President Mobutu the second time, the bulbs popped and our images confronted us in the next day's edition of the newspaper, showing that even a little pushiness gets you somewhere.

And last but not least, I met Sam Nunn. I had fully expected Mr. Nunn to become President of the United States but he has been a disappointment in his unwillingness to run. Sam Nunn came to Zaire a few years ago under some guise or another to do something unspecified, which possibly may not have been politically wise to disclose. Be that as it may, one fine day in Kinshasa, I received an invitation from a Southern Democrat to come to an exclusive group meeting with Sam Nunn.

In my excitement I permitted my Republican husband to go along. When Sam Nunn entered the room, he made a good impression on me. He has an open honest look about him. He shows strength of character and has a no-nonsense sort of purposeful manner. He shook hands with each of us and asked a few questions as he made his way around the circle.

After that we settled down to an informal discussion of issues that interest us Democrats. I like Sam Nunn. If he ran for President, I would vote for him. Not just because I have had my photograph taken with him, either. He represents sound American values. He believes in truth, church attendance, family unity and yes, motherhood and apple pie! He said so, himself. Now if he can only bring himself to support Clinton, I would feel happier.

1975 - Martha Emmert with her first driving license

"Perhaps it is no wonder that women were first at the Cradle and last at the Cross. They had never known a man like this Man – there never has been another ... (He) never nagged at them, never flattered or coaxed or patronized; never made arch jokes ... rebuked without querulousness and praised without condescension; who took their questions and arguments seriously; who never mapped out their sphere for them, never urged them to be feminine or jeered at them for being female ... had no axe to grind and no uneasy male dignity to defend..."

Dorothy L. Sayers

Chapter 31

WOMEN'S LIB

By the early 'seventies, echoes of women's issues and accusations were reaching even the foreign fields. Overseas, we tried to keep informed, but often our New York Times book Review or our Christian Science Monitor came in large quantities several months late, making it difficult to keep up to date on current thought.

Through books, articles and women's gatherings I inevitably became aware of the inequities fueling the Women's Lib movement. One item especially gave me food for thought. Some writers claimed that if a husband dies, the wife cannot touch his bank account -- even to bury him.

Up to that point I had considered myself content to let my husband manage all financial affairs, which he did very well. After all what did I know about money? I had never had any to manage. As a child, the money I had earned had gone to my father. At the seminary all my wages went for board and room. After marriage it took both our wages to survive while Leon earned his degrees.

As a young Christian who was new to a society of church members, I assumed that whenever I disagreed, I must be wrong and anti-Christian. My insecure personality made it easy for me to surrender my independence and as much responsibility as I could (thus avoiding blame). In those days I did not equate money with power, and readily turned it over.

Leon assumed the whole financial burden. He made shopping decisions for everything, much as my father had done with the little we managed on. Being half Scot and half German, Leon is very canny about quality and price. He habitually restricts himself to sales of better quality merchandise. He has several reasons for choice and he is not an impulse shopper.

Then came the disturbing issues of the seventies. How could I mature if all choices were taken care of for me? How did I know I could not handle money? When I traveled alone on speaking tours during furloughs, I handled my travel allowance and expense account very well. I knew that some Christian wives handled all the family finances and the husband applied to his wife for cash. Woman's Lib stirred up a great deal of critical self-analysis within me.

Then came the shocker on July 4th of 1973. A black limousine came to convey Leon to the American embassy in Kinshasa. There he was handed a telegram listing the deaths of his mother Vida, his only brother Walt, wife Ruth, and his only sister, Lois. His father had died previously. It was, in fact, the end of Leon's primary family.

The Emmerts had spent the evening flying in Walt's plane to see the northern Indiana fireworks. Walt had suffered a stroke and the plane crashed in a small lake and sank. The family died on impact.

Our only son, Dan, who had to work that day installing Pepsi dispensing machines, was spared. Three nieces survived their parents' death. Dan lived with Aunt Lois, so the police called upon him to identify the bodies. Twenty-three years of age at the time, and ever since, both he and his father barely tolerate Fourth of July celebrations.

With close friends from the seminary, Audley and Catherine Bruce, Leon and I had planned our twenty-fifth anniversary trip together through Europe that year. Since our passports and visas were up to date, we were able to get on a plane the same night. We arrived in Chicago at midnight the next day, met by these friends. Instead of an anniversary trip, they took us to the farm and stayed with us to help clean, sort and prepare everything for an estate auction.

These were traumatic days and we moved in a haze of disbelief. Walter and Ruth were buried before we arrived home, but it helped us to be present at Leon's mother's and sister's joint funeral in their home church in Topeka, Indiana. This tragedy, which might have brought us closer, seemed to have the opposite effect. It seemed to underline for me all the dangers of dependency.

I saw how a stroke of fate took four lives without warning. I imagined Leon gone, suddenly. What would become of me? I experienced paralyzing fear. I knew nothing about the financial affairs that supported our lives. I had never written a check, never had my own bank account.

I did not drive. When Leon purchased his first car, after a year of marriage, he wrote a check in full for it. This impressed me. A new black Plymouth, bought out-right! My Dad always drove some decrepit truck, which died before the payments were concluded. Daddy then located another truck with a short life span and repeated the whole despairing process. I felt relief to be emancipated from that syndrome.

Before my brothers went off to World War II, I was the right age and had begun to learn to drive. After they left, I took one of Daddy's old cars out and drove it into a ditch. I had to go get my Dad and have him recover the car for me. I did not risk trying again. Soon after that episode, my conversion and call to Christian service happened, dimming all other goals except study and preparation.

Our new car, coming right after my graduation from seminary reminded me that I needed to learn to drive. We did not thrive as teacher and tutor. I got the feeling my driving made Leon nervous and very likely, he would get angry if I scratched or dented the car. Since we lived in Chicago, the probability seemed high of doing both. According to my custom, I gave up trying, disappointed that Leon did not insist I learn.

In Africa, with one pick-up truck per station, I rarely saw a woman driving a mission car. We had one exception—a single lady, who, as school inspector, for whom driving was a job requirement. We women rode in the back of the pick-up, with our children. Whenever I returned to the States on home leave, it always took a while for me not to feel uppity, when I actually rode inside a closed vehicle. It was such an odd sensation after the years of windy, bumpy rides in open trucks.

By 1975, pressured by growing anxieties of dependency, I vowed to correct my situation as speedily as possible. When school ended, together with our 4th term, my opportunity came.

Leon, still suffering bereavement, elected to stay on a few months longer, while I traveled home with Michal Rose, now a middle-schooler. Our first grandson had just been born in February. We were eager to meet him.

Dan and his wife Carmen lived in our Fort Wayne house where he and Aunt Lois had lived. Michal Rose and I moved into the upstairs apartment. This was convenient, especially when I traveled for our Mission Board, since I did not have to leave my daughter alone.

Our grandson, Nathan Douglas, erased any doubts I may have had about being a grandmother. We filled albums with his photos. An adorable baby, he made our hearts sing with hope and joy.

My first job toward assuming more responsibility was to learn to drive. I immediately enrolled in a driving school and proceeded to memorize the rules of the road. In due season, I passed my driver's test and obtained my first license at age 52. I never mentioned my driving lessons to Leon. When he came home later that fall, I met him at the airport. He suffered a shock but has slowly adjusted to it. From then on, back in Zaire, I was able to chauffeur my daughter wherever she needed to be, which solved our school transportation problem.

As another step up from dependency, I wanted a bank account of my own. I opened a savings account and from then on, deposited personal checks I received in my name. By the time I returned to Africa in 1976, I had enough to put in two CD's, to draw larger interest during our absence. For the first time in my life I now had a chance to work with and control a small sum of money. In those days, if you were a married lady on the mission field, your salary automatically went to your husband. Only the single women received salary checks in their names. Each time I approached mission executives about this, they treated it as a joke. I understand the next generation of missionaries, can already arrange it otherwise.

Except for the year I stayed home in Congo, to nurse Michal Rose in 1961 and teach Dan sixth grade, I worked full time as a teacher, or whatever my assignment might be.

Since Leon pays the bills out of our joint salaries, this leaves me managing my fraction of his Social Security. I plan my tithes and gifts for God, support my writing habit, buy greeting cards and gifts, and try very hard to increase our joint estate. I enjoy a Chevrolet Cavalier of 1989 vintage and a library where I can close the door and find peace and silence when I need it.

"No wonder they have said that Thou art 'Love", for if this be not love which follows all my way, dear God, and waits through my forgetfulness, "til I remember, and turns not from me in my soiled and tawdry hour, but haunts me still – yea, even in the uttermost parts of the sea,
And spares, persuades, disputes with me, wooing with more power to break my heart than ever guilty child discovers in his mother's eyes ...
Oh, love me, love me in this lonely perilous world, Love me Lord, among the host of men, in gay hours and in grave, forgive, and wait and love me without merit in me and without stint in Thee,
Though I be unlovable to all but Thee,
To all but thy patient, measureless and perfect love.
O love of God, how beautiful Thou art...
How very full of hope to such as I."

McCall, The Hand of God

Chapter 32

WITHOUT A SHEPHERD

After my life-changing conversion and commitment to Christ, I lived for three years in my hometown, Muscatine, Iowa. I completed my high school work while blessed with a very nurturing Pastor and wife, Wesley and Eleanor McMurray. We had a small, warm close Christian fellowship at church, Lincoln Boulevard Baptist. I learned the Christian walk and saw the Christian virtues in action.

There, in the church, the girl nearest my age, who had been praying for a Christian friend, spent hours with me learning chapters of the Bible by heart and praying together.

The pastor guided me in my prayer life, (I had never prayed before), suggesting I use the Lord's Prayer and add to it whatever was in my heart. He taught me to seek God's will through prayer and Bible study (I had never read the Bible) and to make my own decisions. He was a happy, fun loving young minister, in love with a bride who seemed perfect for her role. I have often wondered how they tolerated our invasion of their honeymoon privacy that first married year.

Suddenly my nursery days were over. The unthinkable happened and our pastor answered a call elsewhere and soon it was time for me to go to the seminary. My pastoring since then has been by chance and by study.

I found myself working in Junior Church, which meant I missed sermons. I suppose the housemother at seminary would have given me pastoral care but she was so strict we only saw her when we broke some unwritten law. She once called me in because she had seen my hand on Leon's knee in the parlor and warned me of evil effects of such behavior. I had no idea what she had in mind.

Often I enjoyed the friendship of Archie, a black student. We would go places together. My housemother (from Texas) called me in to tell me it was not a good practice to be seen together. That did not fit my version of Christianity and I hope I ignored her.

Arriving in Africa with all the years before me stretching ahead for a career beyond my ability, I regretted greatly the lack of a pastor. I comforted myself often by the song:

> *"If I have but Jesus, only Jesus*
> *Nothing else in all the world beside*
> *Oh then everything is mine in Jesus*
> *All my needs and more He will provide."*

I told myself, "I have my Bible, I have Jesus and prayer, it should be enough." I had been a Christian fourteen years, but sometimes I felt like a shepherdless lamb. My hope that Leon would be my pastor somehow did not work out, though, for a time, I kept trying to make it work before giving it up.

No pastor has ever quite taken the place of my first pastor, although some have from time to time been helpful. Some pastors do not know how to treat missionaries. We are only sinners saved by grace, but they put us in a separate category, as many lay people do, and keep a respectful distance from us.

Once or twice the mission board sent out a pastoral counselor to visit with each of us in confidentiality. This was good, but it was so brief, it only underlined our sense of being alone on an island of need with too few resources. Each of us was reluctant to burden a colleague by adding our problems to his load. We needed an impartial ear, one we could trust. This problem still exists, unsolved.

Every fifth year we had a year of home assignment traditionally called a furlough. It gave us a chance to visit family, improve our education and visit the many interested and supporting churches. During our term in Africa we would sometimes in our dreams, equate home leave with rest and spiritual refreshment. In reality, all too often, the only voice we heard raised in the churches was our own, recounting the work of God.

By 1958, well into my first term in Africa, my faith floundered. Measuring my unproven abilities against the enormity of my job's demands, I feared I had jumped into something over my head. With rising panic and without a pastor or confidant to whom I dared confess such disastrous fears, I searched for help among the libraries of my colleagues.

In one of them, God pointed out "Mere Christianity". In my mind, from then on, "C. S. Lewis," meant not only "friend" but "pastor." As I read the successive chapters, life came back into perspective, the commitment I had made, seemed possible of fulfillment. Satan's use of my perfectionism versus my inferiority complex, ended in his defeat rather than mine... I had found a defender here on earth, in the nick of time.

From then on, Lewis served as my Pastor and Counselor and I have been avid and relentless in my acquisition of any words he wrote or said. Until today, he figures very large in his influence on my life and work, much more real to me than many persons I have known all my life.

Of all I have read of C. S. Lewis since, (and I have collected everything possible and reread it annually) I still read, in tears, this passage which fixed his place in my heart forever.

"...If your are a poor creature – poisoned by a wretched upbringing in some house full of... Senseless quarrels... Nagged day in and day out by an inferiority complex that makes you snap at your best friends do not despair. He knows what a wretched machine you are trying to drive.

Keep on. Do what you can. One day He will fling it on the scrap heap and give you a new one. And then you may astonish us all - not least yourself: for you have learned your driving in a hard school."

I felt Lewis' heart was compassionate and loving. He wanted to help simple folk, such as I, whom God had plucked off the street, willing to use us for His good purpose in jobs too great for us, apart from His grace. Lewis brought back all the faith-building truths I needed in terms that comforted and delighted me. He never used the religious jargon that had bothered me so much as a converted pagan. (I could not even pray until I learned King James language.)

The Narnia Chronicles came to me in time for me to read them aloud to my two children over and over throughout their childhood. I still read them. I have made large watercolor reproductions of Pauline Baynes' Aslan, Reepicheep, Puddleglum and Mr. Tumnus, for my library wall next to a map of Narnia. They light my retirement.

In 1963 Lewis died. I had planned by then, to stop in England in 1965 on our way home and try to attend one of his lectures. His death killed that dream. I am glad that I wrote him on his last Christmas, thanking him and trying to express what his books had meant to me. I did not expect an answer. I knew the burden of correspondence we both carried. He answered. This treasured reply is in the Wade Collection. I did not write again. I did not need to. All that I know of his marriage, nickname, "Jack," has been learned since.

I often left after a year at home, more spent physically and mentally than when I arrived from the field. I think I felt this more than Leon who has greater emotional and spiritual stamina than I do. We often traveled separately to reach more churches.

One exception to this pattern stood out in contrast when the First Baptist Church of Minneapolis provided a retreat for furloughed missionaries in 1984. We attended, visited with the congregation informally and listened to speakers dealing with our own spiritual rekindling. They dealt with burnout, with our isolation and other concerns sympathetically. Those few days during one furlough, have figured as a satisfying downpour in a long drought with few showers.

Of course, the truth is that in ministering we are ministered unto. Many times I have felt God sent me to serve in Africa primarily for my own growth and good rather than for the Africans. I learned so much more than I could have taught.

I can not blame the churches, because how could they know without a messenger? It always amazed me that busy Americans, would take time to leap the distance to Africa in imagination and love, writing to us, remembering our birthdays and holidays asking for gift lists, food lists and book lists. What impelled them to faithfully go through the hassle of sending those parcels that so lit up our lives when they arrived for us and our children. How we have thanked God for our faithful churches and the many Christians who made our service possible.

During our final furlough we were invited to our Seminary, Northern Baptist in Lombard, Illinois, near Chicago to serve three months as missionaries in residence. We moved to the apartment on campus in time for classes beginning in January.

We held joint seminar classes on Mission in Zaire/Belgian Congo, usually in the evenings, were available for consultation, spoke in Chapel and hoped to arouse some interest in career work as missionaries. We made some fine young friends among the students and enjoyed the renewed friendship of President Dr. William Myers, who had previously been our pastor at North Shore Baptist church in Chicago.

> *"I learned a very important lesson: one can always push oneself a little bit beyond what only yesterday was thought to be the absolute limit of one's endurance.*
>
> Golda Meir

> *"This thing of being a hero, about the main thing to it is to know when to die. Prolonged life has ruined more men than it ever made.*
>
> Will Rogers

1975 - National Convention of American Baptists. Martha Emmert being congratulated by Dr. Charles Koller and Professor Adam Baum of Northern Baptist Theological Seminary for receiving the Alumnus of the Year Award (Leon also received the award that year)

Chapter 33

HEROES AND HOBBIES

Reading has always been a favorite occupation since before I can remember and when pressures become unbearable, I can always find a book to lighten my outlook. Learning through books is a vocation; rereading favorites an avocation. The hardest possessions to leave behind me when I die will be my very familiar and much read books.

Besides the Bible and C.S. Lewis, I have had help from J.B. Phillips, Thomas Merton, Mother Theresa, Norman Vincent Peale and Schuler. I need large doses of optimism and positive thought for I tend to be a pessimist, and must forcefully try to change. I love being around friends who are cheerful, funny, and optimistic. In fiction, I grew up on Mark Twain, Gene Stratton Porter and James Fenimore Cooper.

I read all the boys' books as well, *Three Musketeers*, *Treasure Island*, and Booth Tarkington's books. I liked Louisa May Alcott and identified with her somewhat in my longing to write someday. We read the Sherlock Holmes books, *Little Lord Fauntleroy*, *Heidi*, *Black Beauty*. I found sad stories about animals unbearable.

I love reading Tolkien and Dr. Suess books and Madeleine L'Engle's series for children. In Africa among the British missionaries, I discovered Elizabeth Goudge and Georgette Heyer, two I have used a lot for escape and relaxation. Pearl Buck, Michener, Morris West, and Nevil Shute could all be relied on for an absorbing read. I was touched by *To Kill A Mockingbird* and *Patch of Blue* and *Five Smooth Stones*. Leon Uris, Elswyth Thane, P.G. Wodehouse, Van Auken, Muggeridge and Jeffery Archer are authors I have accepted as friends and I learned from them.

Since Art was given me to teach, I felt I should have enthusiasm for it. This led me to study and try it out and see what I could learn. As a result arts and crafts have been a hobby for years. I specialize in art pieces made from found materials rather than from new materials. I have dabbled in oil, acrylic, aquarelle, pottery, sand, rocks, driftwood, block-print, batik, tie dye, beaded egg shells, murals, mobiles, stabiles etc. with and without my students.

Flowers are an abiding love and I am an incurable gardener. Much of the pleasure I have derived from living has come from flowers, from orchid corsages to the simplest of wild flowers. I am always ready to see a park or flower garden or botanical display. Since childhood, one flower could occupy my attention for quite a long time.

I always had morning glories, moss roses, petunias and nasturtiums wherever we lived. With flowers, I love plants, bushes, and trees, fruits and nuts and berries. Picking wild berries has been a lifetime pleasure. Picking any fruits or vegetables, I classify as fun. Tramping through woods, along rivers, beside lakes, is a dream of the past. Such walks today would seem to invite disaster from lurking villains.

I am not an impeccable seamstress as was my mother, nevertheless, I have always enjoyed embroidery. I loved the bright colors with sheen. I later learned needlepoint and counted cross-stitch and enjoyed making gifts and decorative pieces for our homes. I have designed and hooked rugs and managed to make two quilts in my life.

For some reason I always had a passion for heirlooms and since none were passed to me I made sure I would pass some on to my children. They are not that interested after all, but I had fun planning and doing it for them.

I learned to use my little Singer featherweight that I bought with my second paycheck from Union Station in Chicago in 1949. I made my baby clothes, innumerable shirts for Leon and Dan and dresses for Michal Rose and me. I sewed uniforms for our students, curtains, drapes and chair coverings for our homes. It is only lately that it sits idle.

If walking is a hobby, I like to walk but I am distracted easily by plant and animal. City walking goes a little faster but I never liked to jog. Letter writing is both a work and a hobby depending on to whom it is addressed. Usually, I prefer hand-writing to talking on the phone and I always prefer handwriting to typewriting. Anything to disturb the sounds of silence is unwelcome to me while trying to think.

I spent a year practicing macro-photography in the jungles of Zaire. I discovered exquisite beauty in the minutest creations.

As to heroes or heroines, people I have looked up to and let influence my ideals – I suppose Eleanor Roosevelt was the first, chronologically. I became aware of politics and public services during the Roosevelt era and they had a great impact on my thinking and feeling about life and the world. Growing up poor and migrant, the chance that I would ever become a Republican was very slim.

Later, I came to respect Golda Meir and Indira Gandhi as women to be reckoned with. Closer home I had as role models my first pastor and his wife, Reverend and Mrs. E. Wesley McMurray, my Spanish teacher, Catherine Miller, my seminary President, Dr. Charles Koller, and later on, C.S. Lewis. I also had my parents as nature lovers and Vida Grensing as a loving Christian mother. My cousin Amber Flannery, who witnessed to me first is far above me in the Christian climb. In every true friend there is a touch of heroism that awes me. I say to myself, " I can never attain that level." I thank God for friends who teach by example and point me higher.

During the UNICEF Year of the child, Frank and Teresa Caplin who collected folk toys for an exhibition contacted me. After months of correspondence, I collected the wire toys of Zaire made by street children. They were quite inventive and accurate with making motorcycles, the Presidential yacht, the concord jet, village scenes, buses, trucks, and so on. This was sent to Princeton to the Caplins and is now with their extensive collection at the Children's Museum in Indianapolis. I do keep art collecting for myself and for my church as an option and as I am able, try to acquire reproductions for framing.

Out of my study and teaching, I have my own favorites purchased from museums where the originals hang. I like Renoir's "*Girl With The Watering Can*," and Murillo's "*Peasant Boy*," Fragonard's "*Girl In Yellow*," reading a book. I love Andrew Wyeth's "*Cornfield*," and "*Jamie*." I collect Rockwell and Grandma Moses and we used drapes printed with her "*Early Springtime on the Farm*," to cool our tropic quarters during our career. I have used Van Gogh as a model in teaching, representing Protestantism. He was fired as a missionary for giving all his possessions away. How different from the early Missionary to Zaire in 1878, Henry Richards who finally sparked the first revival and formed the first Christian church in the Lower Zaire by giving away his possessions when asked for them.

Picasso showed me that I need not be too proud to scrounge for the materials I needed for teaching and making art projects. He regularly raided the city dump with an old baby carriage. "If it is good enough for Picasso, it's good enough for me," I often mumble as I collect from garbage cans and dumpsters.

While teaching Art at the Theological School in Kinshasa I also served as welfare committee chairperson for the International Women's Club. This group included all women from Embassy, business or mission communities, who could use English. I enjoyed the opportunity to make new friends outside the narrow limits of our mission. The Club donated a sum of money for play equipment at the new Pediatric wards being built in Kimpese. We gave regularly for the benefit of women and children in Zaire.

By going to Kimpese myself for a week at a time, I managed to supervise the design and construction of playroom toys and furniture. Since books were not practical, I used murals instead in the playroom and wards.

My theological students provided marvelous illustrations of Noah's story using African animals: a thatched ark and supplies for it being garnered from African gardens and wilds by people (representing Noah's family) from African villages. The mural continues around the four playroom walls.

Each room has a simple text and a couple of mobiles to match the theme. For example, one ward says, "God's love surrounds us." We can not see it but we know it is there as surely as the bright band of colors that climbs the walls, races across ceiling corners, in and out of windows to join finally in an unending circle, like the circle of God's unending love. Besides this ward, there follows the Flag, Numbers, Alphabet, Bird and Map Wards.

An old workman commented, "Mama, we will never, ever repaint these walls. A recovering child asked me, "Where can I learn so I can grow up and paint like you?" Rich rewards for reasonable service.

While still teaching at the Theological School in Kinshasa we had a visitor from the Baptist World Alliance offices in Washington, D.C., Letha Casazza. We toured the dilapidated but historic Sims Chapel. It is the oldest permanent building in Kinshasa built in 1891 by Dr. Aaron Sims of the American Baptist Foreign Mission Society.

The windows full of broken pieces had lost latches. The arches above the doors were open permitting thievery of our light bulbs inside, also unprotected by covers. The yard was ill kept and a pile of trash filled the space behind the Chapel.

Letha Casazza recommended that I try to restore Sims Chapel and put it and its grounds in order. She donated a sum to help pay for glass, carpenter, whitewash and whatever else I had to purchase. It proved a pleasure and privilege for me. With student designs from Old and New

Testament, I filled the windows arched tops with art stain and outline paste for leading.

All of the figures are African. Joseph wears a special hat and cane reminiscent of African Chiefs. The Last Supper is luku and mwamba and the wine is made from palm sap and served in an earthen jug. We did grills above the doors and with sheet copper designed pierced covers with colored glass to cover all the light bulbs. Sims Chapel is a delightful setting for weddings and is now again being used for regular services. A large historical plaque placed there by the Zairian Government marks it.

1972 - Martha Emmert with chimpanzee JoJo, Darling of the Mission Station, Kinshasa, Congo.

My Sacrifice

When I look back on all the years
I toiled in far-off foreign spheres,
Forsaking family, friends and ease,
I managed to adapt to these.

But when Spring came where I had grown
Tho' now I lived in Torrid Zone,
And tropic flowers graced my rooms,
I grieved for distant lilac blooms.

I missed, of course, our teeming shops,
The operas, concerts, even pops,
But oh, when Spring returned back there,
I yearned for lilac-scented air.

And each year's hard detachment brings,
My sacrifice of lilac Springs.
As old year passed into the new,
The lilac hunger in me grew.

And now that I am home once more
And Spring reopens winter's door,
I blissfully restore my soul
With lilac blooms in yellow bowl.

Martha Atkins Emmert

Chapter 34

ANIMALS AND PLANTS I LOVED

Our lives during my childhood depended on hunting wild game for food. We did not hunt for sport. My father loved animals and would bring home orphaned babies when he found them. We have raised skunks and opossums, stray cats, stray dogs, and even white rats becoming involved and interested in their needs and life styles. In the kitchen Mama might have a runt pig warming in a box behind the wood stove or a sickly baby chick to be revived. We were taught to love and respect animal life.

In Africa, as a zoology teacher, my students would bring me whatever they found in the wild. Numerous baby monkeys, toothless and nearly helpless, needing much nursing and care, from the macaque to the red tailed and white curly one. Many times I taught or did housework with a tiny monkey orphan sleeping in my apron pocket. They need to be near a warm body and are accustomed to movement. They cry when you put them down or when they are hungry in the night.

Of our monkeys I can remember Peanut, Hokey, Pokey, and Smokey – there were others.

Of course, like children, the monkeys grew naughty. They would gather eggs and try to climb up a palm tree with an arm full of eggs. They never succeeded. The eggs would drop one by one with a splash.

Smokey, one baby I raised, loved eating off the rose buds so that I had to enclose my roses in chicken wire if I wanted a flower. They would dig up the peanuts in the garden and take bananas away from babies eating them while tied on mother's back.

One of the missionaries had a premature baby and had to boil the diapers and keep them sterile. Smokey gathered the diapers from the line and festooned them in the various treetops. The missionary mother was nearly hysterical. Smokey found the kittens once and carried them to the roof and dropped them down the fireplace chimney, safely, due to the cats' remarkable structure.

When I lost a monkey it was almost like losing a child. They had bonded with me as a mother and could not be driven away. I was the only one they would not bite, but they did not like correction. They loved to pick at my freckles or dance around trying to catch the monkey they saw in their hand mirror. I have a warm spot in my heart for monkeys. I refused ever to eat one. It seemed to me like cannibalism. We loved our monkeys and discovered each one to have a distinct personality.

We had Bambi, a spotted antelope baby and Flipper a dwarf antelope just less than a foot tall equipped with little horns and flipping white feathery tail, hence the name. A mongoose joined our zoo and a wild cat.

Once we had Ntoto, a genet with little bare hands like a raccoon. He nursed at our mother cat's breast that accepted him as one of her kittens. We were given a scaly anteater but it escaped the first night. Anteaters have formidable digging claws.

In Africa, the Weavers had JoJo, a baby chimpanzee. He wore diapers and had a blanket for comfort. JoJo would put his little arms around my neck and snuggle up close. He was irresistible as a baby and became everyone's pet. He would eat a peanut butter and jelly sandwich from one hand and drink cocoa or pop from a thermos held in the other hand.

The African gray parrots with red tails are remarkable birds. Our Jocko learned to whistle, "My Country 'Tis of Thee," to copy our tones and words. He would mimic the dog chasing the chickens, and the noise made by the terrified hens. I have gone outside many times to scold the dog, only to find the parrot sitting there fixing me with his yellow eye. He made the sound of people knocking at the door and the response we made to invite them in. It was very misleading. Parrots are great entertainers and acrobats and can perform for an hour without tiring.

One of our station dogs was part Basenji. Mo could not bark, but hunted swiftly and silently. When she had her babies, she dug a deep tunnel and at the end was a hollowed out nest. Of course, I wanted to see the babies and dug them out, but she made a new nest and carried them back into it. Sometimes she would howl or whine, but she never did bark.

As for the plants, the whole tropical array of flowers opened before me in the Congo. The frangipani, Euphorbia tree, each branch tipped with a bouquet of lovely fragrant flowers, pink, white, yellow, salmon – The wild amaryllis, growing in the woods – The fireball lily of one area – The Amazon lily, white and unbelievably huge. The orchids I knew best were field and swamp orchids. In season, I have had every vase in the house full of beautiful orchids, with red and yellow Gloriosa lilies, which bloomed at the same time.

Of the flowering trees, the yellow cassia was commonest. There is pink cassia, very beautiful and jacaranda, most beautiful of all clothed in a lavender blue mass before the leaves come out. The Royal Poinciana called the Flamboyant Tree in Congo is also a glory to see in a tropical spring below the equator, early in November. The Wenge tree or ironwood, has beautiful lavender clusters drooping like wisteria from branches and often the ground beneath the tree reflected with a lavender carpet of dropped flowers. Then, the wild tulip tree, each branch of scarlet flowers extending above the foliage for six inches or so.

The Baobob, the oldest living thing in Africa, grew in our area. In Congo it is somewhat larger and taller than the Baobob of Kenya plains. There is a living Baobob tree in Boma, which is gigantic, and hollow with a door fitted into it and a plaque on it saying, "Henry Stanley camped inside." The Baobob seeds are fertile with a chalk-like substance. Some children chew on them. For a long time we believed Cream of Tartar came from the white chalky insides, but now we have heard a conflicting rumor. The flower is huge. It is white and hangs on a long stem facing the ground. It has a circle of large white petals crowned with a massive brush of stamens and a very long pistil extending beyond the stamens. It must be about twelve inches from bottom to top, maybe more. Bats pollinate them.

The Baobob tree serves many useful purposes and is an entire ecosystem in itself according to the documentary done on it by National Geographic. We first read about it in St. Exuperay's *Little Prince* while studying French to go to Congo.

I taught Botany for several years in the Congo High Schools. My textbooks, written in France or Belgium, always had examples, which my students had never heard of, like willow and apple and chestnut. Each morning before class, Michal Rose and I would take a large pail with a little water in it and collect the plants that matched that day's Botanical Class Order and Family, to be studied. It was such fun that at those times I wondered if I should have been a botanist. There are many plants unclassified in the African forests.

During our last term I was assigned to do major landscaping of a new post, church, school, chapel, and a guesthouse. One of the joys of gardening in Zaire and Congo is being able to grow nearly anything from cuttings. Take a piece of hibiscus bush, stick it in the ground, and before long you have a new bush. It was the fastest way to reproduce new plants and I filled hundreds of plastic bags of soil with cuttings.

There are several sorrows of gardening in the tropics. There is a dry season of six or seven months which new plants cannot live through without help for several years which means carrying water throughout dry seasons. The rainy season is often so violent it not only kills delicate plants, but washes away whole hillsides if the soil is not fastened down with vines or bamboo or some ground cover such as passion fruit.

If the rain does not pound the plant into the soil, then the tropical sun will cook it. For any kind of flower or tree while delicate, or a seedling, we need to build thatch roofs to protect them from rain and sun until they are sturdier. If that succeeds and they flourish then there is a whole army of insect pests and larva waiting to consume them for lunch. DDT is still used in

Zaire without control, unfortunately, providing future illness for the people.

If trees survive seedling stage, and sun, rain and insects, they still live in mortal danger of dry season fires each year, when hunters burn to flush out food from the fields.

One of the trials of our last term was seeing our baby trees thirsting for a drink during the dry season. We used plastic jugs and carried the water by car from a distance and rationed it out plant by plant.

"No doubt all history in the last resort must be held by Christians to be a story with a divine plot."

C.S. Lewis

African village woman carrying firewood

Chapter 35

A BURDEN BEARER OF AFRICA

Mampasi heard the rooster crowing again, as they do in the Zaire night. The first crow had sounded when the new day had just taken over from what was now yesterday. She spread the cloth around her body over the parts that had worked free. Opening her eyes she saw nothing but heavy darkness inside the shuttered mud shack. She closed her eyes again and tried to settle herself in more comfort on the reed mat on the earth floor.

She breathed the close air, scented always with wood smoke and cooking fumes. To these were added the stale aroma of her soiled clothes revived by the heat of her body. At the third cock crow she must arise, but for now there was still time for rest from effort, time to lie in lethargy and to doze off again before another long day began.

Something scratched in the thatched grass roof and the rooster crowed once more, then lapsed into silence. In the gray indistinct early hours, a half-hour or more before the sun rose at six, she was on her way to the stream with the pail to get water for her husband's bath. Her leathery gnarled feet gripped the familiar ruts and crevices of the hillside path. Her ears heard the chorus of awakening birds now joining the roosters in hailing the new day.

After fifteen or twenty minutes she reached the tree and rock-bordered stream in the little valley. She dipped the pail full before entering the chilly water herself. Stooping, she lifted her long cloth wrapped as a skirt, and threw water up on her now perspiring legs. With hands full of water she washed her face and arms and head. She would have to return later to wet and pound her laundry clean on the rocky surfaces emerging from the stream. Now it was time to remount the bare rocks of the hill and heat the bath water for her sleeping husband. She found the fire stones cold. Gathering remnants of twigs and branches she began her patient fire building under the bucket of water set upon the three familiar stones.

Mampasi noticed the early morning fog climbing the hills. She found some peanuts to shell and grill for their breakfast. She unwrapped a half loaf of manioc bread from the leaves it had been tied and boiled in. Another pan of water with a few tea leaves set in the edge of the fire heating, engulfed and tasting more of smoke than of tea. When it boiled she would add the tiny tin of sweetened condensed milk purchased at market. She ate a few peanuts as she worked, a bite of bread, a sip of hot tea. She heard her husband moving in the mud house. Hurriedly she carried in the pail of warmed water, then returned to boil him an egg as she set the table for his breakfast. When he was dressed and shaved he took his place and began to eat.

He would be walking to work in the dockyard before long and she would be going to the gardens. She missed having a baby. The pleasure of suckling it, the warmth of its little body against her back as she carried it and worked. She missed the joy of its being, the laughs and smiles and companionship. She thought of her three boys now far away in schools. One was in a boarding high school and two were learning to be office workers. Mampasi remembered her girl baby dying suddenly of fever, and of the twins, both dead at birth. Babies were life and sometimes, death to a mother. She had come near to death with the twins but her life had been spared, thanks to God. Now life went on but there would be no more babies.

She was past the age for babies. Today there were weeds to hoe in the garden four miles distant. Wood and food must be gathered for the evening meal. All day long she would collect the twigs and branches, the plants, insects and animals needed. Time to start. She took the clay cruche of water, the long basket with the strap for her forehead and put in her machete and hoe and water jug. She picked up the extra cloth for tying up whatever she collected.

Where her footpath ended at the road, she met her neighbors and friends... the women with whom she lived and worked, and gardened daily.

There was Ngyele, older and feebler and Lendi, young and large with child, Mpidi, tall and strong and Lubata with her baby and a child of five years trailing behind her. They made cheerful company at the beginning of a day, walking to the gardens, discussing matters of village life and family events.

They walked about four miles, crossing the big bridge leaving town and climbing mountain roads, descending others before they left the highway to reach their gardens on the hillsides. There were sweet potato vines and beans growing. Wandu, the bush pea of Africa, stood taller than their heads, with manioc or cassava and peanuts below it. These are her staple foods of the hot, rainy season. Here and there in the gardens a banana tree grew or an orange tree. They put their baskets and water under one of these trees, together with the baby and his sister to watch him.

Around the baby they arranged a loose ring of thorny wild mimosa branches. Among the women as they worked with hoe and hands, there was gossip, laughter, singing and companionable silences as they dug out weeds, gathered manioc greens and cut branches in lengths to carry home. They caught crickets for supper or caterpillars imprisoning them in an empty gourd. At noon they dug a few green peanuts to eat and drank the water, resting for a time, enjoying the baby, watching him nurse in Lubata's arms. When he slept she gently lowered him to the ground while they returned to work until it was time to load the baskets with all they had gleaned and start the long walk home.

Mampasi loaded her basket with her tools and water jug and firewood. She put in the sweet manioc root and the gourd of crickets and caterpillars. On top she balanced a fine bundle of manioc leaves to cook as greens. Mpidi helped her lift the basket on her back. The dry sticks of the firewood rose high above her head. Her back was bent over. She concentrated her gaze on the ground she must walk on with her bare feet. The basket lay on her back and shoulders and was strapped around its flared top to her forehead. The main part of the load seemed to extend above it. She could not turn her head or raise it. She was in harness for the long miles home. They all were.

Slowly they left the gardens and crossed the grassy hill to reach the paved road, and quietly and doggedly began the climbing of the first of the hills toward home. Trucks overloaded with people spilling out on every side lurched past the column of tired women bearing their burdens home. Their slow progress compared to the noisy fuming vehicles that passed them, made them seem part of the panorama of mountain and sky and river. They were a frieze depicting the effort of the centuries of wresting daily life from the earth ... a serious, slow, unending task.

Mampasi smelled the fumes and flinched from the noise of the motors. She scarcely lifted her eyes to watch that which had no bearing on her daily life. Mampasi had never been inside a truck or car. She did not expect to be. Her money, what little she got at the market for her garden produce, went for matches or salt, or petrol for the lantern, or for sugar, or sometimes school fees to help with her grandchildren's education.

She could neither read nor write, but she understood the importance of education, which led to a good job and a salary, making it possible to buy food to eat and live. Yes, today children must be educated. When they had jobs they would feed their elders, house them and eventually provide the money to bury them.

Sometimes she needed money for her church. The women often tried to contribute more than the men. It was a public contest they greatly enjoyed. If it meant going without sugar or salt or petrol or matches, she could accept that. Nzambi, who gives all things, must have a gift from her strength. A gift to carry on His work. She must help to reach other women with the good news of His love. These things she mulled over in her mind as she shuffled under her load, straining upward on the hill. She braked carefully with her leg muscles as she descended. There would be a women's meeting tonight, and she would go.

She thought of what must be done before then. A fire built, the roots pounded, the leaves boiled with all the seasonings of cricket and caterpillar thrown in, and the meal of the day eaten and ended.

Then finally, there would be the joy of singing together at the church with the other women, of studying the Bible together with their literate leader. The sacrificial offering and then needle work projects to finish in order to minister to unmarried girls from the streets who had nothing to do except wait for marriage, since for them no family funds existed for continued education beyond fifth grade primary school.

It was a long day for an African sister devoted to bearing burdens, before she wrapped the night cloth about her once more and lay her weary body upon the floor mat and lapsed again into the sleep she so sorely needed.

"No man (or woman) knows how bad he is until he has tried very hard to be good."
C. S. Lewis

August 1993 - Pastor Kianda, treasurer of Baptists of West Congo

Chapter 36

KIANDA'S STORY

I awakened to pain and the heat of the tropics. Blindly feeling for the worst ache, I discovered that my head and my arm were bandaged. At that, my eyes came open then quickly closed to small slits against the sun's glare. "It must be nearly noon," I panicked, "What am I doing in bed? Why am I not at the office working?" As I struggled to remember, a nurse came in, thermometer in hand.

"Ah, you are conscious now, are you?" She inserted the thermometer under my tongue, cutting off my rising questions. "You are very fortunate to be alive. You were in a terrible auto accident." Retrieving the thermometer, she recorded my temperature, hung my chart on the bed and whisked out.

Thunderstruck, I lay back against the pillow as memory painfully fought its way back. It is true, I had been in my car driving - yes, speeding, to spend time with my mistress during the noon break. Young and beautiful, she symbolized my financial success. Try as I might, I could not recall what had happened, but an accident certainly had happened. My bandaged pains confirmed that.

After a while, my wife came to the hospital room with food, as is the custom in Zaire. She helped me to eat, bathed and cared for my needs before taking the dishes and going home to our children. Exhausted by then, I lay back inert to let the hurt subside. I closed my eyes and thought of the numerous accident victims from the clashes constantly occurring on the busy streets of this capital city.

Emotion knotted my stomach nerves. My mind raced ... I might have died. I am too young to die. Others die young. Look at me, well one day, injured and in the hospital the next. I, Kianda, a successful business man, a good driver of my own car – what if I had been killed? Where would I be, I wonder, after death? These questions had never before seemed so important.

Such thoughts did not leave me. They impressed themselves on my mind to the exclusion of lesser subjects during the hospital stay and even after I went home. I would suddenly recall how close I came to dying and realized how unprepared I felt for death.

After my convalescence, I returned to work and life much as before, but my thinking kept on. As a child, I remembered attending mass with my mother. I tried to recall what I had learned, but only vague teachings of Mary and Jesus and God came back to me. I had outgrown those things so long ago. It was useless trying to remember them.

Then one Sunday a very odd thing happened to me. I sat resting in my yard, under our mango tree where the shade is cool, when suddenly a stranger stood beside me. I looked up in inquiry at him. "Please," he said urgently, "May I have a Bible?" Astonished I stared at him. "Why do you come to me?" I asked. "I have no Bible."

Disregarding my reply, he kept repeating his request. Finally I said, "If you need a Bible, alright. I will buy you one. You may return for it tomorrow afternoon." With that promise, the stranger left me.

After work the next day I went to a church bookstore where Bibles are sold and purchased a copy for him. I took it home and laid it in readiness on the stand by the door, awaiting his return.

The stranger never returned. Every day I looked at the Bible and wondered why he needed it. The next Sunday morning I picked it up and sat down in my chair under the shady mango tree. I began reading from the first page. Before long the Bible gripped me like a living thing. I read and read and at midnight I realized that I had not even paused for food.

The next day I took the Bible to work with me. I closed my office doors and continued my reading. Then another odd thing happened. Once when I paused, I heard a voice speaking words. When it stopped, I waited and wondered, then went on reading, only to find myself reading the same words the voice had spoken to me just before. It gave me an eerie feeling. This happened over and over again during my first reading of this Bible. Never had I dreamed the Bible was such a book as this. I could not stop reading until I had read it all.

I finished reading, shaken by the experience. I pondered what meaning it had for me. My life would never be the same, but how would it be changed? As I meditated, this voice came again, "Go to the Protestant church." I got up, walked the few blocks to a large church I had passed many times in my comings and goings. This day I entered. Right away, a man came to meet me holding out his hands in greeting.

"I am Badianga," he said. "I would like you to meet Jesus, my Lord and savior." He explained that by believing in Jesus and simply asking, I could receive eternal life. As he spoke, faith grew in my heart and as we prayed I accepted Him as my Lord. Immediately I felt like a new and different person.

In the days that followed, I studied my Bible and prayed for guidance. My life continued to change. I gave up my mistress, much as I loved her and became faithful to my wife and children. I felt a deep urge to serve God in a better way.

One day I went to a nearby Protestant mission and told my story and discussed training for the ministry. If I quit my job to go to school, how would I feed my family? The missionary assured me, "If God is calling you, He will provide a way for you to prepare for His service." I believed her.

I closed my office and enrolled in the Protestant Theological School. I did not have gas money, so I walked the three miles, four times a day, between my home and the school. My wife bought wholesale and sold retail to help out financially during the three years until I graduated; then I became the pastor of my first church.

What a proud and happy day it was when I first preached to my congregation at Binza church in Kinshasa, Zaire. First I held a service in Lingala, the popular language of the President. Later on, I saw a need to add two more services, one in French and one in English to serve an international community such as ours in Kinshasa. Instead of one four-hour service, I held four one-hour services. Many attended because of the shorter services. What a joy to introduce other seekers to my Lord.

Truly God has done great things for me and made me very glad. After nearly ten years as pastor, I accepted the job of treasurer for our convention, which numbers nearly 400,000 believers. It is a hard job because bribes and misuse of funds are very common. We are trained to give our first loyalty to our clan, so it is very hard to be true to Christ in this climate of need and old beliefs.

I feel God led in my business training for such a time as this in His church. The American missionaries, who shared the headquarters' offices, encouraged and supported me when I began as treasurer. They helped me make sure that money designated or budgeted for certain work fulfilled its purpose. Sometimes, my fellow Zairians within the church feel the money should go elsewhere.

Today because of political and economic distress, my Christian colleagues from America have been withdrawn from my country. I want to remain faithful to the One who found me, after sparing my life in the accident. The One who caused me to buy a Bible and then to read it. The One who gave me faith and the desire to serve Him. Please pray that my faith will grow stronger and God will keep me honest and true to Him as Head and Chief of my clan.

"Many of us grumble because we are temporarily deprived of blessings our fellow Christians in other lands have never even heard of."

Unknown

1980 - Leon & Martha's (3rd row left) former students who were sent as delegates to the 1980 Western Zaire Baptist Convention

Chapter 37

A CRUCIBLE OF COMPARISON

The parsonage had burned. The African pastor, now destitute, presented his situation before the committee who could help him out. He was a humble, faithful man. He only needed some bare essentials. He had carefully estimated the extent of his loss. He read the list of all his goods with dignity. 5,000 francs was the total estimated value of his loss.

He sat down. The committee considered his plight and his plea. It was decided that his eight other fellow pastors in the area each give 625 francs that would be gathered in from four separate offerings of their people. Thus the burden was borne by the brotherhood of believers. The warm arms of Christian love closed around the pastor in need, providing both comfort and security, and perhaps replacing all his goods.

1 charcoal iron
500 francs of the church's money
150 francs of his wife's money
350 francs of his money

1 pail
1 lamp
1 pair scissors
1 machete
1 pair of shoes
1 pan
2 pairs of pants
2 shirts
1 pan of peanuts
1 pair of sandals
1 small mirror
2 cups

All his goods! I ponder the list. What a pitiful few! For of course, his two shirts and two pants must be kept pressed and ready for his hour of preaching. One pail is enough for one accustomed head to carry on her familiar climb from the spring in the valley; one lamp for one room, where he sits when he studies his Bible. She does not need the lamp, for her work is by the firelight and while her ear strains to catch the murmured reading of her husband, she would not be able to read herself by the light of any number of lamps.

One pan, for meals consist of one hot dish. Whether the manioc leaves shall be seasoned with crushed peanuts, or dried fish, or even a few caterpillars, or a fat, large cricket – it is cooked in her one pan and makes the necessary luku palatable. Two cups – one for him and one for her if no one is visiting. If they do have a visitor, she will not drink.

They owned one pair of scissors, for had he not along with the other pastors, received this shining gift from a generous friend in Chicago? How beautifully they cut. Now how black and charred they have become. But the pastor is very deft with even a broken razor blade. The scissors were a luxury, not a need. One machete that now must be replaced, for with it the ground is cleared for cultivation. With it, the ripe, orange cluster of palm nuts are discovered and cut out, to plummet heavy with oil to the ground. With it, a new parsonage must be fashioned. Yes, another machete must soon be bought.

He owned one pair of shoes for meetings and for conferences. He carried them on the long walks over the hills, and through the valleys and saved them for the time before the public where he speaks for God, wearing his carefully kept shoes. For he would be shod as others who desert their village, attracted by the baubles of many markets, in the cities where such things are bought and sold. As for his wife, one pair of sandals (thongs), were not worn often perhaps, but were kept there, a dignity to have, and rewarding to see on her tired and callused feet, on Sundays when he can persuade her to wear them.

A small mirror is enough. What would a larger one reveal, that might bolster his ego? When there is little chance to improve the image, it is best not to inspect it too thoroughly. There is dismay enough in daily trials.

Was a pan of peanuts saved for the next planting? Perhaps. They must be bought back for the peanut garden is his food store. Peanuts are the meat, the sauce, the dainties that his wife prepares for his travels when she pounds them into a heavy paste with the hot, hot pepper and wraps them in a leaf for his long walks between villages. Peanuts are the daily fare in their simplest form, roasted and blackened by the camp fire, or dug fresh from the ground and eaten raw, to nourish her during the long hours of harvest digging.

Last of all, the money. Her money from the sale of peanuts, or eggs, or fruit, or squash was 150 francs. What can she buy with that? Not a dress length of cloth certainly. Maybe a can of corned beef, or some thread, or a piece of strong soap, or a cup of coarse salt. Not much sugar, but sugar in good warm tea with milk is a luxury that must not be dwelt on. Such tea for dessert, with a little bread, ah well, had he been a schoolteacher or a nurse, perhaps he could have afforded it, but a village pastor does not often indulge in such luxuries. Or perhaps, the 150 francs was being saved for the school fees, for her children must have the opportunity that she never had. They must have the key to economic security found in education. Most likely, it was her nest egg for school fees.

His money, only 350 francs was certainly not great riches, and there was no bank account, and no insurance. Was it his recent salary for the month to buy oil for the lamp, to help support his sister's children, or to get medicine? He had no electric bill to pay, no car insurance, and his travels cost him only the time and strength it takes to walk from one village to another. He needed no batteries for he had neither flashlight nor radio. Truly his needs were small, but it is always wise to save a little for helping someone in genuine need, he ought to be prepared as soon as possible. He would not even think of the books he dreams of, so expensive, so far away. But he had saved his Bible and his hymnbook. They are absolutely essential to his life and work, and he still has the secret hope that God will provide if ever his need for other books becomes imperative.

And the church's money – 500 francs was entrusted to him. In its box locked against theft, the book kept by one member, the key kept by another, and now in spite of all their careful strategy it had been stolen by fire. How long would it take to replenish the treasury again? And the church had yet to pay it's last year's dues to the convention. But this money will be restored with whatever is received in aid from the sister churches. This shall be his first duty.

All my goods; all your goods – have you ever listed them all? Have you ever wrenched free of them and out from under them and known yourself bare of them? One of the most tedious tasks of missionary life is the innumerable listing of contents, the multiple carbons, each time a crate comes or goes across the ocean. One can not pack with a free mind, but what the paper and pencil must be there and each item listed when in confusion and fatigue of packing all our goods even keeping track of the pencil is a major undertaking.

Lists I have typed swim before my eyes -- case number 6. I wonder how many cases it would have taken to carry all his goods. Not even one and we toil on – case number 7. True, much that we bring is not for us personally, but gifts from Christians in America to be transmitted to others by our hands.

Still we do have our share – six pairs of pants, men's used, 4 pairs of pants, boys, used, 8 pairs of shoes, cloth, child's new. We are often overcome with this burden of things. We lose our taste for buying and come away, refusing to buy things we had previously listed as prospective needs, but we always have our mission circles to bail us out later.

Wealth is relative, I know. Our pastor friend is rich in the eyes of many of his flock. We are unbelievably wealthy in his eyes. Less unbelievable, in the eyes of more well paid and better-educated Africans. We get letters from concerned American Christians commiserating with us in our sacrificial self-denial. Still we have our lists to remind us of all our goods, and we have his list. It might be an enlightening project for any Christian to make a list of all his goods and place it alongside his brother's. Go ahead. If you want to face a missionary trial – go ahead and do it. Even at that, you will be spared the packing.

"Christ's achievement in rising from the dead was the first event of Its kind in the whole history of the universe ... He has forced open a door that has been locked since the death of the first man. He has met, fought and beaten the King of Death."

C.S. Lewis

Story of Noah with African Motifs at Kimpese Hospital Pediatrics ward - one of the four wall murals in the children's play room.

Chapter 38

IN REMEMBRANCE OF HIM

On Communion Sunday, have you ever visualized Christians all around the world remembering Him together? I have. Have you ever seen a long line of newly baptized believers solemnly take their first communion? I have. Like us some of you have shared various communions with believers in the far corners of our world. You may recall those experiences. By a remarkable diversity of elements and Christian traditions we are all brought to our moment of self-searching and supplication which is the crucial part of Communion.

I remember my first unaccustomed observance as a newly baptized adult believer in March of 1942 in Muscatine, Iowa. What an odd thing to do, I thought – swallow a bit of bread and drink a tiny cup of juice! Those elements of bread and grape juice every month, upon the first Sunday became a familiar part of my life. Wherever I attended Baptist churches in Iowa, Chicago or Topeka, Indiana, the ritual remained the same. I naively supposed our custom and elements to be universal.

Imagine my surprise when in France, we attended a very conservative New Testament

Baptist church where communion was taken from a common cup of biblical wine passed around to each one. It was my first taste of wine and the burning in my throat surprised me. The church members practiced the holy kiss of greeting, a part of communion as well.

In a European Methodist communion service, I must interrupt my meditation by a trip to the front where we received communion with a dozen or so others as it became our turn.

At some churches the bread substitute turned out to be unleavened wafers or crackers. Not only the elements but the order of service can be varied, I discovered.

Once, when we were in the ecumenical missionary orientation, we learned the Anglicans could not partake unless a bona fide Apostolic successor of Peter administered the service. We solved that by letting the Anglican minister officiate. At the same service, the Quaker delegation sat quietly by, centering their minds on God, taking neither bread nor cup during their communion with him.

Each of us follows what we believe matters most in remembrance of Him. None of the solemn and well-ordered services quite prepared us for the departures from these norms found in our Missionary life.

Go with me to Africa for a communion service under palm or mango trees. See crowds of people swarm in carrying a little stool on their heads, a hymnbook and a Bible. With babies on their backs and children crowding close, they push into the shade out of the tropical sun as the day progresses. The air is scented with many aromas – dust stirred by bare feet, bodies warmed and perspiring from walking miles to get there on time, wood smoke from village cooking fires. See the men gathering on one side and the women and babies on the other. They are all sitting, standing, squatting, finding a small space with a position of comfort for the three-hour service.

Can you visualize this gathering of Christians eager to hear Jesus' words? It is almost like the five thousand feeding on the seashore in Galilee. Bright sun, bright colors, insects buzzing and being slapped at, babies crying and being nursed, dogs and chickens and goats vying for their share in the general clamor.

Finally the crowd is snugly massed together without benefit of rows or aisles. We are aware of stillness. The wine turns out to be Pepsi cola. The bottles stand on the rickety little table used for communion. It prompts a sudden disturbance within the missionary sector. An American child recognizes a favorite and familiar drink and begins to cry loudly and insistently for Pepsi. He is hurried off and muffled inside the cab of the station pickup.

Meanwhile reverent hands measure out the Pepsi very frugally to meet the demand. The bread, chiquangue cut up in small pieces smells strongly of fermented cassava root of which it is made.

Yet though our tranquility suffers at this revelation of Communion in the Congo bush, we see in the faces of those gathered, the same solemnity, the same seeking after God, universal among true believers.

The prayers and hymns express sincerity. They have come to remember Him in spite of the limitations presented by the environment. I never considered how to fill the cup in a land of no grapes, or what might be the bread where no wheat grows. It is like trying to translate the words, "Whiter than snow," into an equatorial language.

The African Christians accept any number of available substitutes in order to keep the spirit of Christ's commands. They use weak tea, tasting strongly of wood fires, or grenadine weakened, or Kool-Aid provided by the missionary. In my mind today, I can see remote African villages, where the communion cup might hold an infusion of bark, or leaf, or root made with boiling smoky water. Perhaps the bread is cassava root or plantain roasted or boiled and cut in tiny bits.

The variety may be infinite, none of it disturbs us, for the essential love and longing and the remembrance of Him prevails. Did you see the new communion set arriving ready to serve on the heads of the deaconesses? Their heads are swathed in new white diaper turbans from White cross. Their uniforms are snowy surgeon's gowns saved out of gifts from American Baptist churches. These women serve both, humbly and proudly. They keep children quiet, they wake up dozing elders, they pass the symbols of His flesh and blood.

I had not been asked to serve communion for many years. Finally in 1985 at Green Lake, at the closing communion of the Missions conference, they asked me to participate in the communion distribution. It is a dignifying honor – to serve communion.

The African instinctively perceives the spiritual truths behind the letter,

> *"All of you are God's children in union with Christ, there is no difference between slave and free, between men and women, you are all one in Christ Jesus."*
>
> Galatians 3:26-28.

Once at Moanza, I observed an old village woman barefoot and bare to the waist, dusty from walking many miles to the communion service. When the tray passed, she took two cups instead of one. I held my breath. A vigilant deaconess arrived promptly, kindly removed the second cup and explained why one is enough. The village lady no doubt felt that if one is good, two is doubly so. Her humility, her innocence in revealing a deeply felt need appealed to me strongly. So did the compassionate care of her sister in Christ. I am sure the Lord saw and remembers her in her thirst for Him.

As we sit in the beauty of a holy place, with the scents of clean clothing and fresh flowers to breathe, with the moving prayers of our communion hymns in our hearts and on our lips, let us remember Him. Let us remember that throughout the world His sheep hear His voice and follow Him as best they can. We are one sheepfold and we have one Shepherd. We are bound in a unity, which as C. S. Lewis said, is deeper than any uniformity. May God unite us by His love as we join Christians all over the world in remembrance of Him.

"The body of Ben Franklin, Printer, like the cover of an old book, its contents torn out and stripped of its lettering and gilding, lies here, food for worms. Yet the work itself shall not be lost, for it will, as he believed appear once more in a new and more beautiful edition, corrected and amended by the Author.

Ben Franklin

1995 - Catherine Miller, Martha's High School Spanish teacher ("The most wonderful teacher I ever had") with Martha Emmert at her 50th class reunion

Chapter 39

LIFE AFTER RETIREMENT

Our first round the world trip ended early in 1989 when we returned to the U.S. for retirement. All of our plans for remodeling our Michigan Home on Lake Huron in the Upper Peninsula had to be re-evaluated in the light of my cancer discovered and surgically removed so soon after arriving in California.

The doctor ordered me into chemotherapy as soon as I reached home. Enroute, we flew to Charlottesville, VA where our daughter lived to pick up our Plymouth minivan they had secured for us. How we have enjoyed that car. Holding eight passengers we dreamed about our family traveling together on vacations. This happened when we drove to our retirement dinner at Green Lake, WI (Baptist Conference grounds) in June of 1990.

We decided rather than leave Fort Wayne where our son and family lived, we should stay near them as I entered chemotherapy in early July of 1989. We researched for a good oncologist and I put myself into the hands of Dr. Sciortino of Fort Wayne and signed up in a research program from the University of

Chicago. These continue to supervise my program. When five years passed safely without a recurrence, the doctor assigned only annual check-ups.

I have tried to forget the chemotherapy, for it was four months of horror to me. The chemicals invaded every cell of my body in cold creeping fashion like an embalming fluid. My tongue tasted of it. My eyeballs peeled after each treatment, so the comfort of reading was denied me. My allergy to the anti-nausea drug caused me to pass out cold on the first injection. About an hour after each treatment, like pushing a button, I would begin to vomit, and continued retching long after my stomach emptied for twelve long hours, on the dot. Just when I began to feel like surviving, it was time for another treatment and I was back to where I started.

During these sessions, my husband had to care for my hygienic needs totally. I had no control over my bodily functions during the exertion of continued retching. I thought to myself, "At last, I'll lose weight." However, the doctor warned that I must eat and drink to wash the poisons out of my body and stay able to support the treatment. Leon did his best to tempt me with liquids and bland foods. I could usually eat baked or mashed potatoes, or poached egg. Chemotherapy changed some of my tastes forever. Cold water feels too much like the icy injected fluid. I am indebted to Leon for his loving care and moral support during those months, which were so difficult for all of us.

When the chemotherapy ended, my hair grew back curly. It was the most expensive perm I ever had. I was gloating to the doctor when he deflated me by saying, "It only lasts a couple of months."

We put our old Wells street house up for sale and found we had to pay for all the repairs and improvements we were moving to avoid. As long as the deed was not signed, we were liable for all damages like water being left on and ruining a ceiling and walls long after we had given up the keys. Finally, however, we were free of it and could move to a new addition, very near our grandsons, farther on East State Street, where it becomes Maysville Road, near the northeast edge of town.

By January of 1990, we decided to return to the west coast to visit those we had intended to see on our way home through California. We drove the southern route and saw many friends, missionary and otherwise, including Leon's niece in Albuquerque, New Mexico, and my brother in Sedona, Arizona. We went as far as Portland and saw the retirement homes of several of our colleagues. In June we were officially retired American Baptists and given our engraved pewter bowl.

By early 1991, I was restored enough to feel as though I ought to be doing something and have some purpose in life beyond surviving. The years of work had not prepared me for unscheduled time. While suffering through those days, I redid all of the photo albums, arranging them topically, rather than chronologically. We still have a great collection of slides that no one is eager to see. This was a major task, and it helped that Leon was gone for weeks at a time, speaking in churches.

In 1991 we attended the American Baptist Biennial in Charleston, West Virginia since we had been unable to attend the Milwaukee convention in 1989. At that convention, Catherine Bruce, my dear friend and former roommate from Seminary nearly died of heart failure. This was a shock and very hard for us to take.

She recovered very slowly from that attack and knew she could die at any time. Her heart suffered severe damage for which nothing could be done, except a transplant. She felt strongly against this option and tried to cut down on her activities.

Catherine had always wanted to visit Israel and when a small group organized a tour led by a pastor friend of hers, she wanted me to go along as her roommate. So in November 1991, we took the tour to Israel and Egypt and I saw and did things I had not been able to do or see on the first trip sixteen years before. In 1994, before Christmas, Catherine died quietly in the night. I miss her beyond expressing.

Early in 1991, I enrolled in Indiana-Purdue University Fort Wayne Continuing Education. I took "*Flower Arranging*" and "*Writing for Fun and*

Profit." It had occurred to me that I no longer had the excuse of, "No time to write." I thought that flower arranging might lead to a part-time job. Throughout my life I dreamed of working in a florist shop. When I applied at the nearest florist, they had a number of part-time experienced workers on call already and did not need me.

I had tentatively hoped that in retirement, I could learn Scrimshaw, but Ivory became an unacceptable product and the Scrimshaw artists I had contacted earlier in Fort Wayne, had gone somewhere else. I ended up selling the best ivory I had collected to work on to Mr. Warren Saint Johns, a tremendously gifted Scrimshaw artist in the Upper Peninsula of Michigan. I traded part of it for some of his work.

My collection of African cloth and quilt pieces is still boxed and waiting. I had thought it might be fun to make decorative cushions or throw pillows to sell, but the decision to write eliminates a great deal of other effort. Each October I enjoy an orgy of making crafted gifts for Christmas mainly for my sister's large family, which I take at Thanksgiving on our annual visit home and distribute. Some of my excess I sell at the Woodshed in Cedarville, Michigan on commission, and every so often a little surprise check comes in.

Another dream I held about retirement to have a real rose garden full of luscious hybrids is falling away. I started out by buying six rose bushes in various colors. One by one they died.

Part of the problem is that we are absent during several crucial summer growing months. Now I stick to hardier perennials that bloom in spring or fall while we are usually in Fort Wayne.

In 1991, our youngest grandson was baptized off the beach in Florida during a youth camp from Faith Baptist Church. That year I succeeded in getting my first two articles published in the National Catholic paper and the local one in Fort Wayne.

With my new friend from writing class, I attended the Maranatha Writer's Conference in Michigan, but left early to go with my nephew to an Atkins reunion in Iowa. This was already 1992 and I had two more published articles.

In March of 1991, we joined First Baptist church and I served on the Religious Art board. In 1993, Guideposts accepted a short piece and later I attended the Wheaton Writer's Conference and met Elizabeth Sherril, a Guideposts Editor, whose writings are popular. I became a part of the first annual Art Camp at the Uptown Baptist Church in Chicago. I boarded with Ray and Corean Bakke and worked in the camp supervised by Brian, their youngest son.

Ray Bakke was our advisor when we were invited to Northern Baptist Seminary, our alma mater , in 1979, during one semester there as missionaries in Residence. He and his wife, Corean, had since then come to Zaire and spent time with us at Matadi. He is the final authority on inner city renewal by the church and of urban evangelism. Due to these circumstances I am given an opportunity to share a week each year with the homeless elderly of the Chicago streets. It is a privilege to get to know them. I have gone for five years now, specializing in junk art. Each year we complete a decorative project to beautify the church with the help of the seniors.

In Fort Wayne, Leon and I were busy putting on a Zaire meal to benefit the Bible School at Kimpese. It made about $1500. There was an auction of artifacts and a series of my paintings of African flowers. Later that year I was commissioned by a friend to paint three large canvases of Zaire flowers and scenery.

One of the joys of being home is that we can usually attend the Emmert apple picking in October at Leon's cousins, Geraldine and Paul Rood's orchard in Covert, Michigan. We drive there through flaming woods and enjoy a vast potluck of family foods. Then we must try not to pick more than we can use. The joys of picking inspired me to write the poem about "Apples" for them in appreciation.

Since 1992 we have had a mini-missionary reunion at Kentucky Dam State Park in March before the season opens. Six couples closely associated during our 35 years in Zaire/ Congo find It beneficial to reunite for fellowship for 4-5 days of talk and prayer and recreation. We have a round robin to strengthen our ties the rest of the year. The first of our number died in 1993, but we just drew closer. We met in California in 1996 to pacify the couples from the

West Coast, but in 1997 we returned to Kentucky.

Our group consists of James and June Clark from Tennessee, Delores and Chester Scott from Arkansas, Marj and Murray Sharp from Arkansas, Jerry and Lee Weaver from California, Rose and Phil Uhlinger from Oregon, and us in Indiana. Marj and Murray Sharp are the movers and pushers of the event. We are in contact by phone occasionally, but do not use the phone as freely as our children and grandchildren do, due to the paralyzing habit of economizing.

An amazing development occurred at the Green Lake Writer's Conference in 1994. The group I joined had a very interesting leader, Lenore Coberly. She surprised me the second day by assigning me to poetry. I prefer reading story books – the longer, the better. However, I complied, and it came surprisingly easy. The first poem I wrote for her about lilacs is my first published poem, "My Sacrifice." It appeared in the *"Above the Bridge"* magazine in the spring of 1995.

In 1994, we saw the culmination of many plans and much prodding as the Board of International Ministries hosted a Zaire Reunion during Mission Week at Green Lake. With three very elderly and revered colleagues present, over 150 of us gathered. We had some children and some grandchildren. The afternoons of the elders were spent together reminiscing about the people and experiences on each station assigned to each day. Everyone overwhelmingly supported the idea of another reunion, perhaps in 1998. Material was gathered and an Anniversary edition of our old Congo/Zaire newsletter was published as a result of the reunion. The get-together meant a great deal to all of us, and especially to our children.

After 73 Years

This old tree that once had much to give
I wonder now, how long it has to live.
I can remember springtimes when it blew
In gentle breezes while its leaves were new.

It's hard to see that young tree in this hulk
It's regal pride, its grace is lost in bulk.
Yet planted firm upon this rock, near bare,
Endures the heat in summer, winter's air.

Could there be some secret hidden source
That feeds its spirit, furnishes life force
And though it's cut off here and broken there
Yet still it's standing, neither young nor fair.

I meditate upon its face and form,
Changed by the years, weathered by the storm.
And as I concentrate, I think I see
Myself upon that rock – the tree is ME.

Martha Atkins Emmert

Chapter 40

1995 – LIVING LIFE FULLY

Retirement has in no way turned out the way we imagined it would. After six years we find ourselves busier than we ever planned to be. We noticed, of course, a dramatic drop in the amount of mail we receive and in the letters we need to write. However, it is still hard to trim down a mailing list of life-long friends, some of whom we only write or hear from at Christmas. We try, but they mean too much not to write to when we hear from them.

Early in 1995 we were invited to join a group tour from the First Baptist Church of Midland, Michigan, who were taking a Caribbean Cruise. None of our ocean crossings on ships (traveling tourist class) had prepared us for the truly excessive gourmet feeding and entertainment we experienced on this cruise. We had been to Haiti before, and knew the heart-breaking poverty of some of these islands, as well as the unforgettable beauty of the waters and teeming aquatic life. The cruise kept us at a distance from the extreme suffering, but for people who knew third world poverty and want, we probably did not get all the joy from it that we paid for. We discovered that a missionary life ruins some pleasures for us.

We came home from the Cruise in time for our March missionary reunion, which becomes more precious each year. In May I went to Art Camp in Chicago with my bags packed for a month. Immediately following the project, we were to take the trip I had longed for – an academic tour with the Wheaton College alumni to visit and study the Oxford of C.S. Lewis and the London of Dorothy L. Sayers.

I met Marjorie Lamp Mead, the study leader of the tour when I visited the C. S. Lewis collection the last time in Wheaton where she works at the Wade Center. My one letter from C. S. Lewis is kept there with many other originals to other simple people, in a climate-controlled vault. Marjorie saw that I knew about the tour and had the opportunity to join. Roger Stronstad, the present editor of the Canadian C. S. Lewis Journal, kindly asked for a written report to publish in the fall issue. I came home with voluminous notes and many photos to help me relive the delight of those days. I met George Sayer, a former student and life long friend of Lewis and his best biographer thus far. How touching to meet Doug Gresham, Lewis' youngest stepson and hear from him of the time they spent together before and after his mother's death.

With regret we left London and the homebound tour to fly to Antwerp, Belgium where dear friends from Zaire days lived. Some came from Brussels to see us there. From Antwerp we took the train to Paris where we were received into the bosoms of two more Zairian families, one a former student, now a family man, and both employed by UNESCO.

With them we feasted on Chikwangue, Saka saka, Nsafu, and other Zairian foods we have no way of obtaining in Fort Wayne. They get it frozen and flown in from Camarouns.

We landed from a relatively cool Europe to a Chicago heat wave. We then drove home to Fort Wayne the same afternoon. Our grandson needed Grandpa to take him to Riley Children's Hospital in Indianapolis where he had chest surgery in 1993. All is well and he is pronounced fit to enlist in the army for his college work and chance to learn a career job after graduation in 1996.

The same weekend, we drove to Iowa for my fiftieth High School class reunion and the first I had attended. It was a three-day affair with orchid leis flown in from Hawaii by a classmate and a cruise on the Mississippi. We have a state senator, three ministers, and a missionary among us. We had a memorial service for those who had died.

My Bequest

Son of my heart, when I am gone
And the Will is read that I have drawn
What is my greatest gift to thee
Since days I rocked you on my knee?
There may be money or house or land
Books read and loved and held by my hand
Albums of memories, pictures of life
Beloved possessions of Mother and wife
But none of these things fill my wish for you
I give you my Jesus as Friend, tried and true.

Dearest of daughters, gift from His love,
I would endow you with gifts from above.
I would fulfill every want you may know,
Cure all your ills, make dreams truly so.
Give you my treasures, my dearest and best.
Things I have made since you emptied our nest.
Some of my clothing, perhaps you can wear –
Rings for your fingers, flowers for your hair.
But oh, my dear daughter, the gift I would give
Is the gift of my Savior, who helps me to live.

And Grandsons so dear, our love and our pride,
Our hopes for the future, to family name tied.
What can I leave you that long will endure
Ease you in troubles – sicknesses cure –
Lead to prosperity, save you from vice
Make you a blessing, your deeds beyond price.

There may be money, but that's quickly spent.
There may be antiques and gifts so well meant.
But nothing I have on earth or above,
There's nothing to match the gift of God's love.

For all of my dear ones, left here on earth
I'm praying from heaven, the gift of rebirth,
So that His spirit might stay in your heart,
And bring you to heaven where we'll never part.

Martha Atkins Emmert

Chapter 41

AFRICA

The vast emptiness of Africa haunts me. Flying over the hills, mountains, rivers and forests, I see tiny villages only rarely. Such a small percentage of land was under cultivation. I had seen the hard woods being gleaned and sold in a steady parade to the ports. The other woods were made into charcoal or cooking bonfires. The forests were dwindling. A tree of fifty years was cut without compunction to harvest the caterpillars of a season for food.

On the winding sand or clay roads, we have driven this vastness, permeated by a hunter here, or a gardener there. Find a spot as remote as possible for a picnic, before it is over a bystander or two will be sure to materialize. The circulation of humans reaches every part, though thin in places. It is a hauntingly beautiful land, unlike in every way my Iowa of childhood.

The land is old, eroded by sun and torrential rains. One finds artifacts of the Stone Age easily on the hills after the rain ends and the dry season burning is over. The trees and plants are all exotic and strange to me. The

Kapok tree sends out roots like flying buttresses, grows thorns all over its trunk and when its seed disperses as the rains begin in October, they fill the air for all the world like a snowstorm.

The beauty of the dry season sunset came nearest to our harvest moon. Huge, orange, and heavy, it hung in blue mists over the silhouette of distant dark hills, truly a sight to treasure. But we went to Africa for the people. Jesus said, "Other sheep I have, they also I must bring ..." and we were sent to find them. In many ways, our Zairian Christian friends have ministered to us and enriched our lives by their love and example. From the classes of twenty years, the most choice students were winnowed out by tests to the very ablest due to lack of schools. From the teaching experience we are one with a host of younger brothers and sisters, strong in the Lord and serving Him throughout the world. These are riches indeed.

Our church leaders and members are dear to us. Though postage is exorbitant, they find ways to send us messages of hope and comfort, though they are the ones suffering these terrible years of anarchy. We must ever uphold them in prayer, for only God can provide for them and for us.

What I learned before reaching Africa seems very little compared to the lessons learned by experience and study while on the job. Because the need insisted on a response, I attempted many things I had no idea how to do, learning in the process.

Asked by our church in Kikwit to come and paint their baptistery I agreed to try. I lived in the pastor's office in the church. I had a barrel of water for use in bathing, a jug of water they had boiled for me to drink. Each day a different family prepared a meal and brought it to eat with me at noon. At 6 p.m., when darkness fell, I closed the wooden shutters against mosquitoes and read my Bible by the dimness of a kerosene lamp.

I did my best to paint a river scene on three background walls of their baptistery. It took many trips up and down to judge the perspective from the pews. After about ten days we were satisfied with the results.

While addressing the women one afternoon, at their request, termites began to fly out of cracks in the dirt floor. The rains had begun. I lost my audience instantly as the women ran and squatted by the cracks, grabbed the fresh juicy protein escaping from the nest into the air.

All of whatever natural abilities God had given me were honored and used to the fullest. I believe that He added some to meet needs I could not, in my own strength meet. One job I had for four years, was that of administering the guesthouse and Private patient wards in the large union mission Hospital at Kimpese, while Leon served as treasurer. This meant handling the purchasing, moneys paid for rooms and salaries of six staff members.

This is work totally uncongenial to me, I would have said. I disliked supervision of men and I feared financial responsibility. Yet for the first time in many years, the establishment came through in the black, financially. Those four years were probably the most tense and trying of my career as I was on call twenty-four hours a day, seven days a week, yet Hallelujah, when it ended, I felt God had made me more than a conqueror. My faith in Him and my love and gratitude toward Him skyrocketed.

While there, I had a safe in my office I used for our money, but also as a bank to keep the savings of a family of basket weavers from a nearby village. I kept their baskets to sell for them to the tourists who stayed with us and by banking for them they could save for large expenses to come. I tried always to encourage the artists and to urge them to do their best work, not descending to tourist quality, but maintaining traditional high standards.

During this sixth term spent in hospital administration, I may have had a touch of burnout. I had some very bad years spiritually, when I felt that God did not hear or answer me. My prayers became a mockery and for some years after, I stopped praying aloud in my devotions and began to write out my prayers in a journal. An old hymn I had learned reflected my feelings.

"How tedious and tasteless the hours
When Jesus no longer I see
Sweet prospects, sweet birds and sweet flowers
Have all lost their sweetness to me.

Dear Lord, if indeed I am Thine,
If thou art my sun and my song
Say, why do I languish and pine
And why are my winters so long?"

A lady pastor I talked to on furlough touched my heart when she said, "You need rest. Do not worry about praying. I promise to pray in your stead for a year, while you rest your soul in him."

I thank God my period of depression gradually dissipated as furlough brought rest, medical care and psychological help. Never did I doubt God's love for me or my relationship to Him, but I missed so much the sense of His soul cheering Presence with me and the several mountain top experiences that revitalized my faith and energies at critical times in the past.

For several years after retirement, I did not feel like thinking or talking about Africa, but now I am beginning to remember, and the trauma of making the break is much less. Home has been so many places and people. My family is so scattered, for my life is intertwined with lives in Iowa, those from Seminary years, while throughout the years in Africa, families, both Zairian and Missionary became ours. Our folk in churches in the U.S.A. throughout our convention, bonded with us as family. One does not retire from a worldwide family, committed to prayer and support.

Life goes on and perhaps I am enjoying the frosting on the cake as I live these years surviving cancer. Each thing is weighed for what it is worth. Priorities are more important and relationships, both old and new, are priceless. I believe I have lived to fulfill God's purpose for me until now, with fault and failure, but with good intent. He can write my concluding chapters as He chooses, for He is my home wherever I may be.

Order Information

Postal Orders should be mailed to:

Martha Emmert
3002 Sandarac Lane
Fort Wayne, IN 46815

Please send ______________copies of *Common Clay*

To: ____

Address:____________________________________

City: __________________State ______Zip
____

Price	$17.95	
Postage	2.05	
Sales Tax	0.90	Indiana Sales only

Enclose check payable to **Martha Emmert**

1949 - Martha Emmert on her graduation from seminary

Mrs. Harry Atkins Sr. (Martha's mother) with Martha Emmert as a seminary graduate

Amber Vincent Flannery, Martha's cousin and first witness of the good news of Jesus Christ

1958 - Daniel, Martha and Leon Emmert visiting tea plantation in Zaire

May 1961 - Danny (10) with his baby sister Michal Rose at Disney World

1979 - Michal Rose Emmert as a High School graduate

May 1984 - Michal Rose Emmert-Hart with her first perm

1993 - Martha Emmert writing memoirs in Upper Michigan

December 1949 - Vida Mae Grensing, Martha's mother in Christ in 1942.

Carmen Emmert with Nathan and Todd (Leon and Martha's grandsons)

Dorothy Bond (Allen) - Martha's first and life-long Christian friend

1975 - Martha Emmert . Morning devotions on the Sea of Galilee

Reverend E. Wesley McMurray and Martha Atkins Emmert after retirement. Pastor Mac was Martha's first pastor, and Martha was Pastor Mac's first convert

Leon Emmert & Martha Atkins Emmert, 1997